Surrogate

Hugo Hamilton was born in Dublin. His father ⸻ ⸻ ⸻ ⸻ German. He became involved in journalism and lived in Germany and Austria during the late 1970s. Back in Dublin, he worked for some time in the recording business and in publishing before taking up writing on a full-time basis. He was awarded a bursary by the Irish Arts Council in 1988. He has had short stories published in the *Irish Times*, *New Irish Writing* and in Faber's *First Fictions: Introduction 10*. *Surrogate City* is Hugo Hamilton's first novel; his second, *The Last Shot*, is also published by Faber and Faber.

by the same author

THE LAST SHOT

Surrogate City

HUGO HAMILTON

faber and faber
LONDON · BOSTON

First published in 1990
by Faber and Faber Limited
3 Queen Square London WC1N 3AU

Photoset by Goodfellow & Egan Ltd Cambridge
Printed in England by Clays Ltd, St Ives plc

A CIP record for this book is available from the British Library

ISBN 0-571-16454-4

No one is himself . . .

Paul Bowles

Berlin

She has been running. What for? Now she has slowed down again; out of breath, close to the side of the buildings, along the mosaic pavement of a street in Berlin. Mosaic pavements make you dizzy, if you've been running.

What makes a young woman run? During the day? In the city? She stopped and looked around to get her bearings. The buildings look the same. Shops and cafés all look the same, like poster repetition on hoardings. And Rosenheimer Strasse sounds the same as Eisenacher Strasse or Grunewaldstrasse. Even the name Berlin sounds much the same as Dublin or London or Boston. If you're still out of breath and weak at the knees. If you've been running.

It makes you look like you're late. Forgotten something. Like you need to get to a bank, or a doctor or an attorney. Like you don't own a car. Dream a lot over breakfast. Say little. As though you know it's going to rain. It makes you look like you've been tricked. Experienced hostility. It makes you look like you've just been attacked. Like you've just escaped from the East. Jumped across the Berlin Wall. Like you've had a taste of freedom. Like you've seen something that made you turn back. Like you once had an idea what you wanted most.

Running makes you look like you've lost something. Or stolen something. Or said something. Told lies. As though there is something you regret. It makes you look like you know something that nobody else does. Like you once had an idea of what you wanted most.

She walked on. She had no more energy to run. She was lost. In Germany, if you don't ask for directions, you must know where you're going. If you're not an *Ausländer*, then you must be an inhabitant. And running makes you look like you're new to Berlin. Because people in Berlin have stopped running in the streets. Running in the street makes you look like you don't belong. Like you're unemployed. Un-German. Surrogate.

1

The street must have been a banking street. She must have strayed into a commercial district of the city. There were blue flags spanned vertically at intervals along the façade of a building. There were trees lining the street along the outside of the pavement. There was a round sandy area around each tree. And stone mosaic circles expanding out from the centre. The trees had a certain distance between them. She passed a litter bin. She passed the entrance to a bank.

She kept walking, or lurching, on. Dizzy. From the stomach. Walking like a woman wading knee-deep into the sea. Moving unsteadily towards the wall on her left. Towards a hollow space in the wall; perhaps that of a cash-card point. Another convulsion heaved her stomach and made her want to vomit. But there was nothing. Nothing but an involuntary unfolding of the stomach, like a handbag turned inside out. Nothing but a dry, salty spit which, after a long time, fell from her lips to the pavement beneath her like a melted five-mark coin.

Nothing matters when you're pale and pregnant. Nothing matters when you're lost. Nothing matters if you've once had an idea of what you wanted most.

She looked up and read the words in front of her; white letters on a turquoise band. *Dresdner Bank*.

Kann ich helfen? a voice behind her asked. Can I help?

She didn't answer. But in Germany, no answer is also an answer.

Breach of Trust

When you see the peeling façade of an old building in Berlin, you want to get at it with your nails. Whenever you see tufts of grass growing up through cracked concrete, you think of a hoe or a trowel. If you see workmen painting, you want to join in. If you see men working on the mosaic pavement, you want to stop and pass them the stones or help arrange them in the sandy base, or hold the spirit level at least. If you see somebody running, you want to ask questions. The way newspapers beg to be read. And the Berlin Wall begs to be seen by sightseers. And everything cries out for an explanation.

A young woman sat on the bus next to the window. She was from Ireland. Her name was Helen Quinn. The man beside her could not help noticing her knees and the probability of perfect thighs beneath her skirt. A sideways glance, which is all that is permitted on buses, confirms that she is desirable, though nothing on her part would have deliberately sought it. But then, the man beside her doesn't know that she is pregnant. How could he? She can hardly believe it herself.

She has not noticed the man beside her. She is preoccupied with the passing buildings and the faces of people in the streets. She is preoccupied with the fact that she is now sitting on a bus in Berlin, pregnant, without the slightest idea what it means to be pregnant. At some stage she must have allowed herself to say: Look, I don't care what happens. Let it come down. And nowadays, you simulate danger; avoiding the consequences like stuntmen falling on cushions. At some point she must have found foresight unbearable, ignored her own advice and said: fuck foresight.

People who behave without foresight have to be helped. They need an explanation. They need to be shown sight of the future. Understood. The way only a confidential telephone number understands. Who can resist understanding a young woman in Berlin looking for the man with whom she lacked foresight? The man who

3

as yet has no idea how close he has come to being a father. Who knows where he is? Dieter. Who can resist helping her find him?

Hadja has been good to Helen. Hadja was the person who came to her assistance. Showed her complete trust. Gave her a room in her apartment without even asking her own boyfriend Wolf if it was OK with him. Hadja was the one who first showed her around Berlin and helped her look for the missing man: Dieter. But without much success.

And then, of course, those who accept help are always expected to reciprocate by satisfying the curiosity of the helper. They are expected to give an honest and open account of themselves, confide fully in their benefactors and allow themselves to be understood. Also, they must reciprocate by listening to, if not accepting, advice. Coming from Hadja, advice is always practical and direct.

Berlin is a big place. It's not too late. You can still terminate and start again.

Hadja is presumed German. Born in Berlin, she speaks German like anyone else because her mother is German and was also born in Berlin. But Hadja's father is Turkish, which accounts for Hadja's name, her equal fluency in speaking Turkish and the strong hint of Eastern heat in her complexion. The auburn colour of her hair is artificial. Her brown eyes are not. They belong to the father's side. She has square shoulders and a habit of jutting one of them forward as she speaks. The family surname is Milic.

Helen Quinn considers her situation from the window seat of a bus in Berlin. Her eyes deceive her. As the bus begins to turn another corner, she is convinced that the pedestrians standing close to the edge of the pavement will have their toes run over by the back wheel. It's an optical illusion. The pedestrians seem unafraid because everything is based on trust. An optical illusion is a breach of trust. A face recognized on the street of a foreign city is an optical illusion. A man who has disappeared from your life is hard to believe.

Hadja is presumed wealthy. She drives her mother's car because her mother now drives her father's car and because he is about to

4

buy a new one and won't even drive that much any more since he is getting on and since most of the family business commitments have now been taken over by Hadja's elder brother, Konrad. Logical!

Could the bus have been taking Helen around in circles? Once again she recognized a street, but soon realized it must have been a familiar shop sign: the Tschibo coffee logo. She wondered how Dieter would react when and if she found him. How does a man react to a pregnant woman? Can men feel pregnant by proxy? To herself, being pregnant felt like a conspiracy inside, something for the first time in her life completely beyond her control. Much like the noises that continue to come from underneath the bus and sound like a wide elastic band stretched to endurance and let go again with a hollow twang.

Hadja lives with her boyfriend Wolf. Musician. Songwriter. Reasonably well known around Germany. His name is Wolfgang Ebers. Plays guitar and saxophone and all kinds of music in the apartment, at all times of the day and night. His friends come to visit at all hours, which at times makes it seem like a public apartment. Hadja often says it's got to change. Wolf will have to find himself some kind of studio or a separate apartment where he can rehearse and play his endless music. She says it's ceased to be a place to live with all these records and tapes and instruments and wires along the floor.

Hadja and Wolf have nothing to hide. They argue a lot, to the point of shouting blindly, slamming doors, throwing objects at the floor. They often argue in the wide corridor of the apartment. They don't care who is listening.

The bus passed one of those places in Berlin that even after a week in the city becomes your favourite sight. Helen has seen it before from other angles, from above, when she travelled on the U-Bahn last; where the underground briefly comes out of the tunnels and crosses a bridge over a disused railway station. Many of the tracks and platforms remain. Others have been plundered. An arch, perhaps the former entrance to the station, stands at a peculiar angle to the platforms, through which the grass grows in tufts. The tracks too have faded under the sand and the weeds, as though everything would eventually be reclaimed.

Is this the way your memory would look, she thought, if you could see a photograph of it?

Berlin was built on sand. In a biblical sense, perhaps not the best choice. At one stage, Berlin was completely covered by the sea. Atlantis reversed, if you like. It's the first thing they tell you when you arrive in the city. They make it sound as though the water has only recently receded where in fact it all happened millions of years ago. And still, whenever you come across road-works, you think you're at the seaside, because they dig up nothing but sand. The workmen often sit on the sand with their sandwiches and beer. The traffic around them sounds like surf. The mid-morning or afternoon breeze in Berlin often comes in off the open sea like another breach of trust. And if you've ever lived near the sea, as Helen did in Dublin, you will always be prey to images of water and maritime weather. The occasional drizzle that covers the city is familiar. The kind of minimal rain that can be detected by day only on the eyelashes of pedestrians; by night, against the headlights of a car. Perhaps, in Berlin, they harbour subliminal thoughts that the city is somehow on lease from the sea. That some day a tidal wave will come back to reclaim the lost sea floor and Berliners will find themselves once again at the bottom of the Baltic.

Hadja and Wolf speak like tour guides, constantly imparting directions. The most direct route to the inner city. The best way to get to the Berlin Wall. Where to find the best pizza, the best curry. Hadja and Wolf sound like the 'what's on' magazine *TIP*. They make you feel like you're at the centre of things. Every new film, play, concert. They miss nothing. They tell you where Wolfgang Ebers can be heard in concert. Everything has a sense of personal history. Everything comes through Hadja and Wolf.

Berlin travel agents know how to set the imagination on fire. They know how to exploit the maritime origins of the city. A bus travelling towards the inner city will pass many travel agents. One of them has nothing on display in the window except a whitewashed wall, two empty glasses on a table underneath a sun-bleached canopy and the mere reflection of blue water dancing on the wall. Travel agents can turn a woman into sand. Turn a man into a camel.

In Germany, the sign that you're moving in with somebody is to bring your coffee grinder. Hadja and Wolf have two coffee grinders, though one, the latest to arrive at the apartment, has become redundant. It is Wolf's apartment. Hadja still keeps her own apartment in Sonnenallee, even though they have been together now for over three years. You need to have something to fall back on in the city.

Luckily for me, she has generously decided to allow me to take over her place in Sonnenallee while things continue to go well with Wolf. In view of the chronic accommodation problems in Berlin, Hadja was only too pleased to give her apartment to one of Wolf's colleagues in the music business.

I now occupy the place intended for Hadja to fall back on.

Hadja and Wolf occasionally make love in the morning, after coffee. Everything goes quiet. The phone is ignored. The sitting-room windows are left open to the sound of traffic from the street below. The smell of coffee covers the whole apartment. Then the sound of a voice, which could equally be the reaction to hot coffee being spilled over somebody's knee. Some time later, Wolf emerges into the sitting room where he begins to play the guitar or blow the saxophone, drowning the noise of traffic. Wolf plays music to keep people away. All day he will keep Hadja away with his saxophone. All day, Hadja pretends not to hear the saxophone. When she goes out, she ignores him.

The apartment door has to be slammed in order to shut it properly. This advice is given to anyone who is new to the apartment. Helen is new to the apartment.

Hadja's directions are simple and unambiguous.

Berlin is a big place. You'll never find a man who doesn't want to be found. What's the use in looking for a father? Get an abortion and start again. See my Turkish cousins, Hadja says. They are all in a desperate rush to get married and have babies.

Think of all the things you'll be missing. Babies make you sidestep everything. Cinema, theatre, concerts. You're young, Hadja says. Attractive. Give yourself a chance. Forget this man Dieter. Forget his baby. Start again.

Hadja knows nothing about Dieter. And little about Helen either.

Nobody has much to say for the other side. The other side of the Berlin Wall, that is. In East Berlin, they say, things are so inferior. Life is inferior. You'd never buy anything over there. Certainly not clothes or electrical items. Nor groceries. Leather bags, maybe. And pickled gherkins. Anything pickled is always worth bringing back.

Hadja and Wolf wouldn't even buy chocolate over there. Occasionally, they take a newcomer or a visitor to Berlin across, on a day trip around Alexanderplatz, drink beer, comment on how different life is over there and desperately try to spend their Ostmarks, which they can't convert back into D-Marks. Nothing can exhaust their money. Until somebody remarks that books are cheap in East Berlin, and they buy up volumes of Kleist and Goethe and Heine.

The newcomer is also urged to take a look at the Berlin Wall itself. It's worth that much, anyhow. The barbed wire. The graffiti. The sentries in the lookout towers with their binoculars. A list of Wall jokes are briefly revived. So are the stories about East German soldiers always going in pairs so that one can shoot the other in the event of an escape attempt. The story of the soldier who emptied his gun and swapped it with his colleague while he wasn't looking, and then heard the futile and furious clicking of an empty gun behind him while he ran away to freedom.

It's a monument that deserves a visit, like the leaning tower of Pisa. But after that, if you settle in Berlin, it is never mentioned again. For most people it doesn't exist. Occasionally, of course, somebody will come along and compare the Berlin Wall to a great love affair that went wrong; usurping the image for a personal biography. Occasionally, too, a statesman will make use of the Wall in a gritty show of courage. Tear down this Wall! they shout whenever they arrive in Berlin on a visit, blatantly missing the point that everyone in Berlin has been trying to forget about it. And in any case, walls are a thing of the past. Dividing lines are a thing of the future. War is a thing of the past, while common agriculture policies are the thing of the future.

There is no lock on the bathroom in Hadja and Wolf's apartment. Whenever Wolf takes a bath, he first runs the water and then walks up and down through the apartment with a towel around his waist, knocking on all the doors and making declarations like a porter in a railway station.

Letzte Möglichkeit zum Klo: Last chance for the loo.

Wolf spends so long in the bath; it's a ritual.

Helen has to have uninterrupted access to a bathroom. In considering her situation on the bus in Berlin, she begins to remember bathrooms everywhere. At home. At school. In particular, she remembers a bathroom in the West of Ireland at the back of a pub in Kildysert, where she and Dieter once stayed. They used to laugh at it. Over the bath there was a holy picture, warped by repeated exposure to steam. The enamel covering of the bath tub was covered in hairline cracks. And once, when Helen was nervous about an exam she was doing, Dieter told her to remember nothing but the bath in Kildysert.

Now Helen realized that all her own personal functions had been taken over by the conspiracy inside. As though all pregnant mothers were surrogate; like commandeered trucks in wartime. Now even her most basic functions are no longer her own.

In Wolf and Hadja's bathroom, among the oils and bottles of lotion, stands a candelabrum with three white candles. It's silver, designed for a dinner table. Beside it, on the window-sill of the bathroom, lies a box of matches.

There is yet another function for Hadja and Wolf's bathroom. Much to Hadja's irritation, the bathroom is being used from time to time by Wolf as part of a studio. He is preparing a demo tape for recording companies; putting some of his songs on tape, which sometimes requires the acoustic separation of various instruments into various rooms, including the bathroom. He admits that this is a primitive way of making a demo tape, but it's equally effective, if you can put up with wires and cables leading everywhere, along the hallway, into the bathroom.

One afternoon, Helen arrived back and found a set of drums in the bathroom, with microphones attached.

There is an anxiety in every woman, irrational perhaps, that her personal bathroom sounds might be inadvertently – much worse, purposely – recorded on tape and, at some later stage, played back.

From the bus, everything you see is enhanced. Berlin looks clean. Hospitable. Inviting. Everything seemed effortless. Not for the first time, she wished she could stay on a bus for ever.

If it wasn't for the conspiracy inside, she might have fallen asleep, as she often did on buses to and from work in Dublin. The conspiracy of human lineage keeps you awake. There was nothing to stop her terminating. Nothing but the fact that she felt she would be refusing to live life. This was the last chance for Helen to stop the world at herself.

From now on, the future would rush at her. Soon she would become a mere ancestor, like her mother and her grandmother; the source of new populations over which she had no more control. She would become part of a forward evolution; expanding internally as though inside her there was a city under construction.

A city full of relatives. Generations of pedestrians and passengers on buses, none of whom would eventually recognize her or each other. Cities full of nieces and nephews and grandchildren politely shaking hands with one another, perhaps somewhere along the line a famous actor, or a notorious murderer.

Luckily, you don't make up your mind on buses. It's a place where you can sit and defer all decisions.

Helen's eyes deceived her again. Against all natural scepticism and doubt, against all credible coincidence, while the bus and all its internal sounds had momentarily slowed down, she saw Dieter outside, just below her on the pavement. He walked past. Back in the direction from which the bus had come. Impossible! DIETER! Only metres away. DIETER, she said, out loud, so that everyone on the bus must have heard her. It could only be him, in his green jacket and that grey bag of his.

She turned and knocked urgently on the window. But the noise wasn't enough to catch Dieter's attention. Only the other passengers on the bus turned around to look at her. Dieter didn't. He walked right past. And by then the bus had already made so much progress that she was left looking behind her. The other passengers were still obediently looking forward.

She stood up. The man beside her instinctively made way, and watched her awkwardly rushing up the aisle, constantly looking behind her, ducking to keep sight of Dieter's back through the rear window. Everyone on the bus was staring at her.

Aussteigen bitte? She asked the bus driver to let her off at the traffic lights. He refused. Didn't answer or even shake his head at first. Only when she persisted, he said: *Nein!* Not until the next official stop. He refused to open doors at traffic lights. Under no circumstances.

I cannot let everyone off whenever they want to, he said loudly, making sure that everybody on the bus heard him.

In Germany, everything works on a consensus of opinion. The bus driver's words were directed not so much at her as at the passengers on the bus generally, whom he needed for support.

Cannot be done, he said. It cannot be demanded of me to open the doors here, young lady.

He was prepared to make an issue of it. Nobody on the bus said a word. He had his consensus.

Helen looked around once more to make sure she could still see Dieter. Then begged the driver again.

I must get off here, she said. Please. *Bitte*.

Nothing worked.

Mein Gott, the bus driver said, appealing for more support. The young lady should sit herself down again and wait for the next stop.

She could think of no alternative at that moment but to faint. She slumped downwards on to her knees, convincingly. Her head fell against the front seats without injury. She collapsed like a doll, lifeless. Perhaps it was too choreographed. But effective, none the less. Passengers jumped up to help her. The driver instantly lost all his support.

Can he not see that the young lady is ill? somebody shouted.

How was I supposed to know that? the driver said, to defend himself somehow. She could have said something.

A man and a woman simultaneously took her arms on both sides and helped her to her feet. The consensus of opinion was all in her favour now. Comments were being made at the back of the bus about the driver's intransigence.

Immer wieder! Always the same smallmindedness, somebody said. The BVG will never change.

The bus driver had already stopped the bus. His defence was to push his palms towards the passengers in disbelief. That such a thing could happen on his bus. He didn't make her sick, he pleaded. But then the man holding Helen by the right arm raised his voice.

Now make you at last the doors open.

Without a further word, the doors opened with a familiar mechanical sigh and she was being helped down the steps to the pavement. She held one hand up to her forehead. It was convincing. Everyone asked if she was all right.

On the pavement, she was being revived with gentle phrases. Pedestrians stopped to see what the matter was. The bus driver stood on the steps looking down anxiously as though he was going to be held responsible. After all, it was one of his passengers.

She kept looking back, anxiously, feverishly. Something back there made her ill, they thought. And then, abruptly, she freed herself from their solicitous touches and ran away.

She could no longer see Dieter, but she was certain she knew what corner he had turned. She kept running. Pedestrians made way. Behind her, where the bus had been held up on its timetable, the passengers were shocked.

Sowas, some of them said.

There was little more that could be said. Whatever support she had briefly gained was now returning unanimously to the bus driver. He felt entitled to his impatience. Shut the doors again with a furious sigh and regarded the whole incident as a full restoration of his authority.

What did I say? he announced, both to himself and to the general travelling public. One cannot allow oneself to be taken in by them.

She ran until she got to the next corner. She had kept it in sight all the time. She turned into a new street and saw nothing. Not what she expected; not Dieter's broad back and his green jacket. All she saw was another street, with more old houses, some of them with peeling façades, some with scaffolding outside.

She continued to run until she got to the next corner. She could hardly run any more. Again, she saw nothing. He was gone. There was something else wrong, too. Every time she turned a corner she expected to see the wide blue band of ocean at the end of the street. Another breach of trust.

She was out of breath; exhausted. She came across a corner café

12

with tables and umbrellas and coral white chairs outside. An area of the broad pavement had been sectioned off with plant-holders and walls of shrubs. She was gasping, and sat down for a moment in one of the coral chairs. She had lost him again, she thought. A waiter came out to her table and without looking at her said: *Bitte*, what will it be? She shook her head and got up to walk away. Kept walking again until she came into another street. This time a commercial street. A street with mosaic pavements and banks and trees along the outside.

Her movements were awkward. Slowly, she made her way along the pavement, looking at the recurring pattern beneath her feet, like a diver alone on the sea bed. She felt ill, really ill this time, and leaned against the wall with her elbow. A flash of turquoise entered her mind. The name Dresdner Bank stood out clearly in the wall in front of her. She looked down and saw a five-mark piece on the pavement at her feet. But nothing matters when you're sick.

That is where Helen first met Hadja. Hadja had just come from the bank, and instinctively asked if she could help.

In Germany, if you're offered help, you need it.

2

Stone, Scissors and Paper

Hadja is a born manager. She knows what's required. Knows what she wants and how to get it. She also knows what other people want. Hadja can identify what people most want. She's a natural organizer. A ringmaster.

The results of mismanagement and flawed ambition are littered everywhere around her. And seeing so much helplessness, Hadja quite naturally rose to her role of guide and helper. She has ambition for the world. At the Free University of Berlin, Hadja studied German and philosophy. It was immediately clear that her aptitude for both became a mere constituent of a more dominant talent for management. A fundamental curiosity about people, matched with a flawless imagination and the sharpest ability to perceive herself in somebody else's shoes, gave her an immense headstart. She sees how people prefer to be manipulated. How they rarely know what they want. And if you can identify what somebody wants, you have them under your thumb.

As a schoolgirl, Hadja once had a strong fantasy which was to come back to her again and again in dreams and daydreams until it became part of her nature. It went back to an occasion when her elder brother, Konrad, brought her to see the circus Roncalli. Nothing ever inspired her imagination more than the women she saw riding horses around the ring, standing barefoot on their backs. At any time of day or night, Hadja could see herself standing on horseback. She could feel exactly what it was like without ever having the need to do it in real life. It was so easy. If she lost balance, or if the horse travelled too fast for her, she would always land on her feet. She would just wait and imagine the horse coming round again and then jump on. Even when Hadja was older and took up horseriding on holidays in the South, it wasn't necessary to try it in reality. The fantasy was enough. And when this fantasy was superseded by other desires, the image remained with her. Hadja would always land on her feet.

Perhaps it is this pilot vision that gives Hadja such command over people. Perhaps the considerable wealth and security which exists in the Milic family helps. The perfect home in Charlottenburg, Berlin. But Hadja firmly discounts both inheritance and wealth as assets. Seeing how often people waste and mutilate their own resources, she believes the only important thing is to have your head screwed on properly; that's what counts.

Hadja, for the moment, prefers to pursue a career in the arts. Creative management. She works with Wolf.

Occasionally, Hadja will meet somebody like herself who has fallen on their own two feet. She admires them for a while, until she begins to detect weaknesses. Weaknesses should be corrected. She likes to bring out the best in people. When it comes down to it, Hadja really prefers dealing with people who can be perfected. People with inadequacies.

I met Hadja through Wolf. Does that make me inadequate? I would dispute it. Put it down to Hadja's unique ability to cast all people she comes in contact with as problems. Minor characters.

What am I doing in Berlin? Right now, I feel adequate; heading for a problem.

Afternoon. Fading light. Hadja looks out over the city through the open window of the sitting room. Their apartment is situated in a corner building; the sitting-room windows overlook the street. Wolf is talking to her, but Hadja doesn't need to look at him to hear what he's saying. Some of the shop lights in the street below have already come on. Some of the shop lights have been on all day. Already, at intervals, small groups of people emerge up the escalator and up the steps from the *U-Bahn* station. From where she stands, it looks like a hole in the ground. The reason she can read the clock outside the *U-Bahn* station is because she already knows the time. The reason she can read shop signs such as AMBAUM BÄCKEREI or METZGEREI BÖSER at a distance of over three or four hundred metres is because she has often passed them on foot.

Hadja doesn't always need to hear Wolf to know what he's saying. The reason she is looking down at the street is that she can hear the traffic instead.

The Tischtelefon lights have not come on as yet. The reason is that Tischtelefon clients don't normally appear until evening time, or even later, at night. At night in Wolf and Hadja's apartment, if the lights in the sitting room are left off and the curtains left open, the room lights up with a red glow every thirty seconds. The red heart outside Tischtelefon keeps lighting up, all night, simulating a delayed heart-beat.

People are small. Hadja can see them in the street below. They seem to move by instinct; without much thought. What speeds them up is the fact that it is still quite cool outside. There could be a cold breeze in the street. Hadja knows everything there is to know about people below in the street. She doesn't need to be a pedestrian to know what it's like. From where Hadja stands, people look small and ineffective. They could be crushed so easily. Another handful of passengers emerging from the *U-Bahn* would hardly be missed.

As soon as Wolf stops talking, she turns towards him.

I don't know what you have against it, Wolf, she said. I don't see why you couldn't just for once make the effort and come with me. You'll see, it will be good for you to be seen there. Trust me. I should know.

There is no further response from Wolf. That is his final answer. He is busy putting new strings on his guitar. He should have the light on, but he doesn't need to see what he's doing.

I don't see what's so awful about going to the opening of an art exhibition. You'll meet people who will be useful to you.

Hadja knows what's good for Wolf. She knows how to draw him out. How to misunderstand him.

I don't see why you always turn your back on what's good for you, she says.

This is an old approach. It worked when they met first; when Wolf was still messing about with drugs. Not that he was ever a fully fledged junkie, but he was half-way there. And it was Hadja who saved him. They met in Galway: Ireland. He was sinking. He didn't know what he wanted.

Look, Hadja, Wolf shouts eventually. I know what's good for me. And it's certainly not those arse-licking functions your brother keeps getting himself invited to. I need MUSIC . . . nothing but MUSIC. Understood!

I eat MUSIC, he said, after a pause.

Wolf contains a lot of fury. Hadja leans back on the window-frame to look at him dispassionately. Wolf is winding up the new string on his guitar. The bass string. Keeps plucking the string with his nail, producing a stairway of notes as he winds higher and higher.

If anyone knows what's good for you, it's me. Hadja said.

Wolf looks up at her. Silhouetted. Almost black now against the evening sky. He doesn't need to see her face to know that she's smiling. His fury is complete. He stops winding the string and goes to place his guitar in its case.

MUSIC . . . is all I need. Nothing else.

The reason Wolf says things like that is so he can hear them himself.

He gets ready to go out. He knows there is one thing that a woman hates; that is to be less important than music. Music makes you overlook things. Nobody likes to be overlooked.

Don't you ever forget who helped you find your talent. And who helped you to get out of your mess. Without me, *mein Freund*, you'd still be sinking in the gutter.

Wolf has nothing more to say. The reason you don't say something is that you don't want to give yourself away. He puts on his jacket. He has to leave anyhow. To meet somebody; me, actually. But he uses the exit to his own benefit.

You should listen to me more often, Hadja shouts.

Wolf picks up a handwritten list and puts it in his jacket pocket. Song titles. A performance order. His jacket is suede; brown. He brushes his hair back with his fingers, checks to see how much money he has in cash and leaves the room. But then he comes back moments later because he's forgotten something.

You forgot your keys, Hadja said.

Wolf left. He slammed the door with maximum effect. Hadja can remain so calm, with her back to the city outside and a cool breeze clutching her shoulders, because she has often heard that door slam. It needs to be slammed to shut it properly.

You need me more than I need you, she shouted after him. The reason that Wolf can pretend not to have heard is that he is already out of earshot, bouncing down the stairs with his guitar case. He doesn't take the lift because he can't get away fast enough. He smiles on his way down because he knows what she said.

People are small. The street lights have come on, even though it's not quite dark. Below her in the street, she can see Wolf emerging from the building. He walks along the pavement. His feet shoot out in front of him. From where she stands, Hadja could so easily have spat on his head. He prepares to cross the street. Hadja could so easily have told him when to cross. And where to cross. She has a far better view of the traffic. His head turns left and right and left and right, comically, like a puppet. Then his feet begin to shoot out on to the street. From where she stood, she could have picked him up in her fingers. She watched him walk all the way to the *U-Bahn* station.

When is it good to look small? When you're far away. On public transport. Reflected in glass. Among millions. When you're going towards something and can only get bigger.

When is it good to look helpless? When you want something. When you want to look smaller than you are. When you have nothing to lose. When you want to give the impression that you have everything to lose.

This is the way Hadja makes love. She places herself in a helpless situation. Lights on or lights off is all irrelevant. What matters is the proximity to danger. She likes to begin by pretending that she needs nothing. That she is beyond help. But she likes to be seen through. She likes to hold on to the brass bars at the end of the bed and pretend that she is perfectly secure while edging closer to the margin of helplessness. She likes to be rescued and dragged back by force.

This is the way Wolf makes love. He likes to proceed from the assumption that the world is the greatest disaster ever. That nothing could possibly get any worse than it is. No society less futile, no city more gasping for survival. He likes to assume a furious vision of the world brought back from the march of progress. He longs to shake somebody by the shoulders. Usually Hadja. He longs to shake sense out of her until she lets go of the brass bars at the end of the bed.

Hadja's brother Konrad needs Kristl more than Kristl needs Konrad. Kristl is one of Hadja's old schoolfriends. Her father and mother run the König flowershops. Kristl is an only child, and is

18

expected eventually to take over the business. But she is still a bit wild. Laughs a lot. Speaks with a Berlin accent and cares about nothing.

It's just what Konrad needs. Not that he is getting on badly with his wife, Gudrun. It's only his need for something less intellectual; less meaningful. Kristl is good fun. Perhaps he will take her to Paris with him next time. Konrad needs Hadja to keep a secret. And Hadja knows how to keep a secret.

Only your best friend will tell you what's important. Whenever Kristl wears the green dress, Hadja feels compelled to comment. Even though Kristl is full of lively imagination, there are things in her personality she lacks. Despite a lifelong association with flowers and colours through her parents' shops, Kristl still has no idea about matching colours. It's a weakness Hadja sets right.

Kristl, *mein Schätzchen* . . . that dress with the red and white front suits you so much better.

Besides, Hadja knows her brother's tastes.

You can choose to be helpless if you want. In Germany, if it suits you, you can choose not to understand much German. Pretend you're new to the city. In fact, I understand a lot more German than I'm given credit for. But it pays not to know too much. It pays, for instance, not to know how to find an apartment in Berlin, because Hadja eventually gave me the use of her own. There must be something attractive about a man in difficulty with accommodation. A man with difficulty paying his fare on the *U-Bahn*.

There is nothing ambiguous about public transport in Germany. In Berlin, everybody must have a ticket. If you don't know what to do, then you ask. I hold up a blank, unfranked ticket. They look at me doubtfully at first, and then realize that I am not German. They realize that they have overestimated me and given me more credit than I was due. With dramatized patience, they take my hand and show me how to frank the ticket properly.

You must make the ticket in, like that . . .

I nod with obvious fascination. I'm good at letting on I know less than I do. I nod with the same fascination when Hadja explains that in her old apartment in Sonnenallee, the main entrance doors are closed at nine o'clock sharp and kept locked from then on until seven in the morning. Only residents with keys can come and go. She warned me always to remember the key and to make sure that visitors always arrive before nine. I'm good at letting on I don't need to be told something twice.

It is the same appreciative nod that I give all my visitors at the apartment in Sonnenallee. The same absorbed interest that I give all German women. I like to be underestimated. To walk into situations without any premonition. I like my eyes to appear wide open. As though I know nothing.

This is how I make love. I like to pretend it is the first and last time ever. Most of the time, in fact, I don't have to pretend.

Everything should happen once, and then never again. If only it would happen to me once, I always say. Just once. Unrehearsed.

This is something I did once. One morning, I left the apartment early with a friend who happened to be staying with me. We were on our way to the city centre for breakfast somewhere. Along the way, we passed by bakery shops and cafés with the unmistakable air of fresh rolls lingering on the pavement outside. We ignored them all because we had to meet Wolf in the city. But I was in no rush, and at one of the bakery shops, I stopped and said: Watch this.

I walked to the door of the shop and opened it. Out came the warm gust of fresh baking. Inside, at the counter, a number of customers were being served.

Auf Wiedersehen, I said. Without actually entering the shop itself. In fact, I had never been into that shop in my life before. But the words *Auf Wiedersehen* immediately set off a chain reaction of greetings whereby all the women behind the counter began to say *Auf Wiedersehen* automatically, without thinking.

Auf Wiedersehen! . . . Auf Wiedersehen! Dankeschön! Auf Wiedersehen!

Something else that happened to me once. I had a girlfriend here in Berlin. Gabi. It was assumed that I couldn't put two words together in German. That I was ignorant. Foreign. At one point it looked like it would go on for ever. But then, one morning, she phoned a friend of hers in Hamburg for a long conversation. I wasn't meant to understand any of this. I understood everything. And it's frightening sometimes to understand things you're not meant to understand. Because it can be seen on your face that you know more than you let on you know.

That morning Gabi left after breakfast.

Just before the doors close over on the *U-Bahn*, you hear the words *Zurück bleiben* – Stand back. You turn around and wait for the next one. There's no problem. *U-Bahns* are frequent. You wander around the platform. Sit down. Lean against the wall. Or stand with your legs crossed like a pair of scissors looking down at the half-smoked cigarettes lying around the tracks in front of you. Nobody minds waiting. The worst thing is to have the doors shut in your face. To be told to stand back.

Twice so far, Helen has been over to Steglitz, the district in Berlin where Dieter's mother lives. Each time, Frau Penzholz was out. Or not answering maybe? This time, Hadja offered to drive her over. Hadja would rarely have any reason to go to Steglitz. But she's curious. Detective work suits Hadja. There might be some excitement when the Irish girl confronts her boyfriend Dieter. Besides, Thursday night; might do some late shopping afterwards.

They choose tea-time. Frau Penzholz lives on the fifth floor. They are breathless when they arrive at the door. At the sound of the bell, a number of small dogs begin to bark inside. A minute later, a voice behind the door tells them to be quiet. Frau Penzholz shuffles around behind the door, talking. It takes a long time before the door is opened. Perhaps she was examining the girls through the glass eye in the door.

Dieter's mother is old. Berlin is full of old people. She asks them to come in. She tells the dogs not to be so excited, but it becomes obvious that she has no control over them. There is an opened bar of chocolate on the coffee table. The sofa is full of dog hairs. Another opened bar of chocolate, same variety, lies on the arm of the sofa. Frau Penzholz broke off some of the chocolate and gave it to the dogs, each standing on hind legs to receive it.

Ach, ja! The girl from Ireland, Frau Penzholz said eventually after Hadja explained the reason for their visit and how they were looking for Dieter. But it soon became clear that Frau Penzholz knew nothing about Helen. And even less about her own son Dieter.

Ja – Dieter? Frau Penzholz said. I don't see him any more. Not even a postcard. He lives in Ireland now, I think.

What infuriates Hadja most is information that is out of date. Old facts.

What infuriates her more is the way that Frau Penzholz suddenly begins to talk about the war. How things were when she first arrived in Berlin. Hadja has no time for this. Only with persistent and polite reminders can she bring Frau Penzholz back to the subject.

Dieter, ja? Where is he now? Frau Penzholz repeated.

Then Frau Penzholz offered to make some coffee. An attempt to keep the company she had received out of the blue. But Hadja was impatient and declined. The dogs kept sniffing around her feet. Hadja later described dogs at your feet as something worse than flies around your face. Hadja got up to leave and told Frau Penzholz that, regrettably, they were in a hurry. No old person wants to hear that. Helen would have stayed longer to hear anything that Dieter's mother had to say. Anything about Dieter. But Hadja was driving.

Before they left, Frau Penzholz took two unopened letters from the top of the TV set and gave them to Hadja. Frau Penzholz seemed to have remembered the letters just at that very moment.

These letters have come for Dieter, she said. Perhaps you can give them to him when you see him. He doesn't come here any more.

The letters were stamped in Ireland. Both sent by Helen.

They shook hands with Frau Penzholz.

Say, girls, Frau Penzholz said at the door. When you see Dieter next, will you ask him to come and visit his mother again some time?

Afterwards, Hadja stopped to have a look at some clothes in a boutique in Steglitz. She held some dresses and blouses up against herself and looked in the mirror. Occasionally, she held up a dress to Helen and said: I think this one would suit you better. But Helen didn't have her mind on clothes at that moment.

There are two kinds of people: those who initiate, and those who wait. Those who manipulate and those who like to be manipulated. There is no doubt which section Hadja or her elder brother Konrad fall into. But there are those, too, who benefit from being manipulated. They seem to know what they want and to get what they want by yielding; pretending that they need care. Sometimes it's not quite clear who's doing the manipulating. It's like the children's game of STONE/SCISSORS/PAPER where each item has the material power to beat one of the others. It's all in the draw.

While Hadja was still attending the university, she became acquainted with an Iranian student named Sulima. *Die Perserin*, Hadja often called her. Normally, Hadja has a tendency to avoid too much contact with Eastern people, since she is already so closely involved with Turkish people. But Sulima's case was irresistible.

Sulima had been promised in marriage since birth to a man from Iran who happened also to be studying at the Free University of Berlin, and was therefore in a good position to keep an eye on her. Massoud, a man with black hair, black eyelashes and a short black beard, was older than Sulima. Whenever they met, he treated her like a younger sister. Reproached her occasionally for not wearing more traditional dress. And even though they lived in separate apartments, in different districts of Berlin, Massoud had a consistent power over Sulima, which Hadja was determined to break from the start; first by talking intellectually about the virtues of Western freedom, and eventually, when Massoud showed himself to be unreasonable, by direct action.

Sulima was afraid of Massoud. Said she hated him and had no intention of ever marrying him. She longed for the same freedom as all Western women in Berlin. And Hadja took it upon herself to show Sulima how to attain that freedom. Very soon, Sulima had less and less contact with Massoud and began to expose herself to the unlimited choice which Berlin life offered. Massoud was ignored. Even officially snubbed, as soon as Hadja established beyond doubt that Massoud was sleeping with other German students. Hadja was able to get another friend to confirm this. She did everything with the greatest discretion and soon won Sulima's complete confidence. With encouragement, she finally persuaded her to take her own German student lover. It worked. Hadja felt almost proud of her achievement, even though Sulima remained tacit about the whole event and refused to discuss the matter with the open candour due between Western women.

Sulima's romance with the German student went on. Weeks and months. Now and then, Sulima was seen openly walking around with him, his arm on her shoulder. Massoud kept his distance for some reason. It was only when Sulima decided to change her hair that the trouble started. She went for a short, spiky, provocative cut. The style of the day in Berlin.

Massoud blew a fuse. He stopped Sulima early one morning at the entrance to the university. He seemed to have waited there overnight. Hadja just happened to be there with her.

You can't do that, he shouted. You have no right to cut your hair without my permission. I am your future husband. I won't allow it.

He looked angrily at Hadja, as though she were to blame. Hadja looked back with the same hostility, ready to take the blame. She couldn't believe what she heard. And for a moment it seemed to become an issue entirely between Hadja and Massoud. But then Massoud turned back to Sulima and shouted.

Go home, he said. You will not leave your house again until your hair has grown.

Massoud was shaking. Fidgeting with his sleeves as though he was about to hit Sulima right there at the entrance to the university. Hadja was half hoping he would.

Sulima stood back, frightened at first. It was touch and go. But Hadja's subtle influence paid off in the end. Sulima threw back her head.

We are all free to do what we want, she said.

The words sounded like music to Hadja. She couldn't have put it better herself. But coming from Sulima, it lacked conviction, the way things always do when quoted.

Massoud smiled. That was his way. He just looked into Sulima's eyes with a broad grin, meant as much for Hadja as for Sulima.

Hadja felt it was her victory. At last, she could trust Sulima to look after herself. Sulima had joined the West. But you can never be sure who's who in victory. It's more like the draw; STONE/SCISSORS/PAPER.

In Germany, if you look into somebody's eyes, it means you are hoping to find something there.

24

Hadja knows how to control eye contact. Sometimes she and Wolf exchange nothing but eye contact for days on end. She has now become Wolfgang Ebers's official manager, concert promoter and agent. She is kept busy. She knows best how to strike a deal, when to make eye contact and when to unsettle negotiations by looking at your ear or at your chin instead. The reason that Hadja looks at your chin or your shoulder instead of your eyes is that she wants to see what you're made of.

It is always easy to look into Wolf's eyes when he's playing music. It's a luxury. That's because there is nothing there but blue infinity.

Helen has a habit of looking straight into people's eyes. At the bakery. At the launderette. Everywhere. It's not something she controls consciously.

Helen and Hadja are sitting at the table at the Bar-o-Bar café. Evening. Wolf is due on stage later. The two women are presumed German.

Leaning at the bar not far away, looking into the street outside, is a tall man in black leather trousers. Without taking his eyes off the street, he can find his glass of beer and lift it up to his mouth. He moves by instinct. He is studying the two women. The reason Hadja knows she is being studied is that the man in leather trousers seems to have been consciously ignoring them. And every time he does briefly look down at them, Hadja happens to be looking away at the band instead. Helen's eyes are easier to engage. She looks at the man in leather trousers as though there is something familiar about him. He has a white face. Long dark hair. He could hardly know that she was Irish.

Moments later, he pulled himself almost wearily away from the bar and came over to their table. He lifted the packet of Lord and began to take out a cigarette for himself, saying: May I?

Nice weapon that, he said, replacing the lighter on top of the cigarette packet.

He took a long, hard look at Helen and blew the first lungful of smoke across the table at her. He doesn't know she's pregnant. How could he?

Wolf and I arrived at the Bar-o-Bar. I was introduced to Helen quite briefly before I had to go and set up the gear for Wolf.

The man in leather trousers shifted his position. The reason you shift your position is to see something new. He turned towards the bar itself. He must have seen Wolf and myself talking to Helen and Hadja. He drank up quickly and paid for his drinks. Before leaving, he stopped at their table again and leaned right over to face Helen. A sweet smell of drink hit her nostrils. He spoke in German.

Well . . . How is it, *meine Damen*?

He was looking at Helen.

Anybody like to join me for a drink over at café Bleibtrue? he asked.

It was Hadja who answered.

Interessiert uns nicht, she said. Not interested. We're staying.

That's where I first met Helen. Later, after Wolf came off stage, we sat around the table for a while and talked.

Helen and I immediately had things to compare. We talked about Dublin. Berlin. Music. If I really want to know what somebody is like, I ask them what music they listen to.

Out of the blue, Helen asked everyone to meet for breakfast next morning. Café Trödel. You know it?

How was I to know she was pregnant?

26

3

City Breakfast

I got up early. It was raining. To me it always sounds like a silent engine outside. An engine freewheeling without a hum. I think that because the rain has a steady revolving sound like a cement-mixer somewhere almost out of earshot. The *Innenhof*, as I still call it, simply because I have not yet translated the term into courtyard, sounded damp and hollow. The workmen on the far side seemed to be sheltering like rare birds in the scaffolding which has clung for weeks now to the opposite wall. Their work sounds were absent. If somebody had asked me at that moment what the weather was like outside, I would have answered there and then: It's freewheeling.

I moved some items around the apartment, put on my jacket, shut the door behind me and walked down the stairs. On the last flight of stairs near the bottom I saw the Turkish woman with her headscarf and pink overall dusting the banisters. She stood back and smiled. Turned her cloth inside out to begin a fresh approach and said: *Guten Morgen*. She seemed pleased and eager to grasp every opportunity to practise her German. There was gold in her teeth. Curiosity in her eyes. The *Hausmeister*'s door had been left open. *Hausmeister* simply because I had yet to translate his title to caretaker, and yet to discover what the *Hausmeister*'s true function is in German society. The sound of an aluminium tray falling to the floor came from inside the *Hausmeister*'s apartment, but that was simply because the Turkish woman had not yet said: *Gesundheit*, and I had not yet identified the brash noise as that of the *Hausmeister*'s declamatory sneeze.

To get out on to the street from my apartment in Sonnenallee you have to cross the *Innenhof*, where you get a preview of the real weather, then walk around through the archway where the bins are kept and out through the main doors. These are the doors that are kept locked at night. As I passed through, I saw young Herbert crouched down in the archway doing up his shoelaces. Herbert was wearing a short yellow rain mac outside his schoolbag, which made him look a bit like a hunchback. In crouching, his bare back and light blue underpants had become partially exposed. The Hertie tag on the underpants stuck out. Herbert is twelve. Lives on the first floor with his mother; without his father. I often see him delaying on his way home from school, gazing in shop windows, hiding in doorways and sometimes stalking old women. I know what he's at usually because I used to set myself the same impossible missions when I came home from school; trying to arrive back at base without being spotted by a single neighbour. Sometimes I can hear Herbert running or howling like an ambulance on the stairs or through the courtyard until the *Hausmeister* or somebody else grips him by the shoulder and reminds him to observe the communal respect for silence around apartment blocks. I feel personally addressed by such reminders. At one point I struck up an arm's-length friendship with this boy Herbert. As close as you can get to a twelve-year-old boy who is slightly cross-eyed and stares through his glasses at your navel. As close as you can get to a boy with no father and whose mother was obviously shocked to find out that I had once bought Herbert a Toblerone. She forbade any further communication. Had she discovered that I was a non-German. An *Ausländer*? Or had she imagined that a stranger like me would replace the father figure which the boy lacked? Or does she imagine that I'm some kind of pervert hiding behind an affable grin?

Hallo, Herbert, I called, in spite of the mother's caution. It was like saying hallo to myself in the past; myself as a boy with Hertie underpants and steamed-up glasses. Herbert did not respond.

The cars in the street sounded like strips of adhesive tape being pulled away from the surface. That was simply because I had a cap over the tips of my ears and also because I find cars a bit hostile at times. Hostile because I don't own one and I had not yet identified a car as one of my desires. Because I simply have not yet fully identified my desires. Because in order to identify your desires you first begin by eliminating what you want least in the world. I remain very much a person of ambiguous needs and ambiguous desires, learning more by mistake than by success.

As I walked through the rain along Sonnenallee, I realized that the Irish girl, Helen, had not told me her second name. It occurred to me that I may already have forgotten it. In my head, I still had no concept of her other than the Irish girl at Bar-o-Bar, much sought after by tall men in leather trousers. I'm like most people. I like what other people like. And being in bars at night gives you other people's desires. Over breakfast, it might be easier to conceal your desires.

I admired the way Helen suggested breakfast. How about breakfast tomorrow? she said. Café Trödel? The suggestion was put to everyone at the table in Bar-o-Bar, Wolf and Hadja included. But when nobody responded except me, it seemed as though a trap had been set. Helen seemed far more honest. She has lively eyes. Eyes that ask questions. And a perfectly plausible motive for breakfast in Trödel. An exchange of biographies.

Descending the stairs into the *U-Bahn*, I felt the rain stop and the warm, dry air take over. I took off my cap. The *U-Bahn* in Berlin has its own dry climate which belies the weather above ground. The smell reminds me of a new leather handbag. But that's simply because I don't really know what a new handbag smells like. The *U-Bahn* has a smell you can't really identify. It smells like nothing. Like nothing on earth. The way water tastes like nothing even though it kills the thirst. And travelling on the *U-Bahn* is like going somewhere, even though it isn't.

In Germany, everything must be declared.

Nothing can be permitted to remain ambiguous. Nothing is without status. As such, the smell of the *U-Bahn* is declared neutral. *Wurst* may be declared cheap, tasty or, at times, tasteless. Clothes can be declared *geschmackhaft*: tasteful. A good film can be declared *stark*: strong. Eggs can be declared high in cholesterol. Cigarettes can be declared low in nicotine. Too many questions can be declared unhealthy. Passengers on the *U-Bahn* declare themselves honest, holding out tickets. Declaration eliminates stress. The day will be declared rainy; dirty; not nice. If the rain stops, the rain will be declared over, *vorbei*, the way history is declared over, *vorbei*, forgotten. The way umbrellas are declared unnecessary.

People declare themselves hungry. Tired. Lonely. Misunderstood. In love. Desirable. Old. New. Clean. Men will be declared lovers or boyfriends or husbands or fathers. Nobody can escape declarations; everything has to be given a title. Because declarations reduce the risk of misunderstanding. Because declaring what you want and what you are is a way of life here. And the worst pain in the world is not having a name for something.

When I entered the glass door of café Trödel, I could see immediately that nobody had arrived before me. I could declare myself the FIRST.

Berlin can no longer be declared the capital of Germany. Even though some people still like to call it the capital. Berlin is a city in East Germany. The part we keep talking about is called West Berlin. West Berlin is an island. It goes to show how things degenerate; how temporary titles are.

The reunification of Germany could be declared an old song.

Dieter could be called a Berliner, because people on both sides of the wall call themselves Berliners. But really, anyone can declare themselves a Berliner. Dieter, the man whom Helen has been looking for throughout Berlin, could be declared a strong swimmer. That's because he is well built, tall and glides through the water like a seal. Also because he has won trophies for swimming, when he was at school. In Ireland, he tried to teach Helen how to swim but she has to be declared a bad pupil. Her behaviour in the water is unnatural. And the sea around Ireland is too cold to learn in. Helen preferred to watch Dieter swimming because he could be declared a natural.

When something happens, all titles suddenly become shuffled and rearranged. All former titles and declarations are wiped out and replaced by new ones. Dieter has to be declared missing. Berlin has to be declared deep.

Helen's behaviour in Berlin has to be called unnatural.

Everything depends on what you call it. A name is like a cage.

Wolf and I talk about this kind of thing, late into the night, drinking, watching the room light up red at intervals of thirty seconds when the throbbing *Tischtelefon* sign comes on. Wolf's eyes light up like red cinders. His leg swings with excitement. Thinking must be like singing.

The wrong title can kill you, he says.

You should hear some of the things Wolf and Hadja call each

other. In public, she calls him a singer/songwriter. In public, he calls her his manager.

Titles are designed to subjugate, Wolf says.

What do you mean? I ask.

If you don't have a name for something, you're finished, he says.

Go on.

Things are dangerous until they are described. If you don't have a name for something, then you don't know what's happening, you're ignorant. It's the way the human mind originated, way back in primordial times, he says.

Wolf has an advantage over me there. He's been to the Free University of Berlin.

Way back, he says, all these primitive creatures ran around frightened of everything like stones and trees, wind, thunder, distance. Everything was a potential enemy. The way it was, if you passed by a jagged rock one day and later the same day a snake bit your wife, how do you know it wasn't the jagged rock you have to thank for it? Everything was crazy with fear and ignorance. Until they began to conquer the environment, explain things, declare a stone a stone and a tree a tree. It was the first real scientific approach. And anything they couldn't explain or find a name for, they simply called it God.

Hadja's father could be called a property developer. He owns several houses in a quarter of Berlin called Kreuzberg. Most of the buildings are in streets which are earmarked for redevelopment. Kreuzberg is a district of Berlin which is often affectionately called Klein Ankara: Little Ankara, run down, almost completely destroyed during the war and now inhabited to a large extent by immigrant Turks. One of Hadja's father's houses, the one in Grossbeerenstrasse where Hadja collects the rent, is occupied exclusively by Turks; some not even registered in Berlin. They could be declared illegal immigrants.

There are many Berliners who would declare themselves great Turkey fans. *Ich bin ein Fan*, they say. Lots of Berliners would give anything to go to Ankara or anywhere else in Turkey, but would never even consider going to Klein Ankara.

Cakes in Germany can be declared superior. The German tourist abroad can be declared a true explorer because he comes home with first-hand information and accurate comparisons. There is nothing in the world like *Apfelstrudel*, or Berliner balls.

Superiority is something that is universally respected. On the building site in West Germany, superiority belongs to the worker who can declare himself most eager to get the job done while at the same time declaring his colleagues less intelligent, clumsy and slow. This is not the way to get things done, he must repeatedly say to his colleagues around him, and then proceed to show them how it's done properly. It's a matter of presentation.

What is the point of intelligence? Wolf leans back in the sofa and holds up his bottle of Schultheis, ready to drink. For a moment I think he actually expects me to answer.

He leans forward again and takes a drink, and I'm left waiting and listening to the air bubbles jumping back into the bottle.

It's the ability to identify something by name, Wolf says. It's like putting a flag on the Matterhorn. Hitting the nail on the head. It's like calling a terrorist a terrorist, which doesn't make him disappear but it makes everybody feel that much safer in their beds. Taming by naming, if you like. The sky was made safe by calling it Heaven. Lions were made safe by calling them wild beasts. And everything else that couldn't be grasped, like infinity, space, death, was all lumped together with God. Some name had to be found for the unknown. Because they always felt safer knowing that there was something superior, something larger than themselves, the way we still like to think there is something bigger than us.

If you want somebody to disappear in Germany, you call him a name like *Arschloch*, or maybe *Schleimscheisser*, which is about the worst thing you could call anybody. No matter what Wolf calls Hadja, she never disappears completely.

West Berlin could be declared claustrophobic. Claustrophobia is a condition which affects people who feel threatened by limitations of space. But this has nothing to do with the Berlin Wall or the fact that West Berlin is an island. Claustrophobia in Berlin is caused by the sight of what other people have. The sight of what other people are, what you might have been yourself. Because everything depends on how you measure claustrophobia. In Germany, it is not measured by cubic feet or lack of space, but solely by proximity to other people. By personal space and private property.

Wolf talks about love. He declares it to be nothing but a symptom of claustrophobia.

He holds a new bottle of beer between his knees, making them look like an extra pair of hands. Then he whisks off the cap.

Love, he says, is just another one of these useless, non-specific, self-protective titles which we keep using all the time when we don't know what's happening around us. We feel peculiar so we call it love. And Wolf should know because he is a songwriter deeply concerned with the subject without ever allowing himself to use the word in his lyrics. What we call love, he says, is a mixture of insecurity, nostalgia, lack of choice, flu symptoms, nutritional deficiencies and unsquandered sex drive. Wolf says he can break any word down into unlimited components.

Kurfürstendamm can now be declared the main street of West Berlin. It is also at times called a fashion parade. This is where you will see women wearing priceless, once in a lifetime costumes, which are then put away in the wardrobe and replaced by new costumes equally priceless. This is where you see men with leather handbags. And women linking arms with men who smoke cigars. And all this is observed by immigrant workers who come in to the main street on rest days to see what the city has to offer.

A woman's nipples are private property. But along Kurfürsten-damm, private property causes claustrophobia. Whenever the nipples or legs or quivering buttocks of a woman are lit up through her cotton dress by the afternoon sun while walking along with her cigar-sucking partner, they beg to be shared. It cries out for socialism. Marxism. More private property can be seen walking down Ku-damm in five minutes than a *Gastarbeiter* would earn in a lifetime.

But then, Berlin provides many places which cure claustropho-bia, or at least temporarily alleviate it. For this purpose, there are many sex Kinos and sex shops, because sex is declared recreational and therapeutic, even cardiovascular. Because sex also temporarily reduces or increases the space and distance between two people.

It is a business in which the Tischtelefon establishment across the street from Wolf and Hadja's apartment specializes. Inside, there is a bar and a large salon with numbered tables. On each table there is an antique telephone which allows the customer to make contact with any other table of his choice. Over the phone you can discuss money and methods to reduce claustrophobia. Money is a pimp, Marx said.

It was claustrophobia which first made Wolf go to Ireland. He wanted to see the Atlantic. You can't miss it. He saw it stretched out in front of him, from the passenger seat of a car. *Mensch*, look at that, he said to himself. It wasn't enough. Only someone who suffers from claustrophobia could really know how he felt at the time. You keep searching for words and alternative titles. He said the Atlantic looked like grey elephant hide. It's a title that worked for him. The car went into a dip and the sea disappeared for a while, only to burst across his eyes again as they drove over the next brow. The driver of the car said very little and let him out at Milltown Malbay, where Wolf went for a drink alone. Some weeks later he met Hadja. The wide imprint of the sea burned the retina ever since, until he got back to Berlin and wrote a song about it. The song is called '*Atlanticsucht*': Atlantic-addiction.

You can do that in German. Just stick words together to make up a new title. Like *Schadenfreude*. And *Wahrheitsliebe*: truth-seeking. *Unschuldswunsch*: innocence-wish, or pre-holocaust-longing. There's a new word in Berlin lately. *Überfremdung*: Over-foreignization. Hadja calls herself names for Wolf. Like *Spasspferd-chen*: funhorse.

In the morning, Wolf and Hadja's apartment is filled with the aroma of fresh coffee and the previous night's titles are forgotten. Mostly, Wolf doesn't need titles because he just begins to play music again. And music is like an endless name for everything in the world, and a song is like a slow, revolving title, like an endless loop.

People think fast in the rain. It's a time for quick surveys of limited options. Helen knows how to get to café Trödel; it's not very far, but it happens to be raining convulsively, so she decides to make a

34

quick dash for a canopy at the corner of the street. She has no protection against the rain. It makes everyone else look rain-hostile.

Helen could be declared reflective. Her progress and present situation could be declared unplanned. Lacking in foresight. Her hair would be declared rain-damaged.

She walked out from under the canopy again with the childish principle that the faster you walk the less raindrops you meet. She passed a gift shop and a boutique, both steamed up with inner comfort, and then reached café Trödel, where the warm smell of baking hit her like a pillow. She passed the glass counter with rows of cakes and for an instant wanted to throw herself across them all. Then she saw me sitting in the centre of the café. I must have had a grin on my face.

You're soaked, I said. But that was a poor title for her at that particular moment. She looked as though she had just stepped out of a shower. And people who meet for breakfast look as though they've just stepped out of bed.

Jesus, I know, she said. It wasn't clear what she meant.

Have you been here long? she asked.

No! No more than ten minutes, I said.

I mean, in Berlin?

Oh! I laughed. I thought you meant . . . I've been here for over a year now. It's not bad. I like it here.

Could I be declared defensive? As though under pressure to account for myself?

I met Wolf in Ireland, I said. He gave me his Berlin address and here I am.

Could I be called a compulsive liar?

How about you? I asked. Did you know Wolf and Hadja from before?

No, she said. I met Hadja by accident.

Helen's eyes could be declared any of the following: lively, questioning, trust-inspiring. Open. Sad. She has eyes that seem to have a tale to tell. But they also deflect enquiry. Her questions tell a lot more than her answers.

Tell me, she said. What's Hadja really like? She's been very good to me but I can't make her out at all.

I kept looking down at the table, then back to Helen's eyes, then at the waitress, who always seems to be on her way to the table, then back to Helen's eyes again. Could I be declared equivocal?

Hadja's great, I said. But she's not one to argue with. I've seen her cut people down to size. I've seen her shout it out with a policeman in the street. And I've seen her argue with Wolf, I said. She's dangerous.

Don't I know, Helen said.

You hear them all the time, I said.

They're not easy to live with, she said. All that shouting.

Helen and I were nodding in agreement. I listened and said things like, Absolutely, or, I can imagine. She knew that I was a friend of Wolf and Hadja, but she assumed that I had more in common with her than with them. And people who nod in agreement over breakfast could be declared intimate. Helen said she didn't like staying with Wolf and Hadja.

What brought you to Berlin? I asked abruptly. It forces Helen to make a declaration of intent.

It's a long story, she said.

Well, there's no rush, I said, smiling down at the table.

Food can be declared a distraction.

The waitress arrived with a stainless steel tray with plates, cups, cutlery, coffee, scrambled eggs and tomatoes, rolls and strawberry jam, all of which she arranged on the table in a matter of seconds. She did it all silently, as though she resented the intimacy between people at breakfast. *Guten Appetit*, she said, and disappeared.

I cracked one of the white rolls as though I was carefully breaking the back of some small animal. Helen waited for me to do everything first, then followed suit. I eat without chewing properly. I could be called voracious. Helen chewed thoughtfully, as though it helped her to remember. She's a slow eater. Breakfast can be declared intimate. And people who eat together in the morning look like they've slept together.

Actually, I'm looking for somebody in Berlin, Helen said.

Who?

Scrambled eggs don't need to be chewed.

Well, it's a guy from Berlin that I knew in Dublin. We were

together for a long time. I've got some information for him. That's all.

Helen looked as though she was reading what she said off her plate.

Do you know where he is? I asked.

I've looked everywhere so far, she said. Berlin is a big place.

I'll help you look for him if you like, I offered instinctively.

Helen said nothing. Just kept chewing slowly.

What kind of information? I asked.

The kind of information men don't always want to hear, it seems.

I'll risk it, I said, smiling again.

Could I be declared naive?

This is a description of the missing man, Dieter. Tall. Berliner. Friendly. Good swimmer. Light brown hair. Wearing a green jacket and black lace-up boots. Last seen in Dublin in March. Last seen in Berlin from a bus. Irrational when it comes to relationships with people. Ignorant of the knowledge that he might be a father.

This is how Helen got pregnant. While she was still living in Dublin with Dieter, on her way home from work one evening, she stepped off the 46A bus and walked as far as Kearney's, the grocer shop. There she bought a loaf of white bread and sardines as well as the evening paper. She walked back to the flat and found Dieter was not back yet. She assumed he was out for a walk. Or out on his bike. She placed the bread she had just bought on a wooden board, cut the heel because she felt hungry and couldn't wait, buttered it and began to eat it. She opened the evening paper and began to look at the ads. Articles for sale. Articles wanted. She heard Dieter wheel the bicycle into the hallway and begin to ascend the stairs. She filled the kettle with water. She knew she was pregnant but she said nothing.

Berlin could be declared vast. Berlin could be declared tax-efficient. A sanctuary for draft dodgers. A city of old people. A trendy address. The edge of the West.

Hadja and Wolf could be declared made for each other. Hadja's hair could be declared russett. Her future rosy.

Berlin could be declared hospitable. Turks in Germany could be declared guests. *Gastarbeiter*. Berlin is said to have two skies.

Helen and I could be declared immediate friends. Friends can be declared desperate. The way chance can be declared part of a plan. Café Trödel can be said to be in the past. Helen could be declared advancing. Tauentzienstrasse can be declared too long to walk. Berlin could be declared slow. The time of year, fast approaching summer.

4

Street Light

Things were beginning to get a bit hot over in Wolf and Hadja's place. I could see it coming. I could see it was not a good place for a pregnant woman to stay. It was only a matter of time before Hadja caught on to Wolf and the apartment would become uninhabitable, thrown into open warfare. Wolf had begun to mess around with a student called Lydia; meeting her in the afternoons in cafés, or at night. And because I work so closely with Wolf, I know what's going on all the time. I was there when he first met this woman, Lydia. Wolf tells me everything. The trouble is that Hadja has also begun to realize that, which is why she comes to me whenever she wants to know something about Wolf, and I have to be very careful what I say.

At the end of the month, Wolf has a big concert on at the Aula Max in the Free University of Berlin. The posters have been up for some time now. Wolfgang Ebers: *Liedermacher*. Hadja has been doing most of the work so far. The phone never stops ringing in their apartment, and she is working herself into a frenzy, organizing newspaper coverage, more posters etc. Everything she achieves has to be acknowledged and spoken about, otherwise she is likely to fly into a rage. There is a genuine excitement in the apartment, because this is an important time for Wolf. The Aula Max is a big one. But the tension has also increased hundredfold. Which is why I think Wolf has picked a really bad time to have a fling with Lydia. It's none of my business, but I can see what's coming.

One thing was certain; Hadja and Wolf's place was no place for Helen. I could see Hadja's suspicion. There would be war. I told Helen she could stay in the spare room at Sonnenallee until she found a place of her own. I said it to her a few times, casually. I wasn't pushing her. I just thought things would be quieter in my apartment because I'm hardly ever there. She thanked me and said she would think it over, and I could only presume that she was still thinking of going back home; that she wasn't going to stay in Berlin since she hadn't found who she was looking for. Anyhow, the offer stood and I said no more. But I took the precaution of telling Wolf never to bring Lydia around to my apartment, even in the afternoon. Besides, I didn't want Hadja discovering them in my apartment; the apartment which Hadja had given me. I was too much a collaborator already.

You have to know who your real boss is. I work with Wolf. I'm a lighting operator. I also do the sound for him at times, but my real occupation is lighting. If I wanted to give myself a real title I would be calling myself lighting consultant. Since Hadja has become manager, it is she who pays my wages and she who determines everything I do, so I can't really ignore the reality that she is my employer. I do some odd jobs for her as well, whenever she asks. For instance, once a week she goes over to collect the rent in one of her father's houses and she needs an escort. I'd say she would be a lot tougher than me if anything were to happen, but she likes the idea of male security. And I'm not really in a position to refuse work, particularly when Wolf can't justify a full-time lighting operator yet. So I'm a bit of everything at the moment. Lighting op. Sound op. Roadie. Bodyguard. Rent collector.

I did have a full-time job in lighting with one of the opera houses here in Berlin. But that only lasted for three months. I was in charge of one spotlight, and every night, at a given time, I was expected to direct the spot on one man, the broad-chested Don Giovanni, as he prepared to go to Hell. That was a good job. Working for Wolf is even better.

Before that I worked with a stage and location lighting company with nothing on its mind but lighting fashion shows and fashion photography. We were expected to think of models only in terms of how their legs could be lit up for maximum effect while providing for sufficient shadows to maintain the myth. I was assigned to a photographer who dealt only with women. A little more Bermuda on her left, he would say to me. Or else he'd say: Give her the Michelangelo from the top. His lighting directions were atmospheric. He would assess the wardrobe, assess the girls and then call out lighting instructions which I was meant to understand by instinct. London rain with Ugandan oranges. Or else, if he wanted a model lit from underneath, he would ask for her to be river-reflected. Float her on the Nile, he would say.

With another photographer I once had the pleasure of lighting up the set for the portrait of a prominent industrialist whose left ear had been damaged during the war. He asked us not to show his bad side. So I blew that left ear off altogether with darkness.

Wolf is turning me into a liar. Every lie that he tells Hadja is backed up by my silence. How can he elude suspicion? The truth of his affair with Lydia must be written on his face. Or written on my face.

Lydia has high cheekbones. She is best lit from above. Her blonde hair and hazel eyes might benefit from a blue glare on the left. With proper lighting, I could make her look more pensive, more mature and perhaps more hurt looking. I could give her eyes more substance; make her look older and less like a student. With a strong backlight, I could give her a Polish grandmother, or some Russian origins at least.

Wolf says she looks very different without her clothes.

Nakedness is a sign of intimacy. It can also be a sign of hostility, which amounts to the same thing. Whenever football supporters expose their backsides to pedestrians from passing buses, it must be a gesture of affection and defiance at the same time. Whenever Hadja walks around the apartment naked, it becomes a show of friendship and fearlessness at the same time. A sign of territorial advantage.

On the morning that Helen decided to move out of Wolf and Hadja's place, this is just what happened. The phone rang in the hallway and Hadja went to answer it without any clothes on. It's summer, of course, but that's no reason. Hadja spoke for a while on the phone as though she were fully clothed, and the person on the other end of the line couldn't possibly have known that Hadja was naked, leaning against the wall, occasionally running the flat of her hand across her stomach and occasionally running the sole of her foot along her shin.

Helen was in the kitchen. The door was open, giving her a full view of Hadja's broad bottom as she argued on the phone.

Helen had already been to the shop to buy fresh rolls. She had made coffee and was having breakfast. She had her clothes on, which makes it very obvious when somebody else doesn't. The smell of fresh coffee must have challenged Hadja's nostrils, because instead of going back to her bedroom, she went straight into the kitchen and sat down.

Ah – Kaffee, she said, reaching up into the cupboard for a cup.

Hadja has very large breasts. Sheer size is enough sometimes to attract attention. And they cannot fail to entrap Helen, who has small breasts herself, into a grotesque fascination. Large breasts are hard to believe, even with your own eyes. The same way that hostility is hard to believe, even if it is compelling and you can't stop looking for it once you see it.

Hadja took one of the fresh rolls and cracked it open with two thumbs. Placed a piece of *Wurst* in the middle and began to eat. She groaned with satisfaction at the first bite.

I'm starving, she said. Bouncing makes you hungry, she added with her mouth full. Then she laughed.

Helen found it hard to believe what she heard. She stopped eating, because eating is such an impulsive thing and it's so easy to put a pregnant woman off eating. Helen could only look at Hadja's huge breasts, which were staring back at her.

Scheisse, Hadja said. They promised the extra posters this morning. Now I won't have them until this evening.

Hadja speaks as though everyone is interested in what she has to say. The same way that she thinks her body would be attractive to everyone. Helen sipped her coffee. She had something on her mind.

Hadja, she said. There's something I have to tell you.

Yes. What is it?

I've found a new place to stay, Helen said. Then, almost as though she wanted to retract an unintended insult, she thanked Hadja for everything she had done. But there was also that sense of joy associated with leaving things behind.

Oh, well, that's great, Hadja said. I'm delighted for you. Where are you moving to?

Helen hesitated.

Well, she said. I've been offered a room in Alan Craig's apartment. He's got lots of space and I think it will be quieter over there.

Hadja immediately began to laugh out loud. Her breasts were flung around, even sideways with laughter. She leaned back so that Helen began to think it was Hadja's breasts that were doing all the laughing.

Into Alan Craig's apartment . . . Hadja chanted. This I cannot believe.

Did you hear that, Wolf? Hadja went on speaking and laughing into the hallway. She's moving in with Alan Craig.

But Wolf was already pushing out the first alphabet of notes through his saxophone in the sitting room.

That day, everything seemed to Helen like the end of a film. In the afternoon, she stood alone for a moment in the hallway of Wolf and Hadja's place, thinking quite consciously that this was the end of something. Something was over. Then she walked out and shut the door behind her. She had to shut the door three times. It wasn't that easy. And later on, she stood for a moment in the darker, far narrower hallway of my apartment in Sonnenallee. She didn't have many belongings. She brought some groceries; cheese, eggs, a jar of strawberry jam and some fresh mayonnaise, which, she said, should go straight into the fridge.

Some people would call me a light-jockey. Same as a DJ except with lights. But I prefer lighting operator as a title. My job is to illuminate chosen objects. To present everything with a swollen look.

A spotlight is like an extended eye or an antenna which gives a preliminary, unspoken name to everything it touches.

Berlin bei Nacht. I've seen most of Berlin by night. Sometimes, working in the music business with Wolf, I don't see much daylight at all. I've often come home first thing in the morning; on the first *U-Bahn*, with people beginning to go to work. Things are so silent in the morning. It's too bright. And people make you feel like you're going in the wrong direction. Even if I changed places with them I'd feel I was going in the wrong direction.

On the way home in the morning, I often see people out with their dogs for an early walk. One morning, walking through Schöneberg, I passed a man with two poodles. But there was something about him that made me think he wasn't the owner; something awkward, something in the way he looked into the distance down towards Innsbrücker Platz. He was a Turk. I knew by the cheekbones, brown eyes and moustache. It must have been part of his job to walk his owner's dogs. There was something strained and unnatural about his appearance. He was too tall to own poodles.

Nobody ever looks comfortable doing somebody else's job.

Early in the morning, the first signs of daylight often make things look idiotic and irrelevant. The lights, which looked so good all over the city at night, begin to pale and weaken in the morning. Light is a fraud. In the morning, everything you see is reduced to half its size. Everything swells under lights.

I walked down Tauentzienstrasse with Helen one night. We were larger than life, swollen in the oncoming lights of traffic. We walked slowly, just talking about things; noticing Berlin the way visitors do. The sky must have covered over with clouds, because there was a reddish hue above us, reflecting the glow of the city. The lights of the street must have flooded our faces as we walked. Neon faces. As we got on the *U-Bahn* at Wittenbergplatz, the strong brightness in the carriage seemed to force a universal equality and silence on all passengers.

Frontiers and border checkpoints are always well lit. Available light is seldom enough to demarcate boundaries. There is a strip along the Berlin Wall which hasn't seen darkness in years. The powerful floodlights come on at the slightest hint of twilight, making it look like a football stadium at night.

Everything ages rapidly under light.

When we got back to the apartment in Sonnenallee, we sat down at the round table in the sitting room with a cup of tea. I left the window open and the lights off. Only the light from the kitchen seeped around the door. It was enough for us to see each other and to keep talking about anything that came into our heads. Helen talked about her father and mother. Her brother. Her uncles. I talked about work. Music. Friends I had. One by one, outside in the courtyard, we could see the lights of neighbouring apartments being switched off.

Helen still couldn't believe that the light goes off inside the fridge when you shut the door. She never will. Her brother explained it to

44

her when she was young, but she never believed it. Which goes to show that you can believe something and not believe it at the same time. The same way that you can voluntarily allow yourself to do something you've been telling yourself not to do all along. I told her there was no way out but for her to get inside the fridge and shut the door.

Helen is light-sensitive. She turns her back instinctively on strong headlights as though light caused pain. She flinches when lights are switched on. She knows that light can be used as a weapon because she remembers her brother going out at night when they were down in the country at their uncle's house near a river where the local boys used to go and blind fish with torches and then gaff them. Her brother used to tell her a lot about fishing. He told her why fish usually have freckled backs and white bellies, so they can't be seen from above or below.

Helen has a fair complexion. Curly hair. Large round eyes. A smile that hints towards the left. Wears little jewellery; a ring, a watch and a chain at most. Her clothes are practical bordering on festive. Her hands are small and thin. Other distinguishing features: vertical forehead, white skin and a lot of freckles, mainly around her shoulders and arms. She is light-shy. Undresses away from the light and turns her back. She likes to leave a light or even a radio on long after she falls asleep.

Hadja phoned me early one morning and asked me if I knew about it. I was only half awake at the time but I knew immediately what she was on about. It had to happen. I just act dumb.

What?

This woman?

What woman?

Wolf's woman, who else? Come on, Alan. Don't act stupid.

Wolf's woman?

Come on, Alan, I want to know everything. Am I the last to find out about it? I suppose the whole world knows except me. And you knew all along and wouldn't tell me either.

Hadja, what are you talking about? I still wasn't sure if she was bluffing or not.

You know what I'm talking about, she said. I'm talking about Lydia Stanjeck. That is her name, isn't it?

Look, Hadja, I said. This is none of my business really. I don't interfere with anybody's private life.

Alan, don't move. I'm coming over, she said. I want to talk to you about this. I'll be there in ten minutes.

Not all light is an improvement. If you shone a hand torch at the Berlin Wall under the floodlights, would it add to the brightness the way a glass of water would add to the volume of the sea, or is light something that duplicates?

Hadja was breathless when she arrived at my apartment. Breathless because there is no lift in the block. She came in and sat down at the round table without a word. Some of the breakfast things were still on the table. There was a plate with a ransacked eggshell and some scattered salt. I took them all away and asked Hadja if she wanted coffee or tea. Helen wasn't up yet.

When I came back from the kitchen with coffee in my hand, I saw Hadja sitting straight, rigidly looking down at a photograph she had just taken from her bag. She looked up at me with accusation in her face. But she waited until I had poured the coffee until she stuck the photo out towards me.

Is this her? she asked, looking intensely into my eyes.

I wouldn't know, Hadja, honestly, I said. I don't know why you're asking me these things.

Come on, Alan, don't be a fool, she said. You know everything Wolf does. You're with him all the time. Tell me, is that her?

Look, Hadja, why don't you ask Wolf himself? It's nothing to do with me.

No answer is also an answer. Hadja must have been able to read my mind because she withdrew the photograph and replaced it in her bag.

I don't want him to know that I know, she said. The bastard. I'll get him for this. Whatever you do, Alan, don't tell him that I know who she is or anything. Tell him nothing, you hear?

Everything that Hadja does is designed to give her answers. She looked around the apartment. She saw boxes by the window in which I keep my equipment; spare bulbs, cables, switches, spots, lighting mixer. Beside an armchair, she would have seen Helen's shoes. Hadja looked out over the courtyard. She must have seen herself as the former occupant of the apartment. It must have reminded her of certain things. Early days. But her mind was blocked with one single thought.

Say nothing to Wolf, she said. Is that clear? Not a word. I'll get him for this.

Everything can be turned into an advantage. Hadja has the skill to reverse any disadvantage, no matter what the circumstances.

I wish I could say the same for myself. Instead, sometimes I am convinced that it is the person who acts who becomes the victim. It's the person who operates the lights who gets blinded. There I was throwing the spotlights on Don Giovanni every night for months, but after a while I found it was me who was going down to Hell every time. Same way that I now feel trapped because I know what's going to happen to Wolf. The game is up. Hadja is on to him.

The house owned by Hadja's father in Kreuzberg is a six-storey building with a peeling façade. It is expected to be re-zoned for development in a few years, so there is no point in making any improvements. The house resembles a village in Turkey, a vertical village or mountain village where each apartment holds a family or group of immigrant workers. They have come to Germany to work and support their families back home. Some of the apartments are subdivided into rooms or simply into bed spaces where men with magnificent moustaches sit up smoking and pay their rent without a word. Every apartment has a radio or a cassette recorder beating out the wild pulse of Turkish music. Not all the occupants have brown eyes and magnificent moustaches. Not all of them have work permits in Germany. Not all of them are proud to announce their own names.

Men without names work mostly for Hadja's brother now at various building sites around the city. Otherwise, they don't exist. Not on any list. Not on any payroll. Their rent is deducted at source. Part of their remuneration is the ongoing promise of legal status, which they respect with eager complicity; an intimate collusion with employer/landlord.

47

The least attractive apartments are situated on the ground floor in order of proximity to the toilet, from which a deadly stink emerges to fill the corridor. Passage beyond the main hallway demands determination and swift walking. The most desirable apartments, by contrast, are on the top floor, where the toilet door is kept locked and the key is handed over from one apartment to another with the greatest circumspection. As a result, there is also a slight disparity in the rent from top to bottom. The occupants on the top floor are also further removed from the small courtyard to the side of the house, which is more often used as a dump. In spite of adequate municipal rubbish collections, the residents of this house in Grossbeerenstrasse pile discarded items like broken furniture into the yard. Sometimes it goes so far that the occupants on the upper floor simply have to throw their rubbish out of the window. Eventually, the house is declared a health hazard, when cats, or rats, begin to proliferate among the rubbish, and the municipal authorities assign a group of workers, mostly Turks, to clear it up.

Under the stairs one time, Hadja and I found children playing with a dead cat; poking it with sticks. A dead cat looks even more like a cat, except shrunken.

Hadja normally buys me coffee and a slice of cake with cream after collecting the rent. I suppose it's to erase the thought of squalor.

It's none of my business, I told her once, but I thought she was a bit desperate if she had to exploit her own people like that. Then she spoke clearly once and for all on the issue. I probably wouldn't believe it, she said, but her father was actually doing these people a great favour. Did I not realize, she went on, that each immigrant had the earning power to keep almost a whole village alive back in Turkey?

We never discuss the house in Grossbeerenstrasse any more. Hadja is not one to argue with.

The Berlin Wall only comes into its own at night. Far more festive and convincing, which goes to show that it's really the floodlights that create the frontier. Otherwise, it might be forgotten.

There are more lights than inhabitants in Berlin. Street lights, shop lights which stay on all night, headlights, spotlights on the Remem-

48

brance Church, porch lights, elevator lights and thousands of apartment lights with which people remind themselves of their own existence, their own limitations.

At the back of Tischtelefon, there is a smaller salon with a bar and a stage which presents an hourly striptease act. The lighting is important. It is minimal. A small red bulb, the size of a pearl or a clitoris and set in a corresponding place on the black V-shaped briefs of a dancer, goes on and off to the pulse of the music. It attracts the eyes of the audience, mostly men, mostly with magnificent moustaches and brown eyes in which the tiny red light is reflected. The place is otherwise very discreetly lit. Because things often perish under light. Imagination perishes in the light. Daylight kills.

I noticed a new row of posters right outside the entrance to the university as I walked in. Wolfgang Ebers! Wolfgang Ebers! He looks different in duplicate. And the posters are really superfluous because the concert was a complete sellout anyway.

I spent the morning setting up the lighting rigs. We had hired extra sets of colour spots so it took a lot longer than usual. But it's going to look a lot more impressive too. I just worked quietly beside the sound operator Willy, from Westphalen. Hadja was in early as well.

In the afternoon, Wolf arrived for a sound and light check. He insists on choreographing the sound and light show for the performance in advance, which suits me because everything is perfectly planned out. No room for hitches. It's an important concert. Hadja was everywhere. She's even more fussy than I am. She's a perfectionist. She stood by and watched the whole rehearsal. All afternoon, I couldn't get near Wolf on his own. I wanted to get some kind of message to him. Eventually, I was able to slip into the toilets after him to give him a small warning.

She's on to you, Wolf, I told him. And I wonder sometimes why I was so loyal to him. He didn't seem surprised at all. He remained calm, almost impervious. I suppose he had more on his mind at the time. Perhaps he could think of nothing else but his music.

Wolf, do you hear me? Hadja knows about you and Lydia, I said.

There is a strange loyalty or comradeship between men when they piss in parallel at urinals. There are these duplicitous sideways and downward glances: fraternal acknowledgement. Otherwise there is little else to look at except the tiles in front of you.

I see, Wolf said, staring at a tile only inches away from his eyes. So Hadja knows. Yes ... well just play along with her. Don't worry. Just play along.

When I got back to the rig later on, the Aula was beginning to fill up. Hadja was there already. She was rushing around the auditorium, and when she came up to me, she handed me the photograph of Lydia. Why was she giving me the photograph? I refused it. She insisted. And then I realized that it was a duplicate, one of which she had also given to Willy, the sound operator, and to each of the security men as well.

If you see her, let me know immediately, she said.

I put the photograph away and ignored it. It's none of my business. The next I saw of Wolf was when he arrived on stage with his guitar. Wolf is fond of the light. He wouldn't be a professional singer if he didn't have such a high tolerance for exposure. It's good to work with somebody who is not light-shy.

The Aula was jammed. There were people standing along the aisles to the side. I occasionally caught sight of Hadja near the doors or down at the front of the stage. She had free movement throughout the auditorium. Wolf's fifth song was the one about the Atlantic. I had the list in front of me. Not that I really have time to listen to the songs any more when I'm working. They merely become reference points for specific lighting performance. The Atlantic song gets a cold, blue background while Wolf is picked out in a strong white spot. I can make him stand right on the edge of the Cliffs of Moher. And if I switched off the white spot, he would disappear; the audience would think he had fallen in. Wolf's face is serious as he sings, as though he is singing out into a strong wind that carries a trace of salt.

I noticed Hadja coming up beside me, but I concentrated on the end of the song where the light is meant to fade like an accelerated sunset.

I have her, she whispered. I have the bitch.

A moment later, the song was over and the Aula broke into unified applause. Wolf disappeared in semi-darkness.

I have the bitch, Hadja kept whispering to me. More like

50

shouting. I pretended not to hear her, but I kept hearing the word bitch, so I eventually had to listen.

There, at the door, she shouted as the applause began to die down. There she is at the door.

I want you to put the spot on her, Hadja demanded.

I didn't move.

Put the spot on her, she demanded again.

I can't do that, I said. I pretended to look busy. The applause had ceased.

Put the spot on her, she repeated. I will do it FUCKING myself, if you don't.

It was no time to laugh at a linguistic mistake. I knew she was serious. I did what she asked and turned the spot.

Lydia was picked out beautifully in a thin white beam. The rest of the lights were left on very low. The house lights were out. The applause died out completely and left a vacuum. The sound was switched off, too, which left Wolf without a mike, and nothing to say.

I was almost proud of Lydia, blinded by the force of the spotlight and by the eyes of the audience who followed the light and looked around at her. Lydia didn't move. She stood still. If she had moved sideways by a metre, she would have fallen out of light.

5

Kiss Bite

So far, Helen had done everything right. She had removed herself from Hadja's influence. She had registered her own name as an inhabitant of Berlin, at Sonnenallee. And she had kept up her constant inquiries about Dieter; twice more she visited Dieter's mother in Steglitz, but came away with nothing new.

Next thing was to get a job. Helen was adamant from the very beginning that she would pay her way; contribute her own share of the rent at Sonnenallee while she was looking for Dieter. If the worst happened and she didn't find him, she would start looking for her own place. For the moment, she needed money. Within a week she had a job at Weinstube, in the city centre, close to the opera and the theatre. The Berlin Weinstube belongs to a chain of restaurants around Germany. Helen's job was to prepare vegetables, stack crockery and sometimes to operate the dishwasher. Her hours were from two in the afternoon until half past twelve or one in the morning, depending on how busy the restaurant got. It left her with plenty of time to pursue her inquiries by day.

At first, I let Helen get on with her life. Whenever we met, at breakfast or over lunch, she told me what she was doing. She wasn't getting very far. Occasionally, she came down to Bar-o-Bar to meet us after work. Wolf had a residency at the Bar-o-Bar. I became interested, to see if she had any success. She would not give up. Somehow, she never doubted that she would eventually find Dieter. She had a contagious determination. I began to help her.

I suggested the Polizei Präsidium. The tax office. The AOK health insurance company and any other institution that might have had a record of Dieter's name on their files. I helped her out with the German. Made phone-calls for her. Most of the time we came up with a false trail. There was somebody else by the name of Dieter Penzholz in Berlin; an old man. Eventually, we tracked Helen's Dieter down to a garage called Rennbahn. But he had quit some time ago. Once more it seemed like a dead end. But Helen

52

was determined enough to get up one morning and go there. She was going to talk to every mechanic at the garage to see what they knew. I went with her. I had little to do in the morning. The reception staff knew nothing. I watched the mechanics shake their heads one after another until one of them remembered something. Pension Potsdam. It was a slim lead.

We sat down in a small, busy café around lunchtime to discuss the strategy from there on. We began to treat the whole thing like a British/American detective story. Helen was able to sit back and laugh at her own situation. It was her own determination that allowed us to joke about it. We inserted imitations of the best-known TV investigators. I hummed signature tunes from TV serials. We laughed a good bit. The clatter of cups and saucers and spoons was extraordinary. The espresso machine hissed and exploded in the background. There was no chance that anyone could overhear us.

Leave it to me, I said, with an exaggerated intensity. My voice was artificially deep and brave.

Helen laughed.

No, Alan, she said, artificially worried. You can't go alone.

I'll find him, I said, looking straight out through the plate-glass window into the street.

A detective's only weapon is his imagination. The purpose of the imagination is to reconstruct. The purpose of a joke is to clear the way.

Let me go with you, she said, grinning.

Somebody shouted, *Zwei Mocca und zwei Espresso*. The clatter of cups started up again. I shook my head.

No, Alan . . . Don't be a hero, she said. Then sniggered.

The purpose of a joke is to tell the truth. A disguise for honesty. The purpose of a joke is to provide mutual trust and something to hide behind. *In risu veritas*.

Helen reminded me that she would soon have to make her way to work. It was half past one. I told her it would only take five minutes to get to Weinstube from there. Then we spoke seriously for a moment. I told her I didn't think I should go to Pension Potsdam with her. It was probably better if she went alone.

I mean, I don't think it's a good idea for Dieter to see us arriving together. You never know, he might start getting ideas about the two of us.

Don't be stupid, she said.

Well, after all, I said. We are sharing the same apartment, aren't we. He's entitled to have his suspicions.

What? she said, verging on anger. He is the last person entitled to ask questions. It's me who'll be asking the questions.

What are you going to say to him?

I don't know yet, she said.

Are you going to tell him about us, then? I asked.

Helen looked at me. She didn't seem to think it was relevant. She drank the last of her coffee. The espresso machine sounded as though it was in pain.

To be totally honest, Helen, I said. I don't understand how Dieter can do this to you. It beats me how anyone can treat you like this.

The purpose of honesty is to say far more than you meant to say. To show your hand. Helen looked at me again. At my eyes, that is. She was going to say something, but she got up to go instead. I watched her walking down the street towards Weinstube. You forget that she's pregnant.

The following day, Helen made her own way to Pension Potsdam to find Dieter. I met her in the evening at Bar-o-Bar. She came in after work and I saw her sitting down. She looked tired. As soon as I had a free moment I sat down with her and got her an apple juice. She can't drink beer.

She told me how the people at Pension Potsdam had been very offensive. She hadn't understood what they were saying to her. Dieter was no longer staying there; she gathered that much. But the porter on reception refused to give her any information. He kept demanding money: 200 marks. He showed Helen Dieter's bag, which he was keeping, apparently against arrears on the bill. It wasn't the first time Dieter had left a hotel without paying. That much didn't surprise her. But she couldn't understand why the manager wouldn't let her examine the bag to see if she could find a new address for Dieter. The manager just kept throwing his arms up and saying: *Interessiert mich nicht*: doesn't interest me! He wrote the figure 200 on the reception counter with his index finger and said no more.

I'll go down and sort them out, I said.

The purpose of bravery is to go too far.

Information is worth money. 200 DM.

Germany is a country with a vast trade in information. The Gross National Product is entirely based on the commercial exchange of information. A person will pay anything for the right facts. People even pay not to receive information; they pay to be kept in the dark and go to the opera or to the Schiller Theater. Vast industries have been built around this internal trade in facts. Employ the theory of relativity and it seems as though all property and ownership status remains completely static. It's not property that changes hands, but information. It's the only thing that changes your position in the world. It's what makes people lucky or unlucky. Lucky people are obsessed by misfortune. Unfortunate people are obsessed by luck.

What is the purpose of pregnancy? Is it self-preservation? What is the purpose of sex? Self-preservation or an exchange of information? Eugenics?

Weinstube is the name of a restaurant chain in Germany which sells information. Its first and foremost purpose is to sell German wines from the south: Mosel, Rhein, Niersteiner. But it also sells ambience and food, the purpose of which is purely informational. It's like selling Germany to the Germans. The information is chunky, traditional, warm, *gastfreundlich*. The entire Weinstube cellar gives the impression of weighty, timbered interiors, much like a medieval banqueting hall, with heavy oak tables and chairs covered with embroidered cushions.

The waitresses are costumed in traditional *Dirndl*. Over the *Dirndl*, they wear white aprons stippled with the crested name of Weinstube. Their white blouses are ruched naturally around the shoulders and around the bosom. The overall effect once again is one of bulk and generosity. Nowhere does the copper lighting work better than in emphasizing the maternal warmth in the cleavage of the Weinstube waitress. The Weinstube waitress has the skill to open a bottle of wine by gripping it between her knees. The uncorking sends a ripple across the bosom. Helen would have got a job as a waitress if only she had more German.

But Helen works behind the scenes, in the kitchen. At no point does the information from the kitchen spill over into the restaurant. At no point will it be necessary for the kitchen staff to enter the restaurant. At no point will the waitress be required to enter the kitchen. The carrots will be chopped at an angle. The bread will be laid in a stairway of slices in the bread basket. Food is a logo. The parsley must not be forgotten. The dishwasher will at all times be set on the operational setting A. At no point will hygiene regulations be circumvented, white chef hats be removed, food be recycled, dishes reheated or harsh words spoken through the serving hatch where they might be overheard in the restaurant. The kitchen staff will remain anonymous. Separate staff toilets ensure segregation according to bylaws. Hygiene is nothing but information. How can you boast something that goes without saying?

The information from the restaurant continually flows back into the kitchen, particularly after ten in the evening, when everybody emerges from the opera and the theatres. There is a babble of conversation, laughter, wine glasses and the music. Mendelssohn; Chopin; the mandolin concertos; violins; flutes; piano duets. Corks pop. Glasses ring. Women laugh. Men say *Bitte*, *Bitte*. The waitresses call numbers through the serving hatch, and once again the Pachelbel Canon, a distant, high-pitched, dropping violin, much like the sound extracted from a wine glass by rubbing a moist index finger around the circular rim. The kitchen staff is made up of two men and two women: Lothar, the German chef; Assar, the commis chef; Fatma, the woman who operates the dishwasher; and Helen. Helen's job description is *Aushilfe*: help out. Kitchen work eliminates gender. You forget that Helen is a woman.

I called around to Weinstube to collect Helen after work. I promised to walk over to Pension Potsdam with her, to see what the problem was. Why they wouldn't give her Dieter's bag. Maybe there was some way of bargaining with them. Maybe I was going with her not so much to achieve anything as to prove that there was nothing to be gained.

The restaurant was closed by the time I got there. Helen came out through the heavy oak door and we walked along the half-wet pavement together. It had rained earlier, perhaps selectively, because there were wet patches and dry patches. We had a strong purpose together, Helen and I. A strange sense of determination which combined us like a couple, with a story, or a mutual biography. Even though we were out to look for the father of her baby, we must have looked much more like partners, walking along the empty streets of Berlin. It was late. People were asleep. The lights were out and shutters were down. Though nobody ever seems entirely asleep behind shutters at night. You got the impression that everyone was waiting for dawn, awake in the dark, listening to people passing by in the street below, talking.

Helen talked about work; Weinstube, what else? She described the methodical task of slicing twenty or thirty loaves of caraway bread first thing every day and laying them in ascending order in baskets. The repetition of preparing vegetables and stacking delft. She described it all with great enthusiasm. It was the MOST boring thing on earth. The WORST thing was clearing the plates. They don't even TALK to each other in the kitchen. Helen seemed excited to tell me about it. Even the most menial things make thrilling information.

You should get out of there, I told her.

I'd love to, but I need the money, she said.

You deserve better than that.

There was a smell of rain in the streets. For some reason I thought rain smelled like new electrical appliances; a new toaster or a new heater. A car ripped through an adjacent street. We passed by a joinery with high gates. A guard dog threw himself against the gates as we passed, and Helen got a fright. Through small openings in the gates, we could see the dog inside, barking silently. He must have had his larynx removed.

We walked on. We were getting near Potsdamerstrasse. There was something on my mind which I wanted to tell Helen; something I felt had to be said. I had said it before to myself. Then I stopped, and she walked two or three steps further before she realized, and turned.

I really don't know how anyone can do this to you, I said.

She seemed to have anticipated it. She smiled.

I don't know how he can treat you like this, I said. I mean, why couldn't he at least tell you or talk to you about it instead of disappearing and hiding out like this?

It seemed amusing to Helen even to begin to discuss this in the street, in the middle of the night. But then, she must have guessed the real question behind my inquiries. Why was she willing to accept it? How could she put up with this? We stood there looking at each other.

Alan, you don't understand, she said. Dieter must have something on his mind. He doesn't realize he's a father yet.

So what's he running from then?

Who knows? she said.

He's a fool if you ask me, I said. Any man would give his right arm to take his place. I can tell you that much.

In Helen's defence, I felt entitled to attack Dieter. I got to like her. I hated to see her being pushed around. She acknowledged my point and stepped towards me, taking hold of my arm.

It's funny, she said. But you can't just forget somebody overnight. I don't know what it is. Maybe it's the baby. Maybe it's just me. But I feel I've got to find Dieter at least and tell him. I've got a duty at least to let him know, even if he doesn't want to know.

Well look, Helen, I said. I want you to know this much. I'll do anything to help you. I mean that. I want to help you out. But I'm not going to watch you being messed around. I draw the line there. I'm not going to look at him treating you like a piece of dirt.

You're a different person altogether, she said, staring up into my eyes.

Helen is a bit smaller than I am. She placed her head against my chest and put her arms around my waist as though she was going to measure me. She pulled tight and let go again. I placed my hands on her shoulders; it was the only place to put them, in the middle of the night in the street. She looked up at me, took my jaw in her hand and kissed me. At first it was a thank-you kiss, but then it was more than that. Helen's lips are cool and warm simultaneously. Her lips are soft and full, moist and dry; exaggerated in the imagination, when you close your eyes. They taste like elemental metals. Red is a primary colour. I thought her hair smelled of food; Weinstube, maybe?

A kiss is louder than words. You forget that people are asleep. You forget where you are. And who you are. I embraced her firmly, then more gently, afraid of crushing something. You forget that Helen is pregnant.

Around us, there was nothing but parked cars and silent apartment houses. And people sleeping furiously.

Helen leaned back, smiled at me and looked straight up at the sky. You forget about the sky. Then she leaned forward again, opened her mouth and bit the side of my face. I felt her teeth grip the left rail of my jaw. I pulled back.

What's that for? I said.

At night in the city, voices often come and go like that in the street, drifting in and out of sleep before moving on again. We walked on along Pallas Strasse; Helen was holding on to my arm. We turned the corner into Potsdamerstrasse with renewed purpose.

We got little satisfaction at Pension Potsdam. The porter was hostile from the start. He gave the impression that he met people like Helen and myself every day and that life was too short for words. He sat sideways behind the reception with his feet stretched out. A small desk lamp lit one side of his face only. He refused to be drawn into a discussion about Dieter's bag and kept repeating the sum, 200 marks. Whenever I talked, he turned questions on me. Would I expect to get free accommodation? What supermarket would let you walk out with 200 marks worth of credit? *Nein, meine Herrschaften,* he said.

I had an idea. I told the porter that Dieter was a schizophrenic; he probably didn't know what he was doing. The trouble was that we had to find him to tell him about the bag. Naturally, I told him, the 200 marks would be paid. There was no question about that.

The porter smirked. Anything you say to a porter at night, he seems to have heard it before. He said it didn't interest him what I had to say. Somehow, he knew that if we had a look inside Dieter's bag, we might very well change our minds and decide it wasn't worth retrieving.

Pension Potsdam was as grubby as Helen had described it. The wallpaper was beige with stippled brown leaves. The door-frames were brown. In the narrow foyer, there were tan-coloured leather seats and a standard lamp on a table with a light blue shade. You have to know what you're doing when you choose colours like that.

59

There were two women sitting in the brown seats when we arrived. They were obviously dressed up and ready to go somewhere. They had a purpose. One of them was smoking. Both were listening to the discussion over Dieter's bag as though it were the most trivial subject imaginable. They looked at Helen, up and down. Could have told her she was wasting her time. They had seen everything worth seeing. Their appearance seemed to say a lot more about Dieter. The kind of man he was. Pension Potsdam said everything.

I urged Helen to go. She looked at me to see if there might be something else I could do. I asked her whether she realized what kind of a place this was. Had she any idea where she was? In a final effort, I offered the porter a deposit of 30 marks, which was all I had in my pocket, just to have a look in Dieter's bag for some address. But the porter didn't listen.

I turned back to Helen like an obedient translator, and shrugged. Let's go then, she said. Back in the street she decided she was going to try and get an advance on her wages from Weinstube. I asked her if that was wise. It seemed like a high price for a bag which Dieter was very reluctant to collect himself. It's not the bag. It's the information that Helen wants.

I told her I would lend her the money. She wouldn't hear of it.

You have to know what you're doing when you're pregnant. So far, Helen did everything right. She attended her gynaecologist regularly. She looked at the calendar. She inquired about maternity leave. Checked her legs to see if there was any hint of varicose veins. Stood sideways in front of the mirror and held her stomach in her hands. She thought about progress. The expanding future. She thought about her mother. Home.

Helen asked for an advance at Weinstube and was told it would take some time because these things were all processed at headquarters. She pleaded for an exception. Could they not manage 200 marks out of petty cash? But the manager said it was strictly against the regulations. He was sorry. There was nothing he could do. Helen went back to slicing bread.

Even the toxic smell of caraway seeds can be reassuring. Even the sound of searing meat in a frying-pan can take your mind away. Even the sound of Pachelbel's Canon can make you glad. Even the sight of a crumpled blue serviette bearing the Weinstube crest and left soaking in a half-finished bowl of french onion soup can make you feel at home. Laughter spilling in from the restaurant outside can make you float. Kitchen work can make you forget. Even a smile from the commis chef is better than nothing.

Even a poor joke conceals what goes on inside. Even minutes turn into hours.

It would have been weeks before Helen got any kind of an advance out of Weinstube. By then she would have been due her first month's salary. I decided to fork out the 200 marks and collect Dieter's bag myself, just to get it over and done with. The money wasn't important. I was glad to be able to do something decent for Helen, but at the same time it feels bad to get ripped off over a bag. Especially when it's not even your own bag. I took a good guess what was inside.

Later that night, I stood outside Weinstube waiting for her to finish work. The last remaining guests were leaving the restaurant through the oak door. I saw a woman accompanied by a man who had his coat loosely thrown around his shoulders.

Dieter's bag was on the pavement. I knew Helen would be pleased when she saw it. I didn't need to open the bag to find out what was in it. I was pretty sure it could be nothing else but some dirty laundry. For Helen, it would be something tangible.

The manager came to the door and told me to wait. *Abwarten*, he said with his flat hand held up. I was far too early; Helen would be at least another twenty minutes. He didn't like me any more than I liked him. He closed the door again and went down into the restaurant. He looked to me like a person who was given too much information too soon. Maybe the *Aufklärung* was premature. *Aufklärung*: clearing up, is German for the facts of life. He looked troubled.

I waited outside. Not far from where I stood, there was a luxury tour coach parked at the side of the street. All the lights were on but there were no passengers inside. At first, I made a connection with Weinstube and thought a busload of passengers would soon emerge from the restaurant. But no other guest came out. It seemed the bus was just parked there temporarily before picking up passengers somewhere else for a night journey across Germany.

There was a woman on the bus systematically stripping white headrest covers from the seats. She was talking all the time to a man who sat in the driver's seat with his feet up. I couldn't hear anything. But now and again I could see her stopping to emphasize a point. After a while, she went to the back row of the bus again and began fitting clean white covers over the headrests, right to left. Always right to left.

You forget how stationary everything has become. Even the sight of a stationary bus makes you want to leave. Even the sight of systematic work can make you want to walk up and down the pavement, impatiently. Even the sight of a bag that doesn't belong to you, on the pavement, can make you look like a traveller.

The bus moved away. Helen eventually came out. She embraced me instinctively. Then saw the bag on the pavement and said: You shouldn't have. She thanked me with a kiss. I'll owe it to you, she said. I expected her to fall on her knees and root through Dieter's bag immediately for clues. She restrained herself. I picked up the bag. She took my arm and began to walk down the street.

Let me buy you a drink, she said.

That was something else I found attractive about Helen. She says thanks once and leaves it at that. She doesn't go on continuously feeling indebted. She gets on with things. We had a few drinks at a small bar on the way home. Helen even decided to risk some beer herself. We talked about the manager of Weinstube. She said he was the MOST unimaginative person she had ever met.

At last she opened Dieter's bag and had a brief look at the contents. As I had expected, there was no clue and no indication of any other address. It revealed nothing but crumpled clothes and some magazines. The only item of value was a hand torch. I wondered how soon the clothes would enter the laundry chain and find their way into my cupboard as part of my clothes.

We returned to the subject of Weinstube. I told her she should get out of there. It was no place for her. I told her she wasn't made for that kind of work. And besides, she was pregnant. She shouldn't spend so much time on her feet.

Nobody was made to work in Weinstube, she said. Nobody was made to have babies.

The purpose of drink is to lose your reason.

Why don't you quit working? I said. Hand in your notice. You don't need the money that badly.

I'd love to give it up, she said.

This is how Helen makes love.

She shouts. She thinks. Dreams, occasionally. Throws things around. Then she becomes incredibly calm. She is unpredictable, abrupt, even violent. Sometimes she pretends to scream.

I made sure the window was closed. The neighbours around Sonnenallee are sensitive. Light sleepers.

Helen stood against the wall of the bedroom and allowed me to kiss her. She clasped the back of my neck with her hand. After a while, she pulled away and began to kiss my face. And suddenly she bit my cheek, right under the eye.

Jesus, Helen, don't do that, I said, moving back.

She laughed. Showed her teeth.

Helen, don't bite, I said. Angry.

OK, I promise. I won't bite.

She jumped away on to the bed and began to take her clothes off. She does things quickly without actually rushing. She jumped off the bed and opened the window, stood there for a moment and then jumped back on to the bed. She was kneeling and held a pillow against her. She was waiting for me.

You shouldn't be jumping around like that in your condition, I said.

Why not?

Well, I can't help thinking you'll damage something.

What?

The baby, I mean. Shouldn't you be careful?

She jumped up and threw the pillow at me. I managed to close the window again before she started shouting. I sat down on the bed and kissed her again. That calmed her. Helen keeps talking. She has a warm voice which exaggerates trust. She says anything that enters her head just to keep talking. A trade in information. She likes to keep her eyes open, too. When she shuts her eyes, it is to see me. When she stops talking, she wants to hear me.

I'm afraid I'll crush you, I said. The baby?

Don't be crazy. Relax. I'm still very small. It's tiny. Nothing will happen. I swear. You can't even feel the bump.

Where there were windows, they were shut. Lights were out. Voices merged. The streets of Berlin were empty. Even the absence of sound can be significant.

Helen kicked. Bit my shoulder. And shouted. She was first, and had the privilege of waiting for me. Even at a standstill, you keep on moving. Even the neighbours must have finally gone to sleep.

That's it. I have taken Dieter's place now.

In the morning, I told Helen not to go into work. Give it up, I said. It makes your hair smell. I'll ring up and tell them you're sick.

Arbeit macht frei, she said, laughing.

Rubbish, I said. *Arbeit macht krank!* I'll tell them the work makes you sick.

She took a shower and went back to bed. I brought her some tea. She couldn't look at food. All she wanted to do was to re-enact the past. She pulled me in beside her. The purpose of repetition is to believe what you see.

6

Privacy, Posters and Infidelity

Wolf and Hadja are at each other's throats.

Since the incident at the Aula, the strain is registered everywhere. But it also seems that neither of them is fully resolved to make it up. No point in a hasty reconciliation. For some reason, harmony is being postponed. Even though Wolf repeatedly declares that he has nothing more to do with Lydia and that all contact with her has been broken off, Hadja will not believe him. She doesn't care. Or does she want to make him suffer for a while? Make him pay for it?

Their stormy arguments begin early in the morning and go on till late at night. Even my presence doesn't hold them back. Being in the privileged role of Wolf's right-hand man while he works on putting together his demo tape for the recording companies, I become the first-hand witness to many of their inflamed and passionate rows. They stop at nothing.

Hadja has withdrawn all physical contact. Wolf is depressed about it.

What can I do? he says. She will not talk to me about it. She will not let me explain. She will not make love to me. Not even a kiss.

Cheer up, Wolf, I said. There's an election on in Germany.

But Wolf didn't see the joke. In fact, it was probably the worst thing I could have said at the present moment. Right now, Hadja is helping her brother Konrad by putting up election posters around Berlin. Konrad belongs to the SPD. He puts his resources at the disposal of the party. Hadja owes her brother a favour. The SPD will owe Konrad a favour.

Wolf owes Hadja a favour. Instead of putting up posters of Wolf, Hadja is now arranging to put up posters of Helmut Schmidt. It's more than Wolf can bear. The strain is registered in the angle of his head. The frequency with which he looks downwards at the floor. The progressive contradiction in his behaviour; switching on the overhead light in the room and moments later switching it off again. The energy and confusion with which he announces the temporary loss of vital implements such as screwdrivers, plectrums or Sellotape. The frequency of certain words like *Scheisse*. The speed with which he now eats food and swings his leg while eating. The excessive trust and admiration he awards me in technical matters. The furious pace at which he throws himself into his work. Can Hadja do all this to him? It's just what she wants.

You should have thought of my feelings, she accuses him once more, after dinner.

Gastronomic satisfaction fuels domestic strife. Full stomachs make heavy minds.

You can't talk about feelings, Wolf responds abruptly. His hostile look across the room from his lounging place in the armchair is laden with nutrients. A suppressed belch reduces the impact of his words.

Food kills.

Feelings, he repeated. Don't talk to me about feelings. You have as much respect for feelings as a new *Autobahn*.

Scheisse! Hadja shouted across the room at him, with feeling.

That's it, Hadja said. You have no concept of my sensitivities, have you. All you think of is yourself and your music and this Lydia woman.

Look, Hadja, he shouted back. Do we have to go through this all again? It's over. Understand. It's over. *Fertig – aus! Basta!*

Music aids digestion.

Wolf got up to put on some music. He went over to a bank of recording equipment and began to wind up a spool of reel-to-reel tape. Then he searched through a box for a cassette of suitable after-dinner music. The tapes are all clearly marked in his own handwriting. The length to which he goes to select the music, by process of elimination, demonstrates uneasiness. The intensity of Hadja's eyes in following his movements reflects the intensity of intestinal activity after dinner. It is misleading to attribute raised voices or hostility in the air to the quality of food ingested.

There are hundreds of cassettes in Wolf's collection. There is only one light on in the room. There is only one thing on Hadja's mind. There are wires all along the floor of the living room at the moment. The wires also lead out into the hallway and into the bathroom.

Anyhow, Wolf said, I thought we had a firm policy of non-interference in each other's personal matters.

Non-interference? Hadja shouted. Her brown eyes are wide open. We had a policy of trust and honesty.

I thought we agreed not to harrass each other over small affairs and friendships with other people. I thought we had scope in our relationship?

All right then, Hadja said. I'm going out to do the same. I'll go and find the first Greek or Italian I see and hop into bed with him. Is that what you want? I know they'll be queuing up with their tongues hanging out. Is that all right with you then?

Come on, Hadja, be reasonable.

Is it unreasonable to associate propendent tongues with physical desire? Or to equate desire with appetite? Or to relate opportunity to need? Slept-with men are soon forgotten. Forgettable men are fast food.

Why don't I go out and see what's available? said Hadja.

Wolf has become angry. He wants to discuss this whole thing rationally. Hadja doesn't. To rationalize means to digest. Metabolize. Forget.

Why don't I go out and get some brawny young Muslim, she said, and then, pausing for a moment . . . somebody with a decent recovery rate.

Don't talk such *Scheiss*, Hadja, shouted Wolf.

It is misleading to associate the word *Scheiss* with metabolism. Hadja's arms are folded. Battle formation. Her face bears a smile which could mistakenly be attributed to kindness instead of hostility. Her eyes are hungry. So far Wolf has failed to select suitable after-dinner music. He lurches around the room, followed by Hadja's constant stare. It is unreasonable to associate lack of decision with choice of diet. Perhaps Wolf now wants to find some music which would be as offensive to Hadja as her last remark was to him. Their argument develops like a shower mixer being pushed back and forth by millimetres between the blue and red arrows.

Wolf suddenly tripped when his foot became entangled in the wires along the floor.

Kruzifix! he shouted.

Smiling aids digestion. Their insults have been reduced to a long, piercing silence.

I don't care what you do, Wolf said abruptly but quite calmly.

67

Arschloch, Hadja replied. If only I still had my own apartment in Sonnenallee, I'd move back there right away.

The threat is bare. It has been made before. But it is a threat, none the less, and enough to push Wolf over the brink. He said nothing, and began to search frantically in a box of loose tapes. No insult can go unreturned, and Hadja waited for his reply. Eventually, Wolf seemed to find what he was looking for. A self-assurance not unlike contentment entered his movements. He placed a small spool on the upright deck, fed the loose tape around to a free spool and began to rewind.

He stopped. Played. There was a brash but distant trumpet sound. He stopped and rewound further. He tapped his finger against the machine with impatience. He stopped again. Played. Sound of voices. Fast forward. Played again.

At first there was nothing. Nothing but the tape noise. Ambience. He turned up the volume. There was a slight hiss. Hadja was listening. Then came the clear sound of a door closing. A cough or a grunt followed by the sound of footsteps or movement in an enclosed space, followed by further sounds of muffled breathing. Fabric being pulled. Then a very clear sound rang out. It was the sound of pissing. Unmistakably, the sound of pissing. It was so loud that Hadja looked across the room with shock in her eyes. With gathering rage, not unlike intense personal interest, she began to realize what this meant. It sounded like a cow. Exaggerated and amplified. But there was no mistake. As Wolf looked across at her, Hadja could not escape the clear intuition that this was the sound of herself pissing. He had recorded her private sounds. Now he was playing them back to her. She could hardly speak.

Blöder Schuft, she spat, ineffectively.

She stood up and walked out. Even before the sound of the flushing toilet came across the speakers, she had stormed out of the apartment, slamming the door behind her. The slamming of doors has become ineffectual. So too have most other universal attempts at punctuation. Nothing ends where it's meant to end. Does an argument end when people stop talking? Can it be assumed that people disappear when they can no longer be seen?

It is in my own interest to promote harmony and reconciliation between Wolf and Hadja. Otherwise she might start looking for her old apartment back. Instability between Wolf and Hadja might directly affect the stability between Helen and myself. Hadja might ask us to move out of Sonnenallee so that she can feel more independent. Bear it in mind, I keep saying to myself. I co-operate as much as I can with Wolf and Hadja.

It is in the interest of stability and confidence in the economy that elections are now being held in West Germany. Throughout Berlin, the first wave of posters has already been up on the billboards for weeks. Radio and television networks have been discussing the issues. There is hope in Germany. The candidates speak of new enthusiasm in the soul of the nation. Rationalized planning. Ten times larger than life, they look down from their posters with sincerity, not unlike the implicit trust of parental smiles.

When is it good to look German?

At six in the morning outside the offices of the *Arbeitsamt*, men gather in small clusters or stand alone, some smoking, some with their hands in their pockets, all of them throwing eager glances in the direction of the oncoming traffic. Some of them are German. Others include Greeks, Turks, Italians and Yugoslavs. They are looking for casual labour. Even though the offices of the *Arbeitsamt* don't open until nine, this is the right place to be. It is a pick-up point.

Sooner or later, a van or truck will appear, veering left out of the flow of traffic and stopping along the pavement in front of the *Arbeitsamt*. The men will all surge forward. Their combined attitude will approach cameraderie and friendship, however temporary. A man will jump from the van or stand on the runner step and lean over the open door surveying the group.

He will need eight men for two days of furniture removals. Offices in Friedenau. *Arbeit* for strong, experienced personnel. The word *Arbeit* is like currency.

The group of eager faces look upwards. How can you look stronger than you are? How can you look less eager, less foreign, more intelligent? The man standing on the runner step of the van will choose eight faces. Eight men will pile into the back of the van, which moves off speedily, rejoining the flow of traffic, leaving the rest of the men to disperse again, encouraged that there is work going; disappointed not to have been chosen.

Occasionally, a van will arrive and summon the group of casual faces, but instead of prospective employers, the men in the van will turn out to be immigration officials, who then begin to question foreign faces and demand identity cards. The pick-up point outside the *Arbeitsamt* is no longer the place to be when you have no papers. Surrogate workers must be registered. The casual labour force is a clean race.

When is it good to look like a Turk?

Hadja's brother Konrad has been on the phone. He has asked her to mobilize three or four good men from Kreuzberg immediately. The second wave of Schmidt posters have got to go up around the city now. They need fast workers. The job must be done speedily and inexpensively.

Hadja needs to cover poster sites as arranged in the Schöneberg and Wilmersdorf districts. She goes to the house in Grossbeerenstrasse where she is greeted by everyone as an equal and as an employer simultaneously. She looks German, and also a little bit Turkish, like one of their own. She commands universal trust. She selects three able men, who pile into her car and are brought to the SPD election office in Schöneberg to collect posters, brushes, paste and ladders.

It's more than Wolf can bear. The image of Hadja conducting this work with three Turkish men at her disposal burns his mind. Larger than life posters of Helmut Schmidt distract his concentration.

Hadja's small group works quietly and efficiently, moving from one site to the next. Some of the poster sites are larger than others and have to be pasted up in portions. The left side of the face, followed by the chin, the right side and Schmidt's democratic sailor's cap. Each poster is pasted up with care and attention. In Germany today, there is hope, enthusiasm and longing for the future. There is life in Helmut's eyes.

They spend the afternoon about this task. The posters take between ten and twenty minutes to paste up. There is something intimate in this kind of work. Repeatedly coming face to face so closely with this poster of a leader gives the men a feeling of deep human contact; if they met Helmut Schmidt in the street they would feel they knew him well.

It's more than Wolf can bear. This extraordinary infidelity of Hadja.

When is it good to look hurt?

At the Bar-o-Bar in the evening, Wolf is on stage once more giving the performance of a lifetime. Neither Hadja nor Lydia are anywhere to be seen in the audience. Lydia doesn't come any more. Hadja is making a protest. But Wolf sings as though they were both there, sitting at opposite ends of the bar, separated only by tables, smoke and a short, ill-lit distance. They both make up part of his internal audience, to whom he can sing at any time, whether or not they are present. He needs them to sing to, more than anyone else; he needs their understanding, sympathy. Their demands and needs. Perhaps it is the thought that Wolf sings to Lydia or that she has become part of his internal audience that angers Hadja so much. On stage, Wolf looks hurt, generally misunderstood and wronged. With effective lighting, I can draw this out to maximum advantage. It is my job to exaggerate this hurt.

The applause confirms it. So does the round of drinks, anonymously paid for. And so does the reluctance of the audience to leave immediately. After the show a man approaches me and asks when Wolf is going to record an album. Very soon, I say, continuing to pack up the gear and wind cables, sending him away again steeped in hope and satisfaction. Two women from Munich say they are here in Berlin on a brief visit. They are Munickers who would like to know where they could see Wolf again before they leave.

At the bar some time later, Wolf looks torn apart by thought. When most of the audience have drifted home or on to other bars, Wolf places his elbows on the bar and holds his drink with both hands, the posture of a man about to say something significant into his drink.

Hadja is torturing me, he says. She will not talk. She will not discuss anything any more. She will not make love to me, Wolf says.

He forces me to imagine himself and Hadja together in bed.

Hadja clinging to the duvet, perched on her side of the bed, and Wolf inert on his side, bearing a frozen, tragic expression.

Is she still operating as your manager? I ask.

Ach, yes, of course, he says. But now she is also putting up these election posters for the SPD. This makes more pain for me. I cannot see her doing this to me. I cannot see her torturing me like this any more.

Has she joined the SPD? I ask.

No, of course not, he answers. She's just doing her brother Konrad a favour. Everybody owes everybody a favour around here.

Best to be in credit, I said.

Wolf nodded. Everybody has now gone, leaving only the barman shuffling around with his endless little tasks; stacking glasses, wiping surfaces, rearranging bottles. Wolf keeps nodding.

Right now, Wolf said, with swollen significance, Hadja has all the credit. She wants to extract it all slowly; painfully. She likes to keep the imbalance alive.

Wolf is very productive under pressure of imbalance. Artistically prolific and imaginative. It is in the interests of art that imbalance should remain in Hadja's favour. It is in the interest of imagination that posters of Helmut Schmidt are put up around Schöneberg and Wilmersdorf.

Wolf begins to talk about me and Helen. What about you? he asks.

Is it unreasonable to be so reluctant to talk about Hadja and Helen in the same breath? Is it unreasonable to talk about Helmut Schmidt and Wolf in the same breath?

I like Helen a lot, I said. I would do anything for her. Absolutely anything.

Is it unreasonable to watch the methodical work of a taciturn barman with such fascination? Is it unlucky to say what you feel?

You love her? Wolf asks. She loves you? You sleep together, not so?

Yes, I said, looking into my drink. I think Helen is lovely. She is the best person I have ever met. I only hope this man Dieter never reappears.

What about Dieter? Wolf says angrily, on my behalf. He has left her. Abandoned her. You took her and looked after her when she needed somebody, not so? Dieter has nothing to say. He has no right to reappear.

Is it unreasonable to simplify matters? Is it unreasonable to submit to this urge to tidy up; to wipe surfaces and stack glasses?

Helen is part of my internal audience. Wolf makes me sound like a singer, singing to Helen.

I wish my life could be as simple as yours, Wolf said. I wish I could belong to a simple love like yours.

I understand what he means but I pretend not to understand.

I would love to belong to a love without credit, he says. Here in Germany, everybody seems to owe everybody favours. If you don't have what you want, it's your own fault. You're inadequate, not so?

Wolf is doing all the talking. I nod in agreement. The barman keeps rinsing glasses and repeating things he has done before.

In fact, Wolf adds, we are morally bound to seek satisfaction here. Nowhere is satisfaction more rewarded. More obligatory.

Wolf holds up his glass of Schnapps between thumb and forefinger. He drains it and pauses. Then, with another surge of feeling, he begins to talk slowly and deliberately across the bar in the direction of a row of bottles.

I would love to belong to a minority, he said. I would love to belong to a small race of people with nothing to lose. Palestinians. Kurds. Dispossessed.

When is it good to look drunk?

Impaired hearing is a privilege. Lack of stability is a luxury; a clear advantage Wolf and I have over Helmut Schmidt, larger than life, staring at us from his posters on the way home at Innsbrücker Platz. I have noticed that the light source in Helmut's eyes is reflected by a white square on the left side of each pupil. There is life in his eyes. He looks sober. Two pedestrians along Schöneberger Strasse form part of his internal audience whether we like it or not. We can be nothing but voters returning home late at night. Scoffing at inert posters makes you impotent. Pissing in the street makes you deaf. Aiming at politicians makes you feel empty.

Wolf pleaded with me to join him for a final drink at Tischtelefon. He couldn't face Hadja, he said. So we walked in past the main room where we saw men and women sitting at numbered tables with telephones and pink table lamps and ice buckets, until we reached the recess bar. The principal source of light is the small screen on the far side showing forest carnal scenes in black and white. We ignored these and went to the bar. As always in semi-darkness, it is hard to tell if the place is empty or full of people.

Wolf crouched over the bar and ordered Calvados. Gradually, my eyes adjusted and I could see four or five men sitting separately in low seats watching the forest scenes. A woman came up behind us and placed her arms around us.

Not so tragic, *Meine Herren*, she said.

I noticed that her bare arms were white and fleshy underneath; dripping with slack muscle. It seemed right somehow.

Now come on, *Kumpel*. Not so tragic. You've missed nothing. The show is just about to begin.

Wolf ignored her completely. She deserved more courtesy. I began by nodding, and then said I looked forward to her performance. She looked pleased. Ten minutes later, the forest scenes were abruptly switched off. Lights began to illuminate a small stage with a purple carpet. Brass music rose slowly and discreetly over hidden speakers.

Flesh-coloured music, Wolf said, without turning away from the bar.

The woman appeared on the stage and began to dance. But her limbs seemed to move with excessive force. Did she have artificial hips? I could see also that she had the same loose, white flesh across her stomach. It seemed to have such a soft, slack texture as to be entirely without sensation; under constant local anaesthetic. I was curious. I wanted to pinch it to prove it. We left.

Daylight makes you blind.

It was bright by the time I got home to Sonnenallee. That's what Helen was telling me at around noon the next day when I woke up. She was shuffling around the room waiting for me to wake up, like a child waiting to be allowed to speak. She must have been shuffling back and forward around the apartment like that all morning, waiting.

I couldn't sleep last night, she said. I didn't know where you were.

I was with Wolf, I said immediately. You shouldn't worry about me.

74

I was waiting for you, she said. All night. How am I supposed to know where you are?

Accusation reveals concern.

I thought you would have known I was out with Wolf, I said. Defence reveals capitulation.

I was waiting, she said once more. Don't you think I get lonely here all on my own at night? Do you think I like waiting and waiting all the time on my own?

Helen has big round eyes. She made me feel like Dieter just then and there was nothing I could say. I could only look back at the sad expression on her face. It was the first time it occurred to me that my absence might keep her awake. That endless hours alone in the apartment could drive her mad. Or that her pregnancy was like a confinement. Now that she was no longer working at Weinstube, she had too much time to reflect on things. Too much time spent waiting.

You come home in broad daylight. Drunk as a monkey, she said. The initial intensity of her anger seemed to have softened. From time to time, we did occasionally have these arguments. But they were polite. Nothing on the scale of Wolf and Hadja.

Then you got into bed and started putting your freezing hands all over me like wet fish, she said. You started saying I had a tennis ball in my stomach.

What? I asked.

Cold hands like dead fish, you have.

Repetition means loneliness. Humour means sorrow. Whenever Helen says something serious, perhaps I should think she's being funny.

She went over to the window and opened it, letting in a cool breeze across my face and the brash sound of work from the courtyard outside.

Come on, Helen, please, I said. Not the sound of work. You know I can't bear it.

Serves you right, she said. Not coming home at night.

The sound of somebody else working makes me angry. I sat up in the bed and looked at her.

What's it got to do with you when I come home at night? I work at night.

Helen recoiled and said nothing.

75

At least I'm here, am I not? At least I do come home, which is more than you can say for Dieter.

What's that supposed to mean? she barked back.

Her anger was revived. It tells in her eyes.

If you think I'm depending on you to stand in for Dieter or something, you're all wrong, mate, she said.

Her voice was raised. Hostility reveals attraction.

If you think I came here for some kind of replacement for him, you're wrong. You can't start comparing yourself to him. I don't want a stand-in.

Isn't that what I end up being? I asked, finally allowing anger to form some of the questions concealed in the back of my mind. Well, what happens when you find Dieter? What will you do when he comes back, then?

How can you even ask that? she said, turning away her face towards the window. I can't speak for him or for any of us. I can't speak for the future, can I. For some vague possibility.

Well, you are still looking for him, aren't you?

I have to, don't I. I have his baby.

What happens when you find him? I'll be turned over and dropped. Isn't that right? I'm only here as some kind of substitute for him.

Don't be stupid, Alan. Where did you get that idea? I'm not depending on you or on him, or on anyone else for that matter. Not for anything. Nobody is making any promises around here. While I'm here with you, I love you. What more can I say? If Dieter appears, it's an entirely new situation.

Anyhow, she said. Who says I want Dieter back? I can't speak for the future, you know.

The sound of work in the courtyard was unbearable. I lay back down in the bed and said nothing. Silence reveals how close you come to saying something before you hold back. She began to shuffle around again. Nothing is as convincing as action. I knew by looking at her shoulders, at the back of her head and at the way she moved about, that she had begun to cry. Once more I felt it was I who had deserted her. Once more I felt like Dieter.

Helen, I said, trying to call her over. But then she looked at me with large round watery eyes and began to walk out of the room. I called her back.

Helen, come here. Sit down on the bed.

For the first time, I needed to know why she was crying. Why she was worried. Why she was lonely. If she missed her parents. Dieter. What she thought about me. For the first time, I needed to know from moment to moment what was going on in Helen's mind. For the first time, I needed to see her smile.

In the interest of silence, I asked her to close the window. She sat down on the bed beside me, still reluctant to look straight into my eyes. She was pushing a knuckle against her nose.

It's not me that's crying, she said. I don't know what it is. It's only because I'm pregnant. It must be hormones. It's not me.

I took her hand and began to squeeze it firmly, as though it would stop her crying. I began to speak as though I somehow received the power to fix the future. I began to make promises.

From now on, I want you to go everywhere with me, I said.

Speaking reveals how close you come to not saying something. Promise, and the world promises with you. It was an outrageous promise. I knew it wasn't possible or even practical, but it somehow felt right to say it, and it urged me to draw her down into my arms so that I could feel the trace of her tears across my bare shoulder. Without a word, she got into bed.

In the interest of safety, steel toecaps are worn on building sites. In the interest of efficiency, things are marked urgent. In the interest of democracy, candidates smile. In the interest of stability, laws are enacted, profit is admired, the past is forgotten, promises are made, looks exchanged, belief and logic suspended. In the interest of neighbours, noise is kept to a minimum.

In the interest of progress, neighbours are ignored, clothes are removed, Dieter is forgotten, pregnancy is relegated and voices converge.

7

Polizei

It has been a time of feverish, if not compulsive, activity for Hadja. Apart from everything else, there has been another small worry at the back of her mind. Something like a subconscious ache which wouldn't go away. She had read in a magazine that it was the small unresolved issues that trouble the mind most and that become the greatest stress factors. What bothered her most was one of those minor things. She hadn't seen or heard of Sulima for months.

Now Sulima has become the most vital assignment in her life. Hadja worries that she may have relapsed into the old obedience to Islamic traditions, instead of the new obedience to the Berlin lifestyle. She has been looking for Sulima but can't find her. Hadja is worried that Sulima might still fall into the hands of her fellow Iranian student to whom she is promised by arranged marriage.

Over the six weeks or so since the Aula concert at the university, she has been giving it more thought. Since Hadja rarely goes to the university now, the regular contact with Sulima is broken off. She felt certain that Sulima had by now absorbed enough of the principles of Western freedom not to fall into the trap of this arranged marriage. Somehow, Hadja wanted to be sure her influence hadn't weakened.

For some reason, Sulima wasn't answering the phone. Nor was she acknowledging any of the messages Hadja had left at the university for her. When Hadja eventually went to enquire for her at the pharmacology faculty, she was told that the Iranian girl hadn't been seen for months. She made a trip over to Steglitz and got no answer at the apartment either. It was a matter of concern. A young student all on her own in Berlin.

The urgency of this obsession amuses me. All of a sudden, it has become essential that I should accompany Hadja over to Steglitz again to investigate. I suspect that Hadja is frustrated by some inability to lash out at Wolf and needs to lash out at this Iranian, Massoud, instead. But Hadja says it's a matter of life and death. Sulima has fallen back into the grip of Islam.

Come on, let's face it, Hadja, I said. You're not going to alter the destiny of Islam, are you?

I felt entitled to ask, since she seemed determined to involve me in the matter. I was trying to get out of it. Said it was none of my business to be nosing around other people's apartments. Why me? Why couldn't she ask Wolf instead? Wolf wouldn't be interested, she said.

What makes you think I'm interested in changing the natural course of events? I asked.

Come on, Alan, Hadja said. We've got to help Sulima. She's in trouble. It's up to us.

Us?

You know what these Muslims are like. You know what that bastard Massoud is capable of.

I don't.

Well, I'd hate to imagine, she said. And I'd hate to imagine I was in trouble and nobody even enquired to see if I was all right.

But why does Hadja need me to be involved? And why this recurring hysteria over missing people? I'm not in a position to refuse, and Hadja does not accept my reluctance. She needs me for protection from this mad Iranian, though I suspect it's less physical than moral support she wants. Somebody to back up her legitimate concern. What if he attacks me? she asked. I could see that Hadja's imagination had already developed in leaps ahead of me.

As usual on Fridays, unless I can get out of it somehow, I accompany Hadja on her rounds to collect the rent at Grossbeerenstrasse. It's enough to remind me how compelling squalor is to look at. And enough to remark again how meticulously clean some Turkish apartments are kept alongside the dirt of the courtyard and the raw smells in the corridors and on the stairs. The house is filled with the chaos of music. Every radio and cassette recorder is playing, like a pulse, as though silence would mean instant death. The women invite us in for coffee, but Hadja declines. She has a way of smiling and making these Turkish women laugh and show their gold fillings while they hand over their rent. With the rent, they hand over bits of gossip and small requests, such as new cousins looking for work, all of which they laugh at hilariously, but I fail to understand because they speak in

Turkish. Hadja explains as we go along. She describes them like cartoons. To me, Turkish sounds like gold teeth or gold bracelets.

Afterwards, Hadja deposits the money at the Commerzbank and invites me for the customary coffee and cake. Two cups of Mocca and two *Apfelstrudel mit Schlagsahne*. Enough cream to erase the past. Before Hadja sat down, she briefly went to make another call to Sulima just on the off-chance.

That's it, she said angrily, coming back. This Persian maniac. I just now telephone Sulima and this Massoud answers the phone. I ask for Sulima and he says Sulima doesn't want to speak to me. And then he hangs up . . . *Mensch!*

There is fury in Hadja's eyes. Pieces of *Apfelstrudel* disappear into her mouth with rage. She chews with belligerence and thought. Never mix food and thought, I want to tell her. She drinks the coffee while it's still far too hot. The sting of heat produces a tear in her eye and a rare expression of hurt and helplessness which, in robust people like Hadja, first strikes you as comic. But there is no comedy in Hadja's eyes, and the more you look at her, the more you feel accused.

I knew it, she said. But this will not happen here in West Germany. This is a free city, she said, pointing her fork at my face.

This I will say to you, she said. No woman will be kept in captivity here in Berlin by her future husband. NO WAY! No woman will be a prisoner here under our noses.

I looked around the café, subtly reminding Hadja to keep her voice down.

We will not see this, Hadja said. This cannot happen here in a free society, I will tell you. We will go directly over to Steglitz and demand to speak to Sulima; immediately. *Aber sofort!*

Hadja, I said quietly, looking around once more at the other people in the café. Do we really have the right to interfere in somebody else's private life?

Um Gottes Willen, Alan. We cannot allow this to happen right under our noses. What these Iranians do in their own country is their own business. They can cut off fingers and mutilate each other as much as they like. But here in Berlin, they must behave decently like any other German inhabitant. Sulima has the same rights as any German woman, you know.

But Hadja, be rational about this, I said. You're not going to change anything, are you? You're no match for the wrath of Islam. You're not going to start playing World Police, are you?

Now listen, Alan, she said, with a strong, earnest stare. I cannot stand by when I see something like this. I give a SHIT about people.

But why enforce your idea of freedom on somebody else?

Because I care. Because I give a FUCK about Sulima and I want to help her.

Hadja put her fork down with a clack. She was ready to go.

No woman will be kept in confinement here, she repeated once more, louder than she needed to. And the way she looked at me, I could not help thinking for a moment that it was Helen she was talking about all along.

Hadja got up and picked up her big leather holdall bag from the floor. Such is her determination now that she doesn't need to make sure that I'm following her.

Sulima's apartment in Steglitz is at the top of a relatively new building; post-war, that is. The block has a series of bird features cast in the plasterwork on the outside. Inside there is an elevator, but no intercom system. The landings and stairs are finished in a light blue marble in which further species of bird are cleverly represented, giving the house a slightly cold, tropical dimension. There is no graffiti in the lift, which always makes me want to scratch a little *Swastika* or some other rude curse.

There is no answer from Sulima's apartment on the sixth floor. I began to think that all of this was a big waste of time. But Hadja wouldn't give up that easily, and began to jam her elbow on the bell.

I will be answered, she announced, with raging confidence.

I went over to lean on the banisters and looked down to the bottom of the building. As usual in these circumstances, I discover a peculiar urge to throw myself down. Either that, or I turn around and imagine myself grappling with a tall killer wearing a trilby hat, his hands on my throat, my back arched over the banisters and my elbows resting on the rail with ironic comfort.

Sulima, Hadja eventually called through the door. What is then the matter with you? Why don't you answer?

Hadja has no fear of attracting attention. In fact, this was exactly what she wanted. She began to repeat her pleas through the door

81

as loud as respectability permitted. When there was no response from anywhere, she decided to ring on the nearest doorbell and call out one of the neighbours. With a pedantic flourish of apologies, she begged forgiveness for the intrusion and explained to the nervous old woman only half emerged from her apartment that there was cause for concern over her nearest neighbour. Hadja pointed at Sulima's door. Yes, the woman acknowledged instantly. It had already been noticed by the other people in the house. The young Persian student had not been seen for some time. At first it was assumed she was away, but then they were told by her brother who now lives with her that she had in fact been quite ill. But they were assured that he was looking after everything.

Hadja looked shocked. The idea of Massoud masquerading as Sulima's brother made her want to put her foot through the door. She made clear to the woman how sinister this sounded.

Wie komisch! Sulima does not have a brother, she said.

Another neighbour emerged on to the landing. An elderly man. Berlin is full of them. Voices on the landing bring out more elderly people. Soon, a small group had gathered in discussion, casting occasional glances in the direction of Sulima's apartment. We always knew there was something strange about them, they said. Hadja fuels their speculation and suspicion with hints and expressions of concern. What should be done?

Something is not right here, one of them said.

The imagination of a crowd develops fast. With public opinion now on her side, Hadja once again rang on Sulima's bell, to demonstrate to all that something was wrong. But nobody wanted to transgress the normal rules of conduct. They went for explanations instead. Maybe she was asleep? Maybe Sulima was studying?

In Germany, privacy is absolute. Nothing is more desirable or sacred than complete privacy. Nothing more deserving of violation.

But something is not true here, one of them kept saying. The *Hausmeister* should be summoned.

Another woman who had come half-way up the stairs from the landing below asked if the occupants of the apartment in question were not *Terroristen*? You never know?

Hadja took it upon herself to go down and call the caretaker. I stayed where I was, leaning against the banisters. She came back minutes later accompanied by a small, stocky old man who had his sleeves rolled up and carried a bunch of keys. But he was very reluctant to use the keys, and even more reluctant to transgress the rules of privacy he was employed to uphold. He rang the doorbell instead. The crowd unanimously told him it was no use.

The *Hausmeister* defended himself. He had no authority to open any apartment door. The people on the landing would all agree that except in cases of fire or emergency, he could not simply walk in and make himself at home in somebody's apartment. Hadja explained that it was an emergency. But the *Hausmeister* remained firm. He stood before the great ethical dilemma of his profession.

The crowd on the landing began to discuss the grey areas of the *Hausmeister's* authority. After all, it concerned them as much as anyone else. The infringement of privacy was desirable only in case of emergency, they agreed. But something was not right here, somebody kept saying. What constitutes an emergency? Suspicious foreigners?

Something smells funny, an old woman repeated.

Then it's a matter for the *Polizei*, Hadja announced.

Collectively, they agreed that this was the best course of action under the circumstances, and after the *Hausmeister* had shouted once more through Sulima's door, he resolved to phone the police, for which purpose the nearest apartment of Frau Fuchs was most cordially and helpfully thrown open. The *Hausmeister* went inside, supported by Hadja.

Steglitz. In this predominantly residential area of Berlin, the police have a self-publicized reputation for being on average only one minute and eight seconds away from the scene of a crime. Though this has often been disputed and put to the test by Berlin newspapers, it has never been disproved. Attempts to question or verify the 1.08 min arm's-reach of the Berliner *Polizei* run into confusion because of claims and counter-claims about the order of urgency. This time, it took almost ten minutes.

The urgency of police action is interpreted in order of danger to the common good. When does the state have the right to intervene? When the state is at risk. When the individual is at risk. When it is felt that individual freedom is placed at risk by somebody else's individual freedom. The state maintains the right to protect the individual from himself or herself, whether he or she likes it or not.

No individual shall have the right to devalue his or her own civil liberties. The individual shall forfeit all claim to privacy and other constitutionally enshrined liberties when he/she places himself/herself at risk.

Flashes of green uniforms can be seen at the bottom of the stairwell. The police are heard entering the lift. Here they come, somebody said. When two policemen emerged from the lift on the top landing, the crowd instantly parted to make way. Respect for the law means respect for yourself. The crowd on the landing is pleased to co-operate. Where privacy is the highest prize, so too is its penetration. The *Hausmeister* stepped forward and began to explain the need for such penetration.

We have here a problem, he said, pointing towards Sulima's door, and then allowing Hadja to take over.

Both policemen listen carefully. They seem relaxed. A policeman listens by looking elsewhere. They studied Sulima's door. They studied the geography of the landing, the number of footsteps to the stairs, the position of the small crowd behind them. One of the policemen looked me thoroughly up and down. Then he asked the crowd to stand back a little. Hadja was able to tell me afterwards that he smelled of garlic.

OK, he said. *Aufmachen!* Open up here, the first policeman said loudly, because shouting means loss of authority. He rang the bell and beat the side of his fist confidently on the door, as though sheer authority would succeed where persuasion had failed.

Aufmachen! he said again, forcefully.

They're in there all right, somebody said.

The woman from the landing below repeated her anxiety about *Terroristen*. You can't be too careful.

Something is not true here, somebody said again.

Finally, the first policeman gave the *Hausmeister* the nod that everybody had been waiting for. They stood back. The *Hausmeister* stepped forward with his keys and began to unlock the door. But just before he inserted the key, the door was unlocked and flung wide open of its own accord. The crowd gasped. In the doorway stood the Iranian, Massoud, with a broad smile on his face.

The crowd on the landing set up a low whisper. The first policeman became suddenly angry at the smile before him.

Ah . . . Now you will answer us, he shouted.

But the Iranian said nothing, and continued to stare back with his dark eyes. Basilisk eyes. Everyone on the landing seemed to be touched by his malignant smile. Behind him, in the hallway of Sulima's apartment, they could see a poster of the Shah of Iran with a bullet-hole in his forehead. Beyond that, there was nothing but a glimpse of the bedroom and a lifesize poster of the Khomeini. What can be less private than the Khomeini in the bedroom?

Where is Sulima? Hadja shouted.

Just a moment, the first policeman said, holding up his hand to Hadja. First things first. He asked Massoud for his identity papers. *Ausweis, bitte!*

The Iranian explained that he had to go inside to get his identity card, and returned moments later, still smiling, with two cards, both his and Sulima's. Policeman No. 1 inspected them and then handed them over to Policeman No. 2, who went to radio the names in to headquarters and waited for the all clear while Policeman No. 1 began to ask questions.

Hadja politely intervened when she found the right moment. That's him, she insisted, making it sound as though she was fingering a murderer. That's him. He's keeping a woman here in her own apartment against her will. He's imprisoning a friend of mine, Sulima.

Massoud's smile is diplomatic.

OK. Where is this woman? the first policeman asked. In the meantime, the all clear came back over the radio from headquarters. They held on to the identity cards for the moment.

Let this woman come out and show herself, the first policeman said.

She's sick, Massoud replied. She does not want to come out.

Policeman No. 1 showed his impatience by turning around slowly, almost painfully slowly, towards his colleague, and sighing loudly for the benefit of the crowd. A policeman indicates impatience by looking pleased. A policeman indicates that he means business by looking elsewhere. Without turning back towards Massoud, he raised his voice and spoke in clarion tones almost up towards the ceiling.

Will the young lady come out or do we have to go in? he said.

The Iranian disappeared, left everyone waiting for a while and then brought Sulima out to the door. She looked pale. A little bruised around the face, Hadja thought. Her hair had not been combed for weeks, it seemed. The small crowd on the landing strained to look past the policemen to see her face. Something is not quite in order, Frau Fuchs said, in a whisper.

Hadja greeted Sulima warmly and kissed her on both cheeks. The Iranian seemed reluctant to let go of Sulima's elbow. Hadja placed her arm around Sulima and pulled her away, turning back to Massoud to shout at him.

Why don't you let her out? Why have you imprisoned her in her own apartment? Why don't you let her go to university? You can't do this here in Germany, Hadja said emotionally.

She doesn't want to go out, Massoud replied, without anger.

Ach, what? Hadja shouted. She has no freedom of choice with you. Hadja turned to Sulima again and spoke quietly. Come on, Sulima. You and I can go somewhere and talk about this in peace.

But Sulima moved back, hesitating. She indicated that she would rather stay. The crowd fell completely silent. Another brief hostile exchange erupted between Hadja and Massoud. Why was he keeping her in captivity like this? Did he not see that he was infringing the rights of personal liberty? He could do all this back in Iran, but not here in West Germany. In Berlin, women were free to do what they wanted. But Massoud continued to smile diplomatically, and told the policemen and the crowd on the landing that Sulima was free to do what she wanted. Sulima wants to be obedient to me, he said.

Hadja grunted. She looked at Sulima, and seemed surprised that she wasn't insulted. The crowd on the landing seemed to resemble a people's court. Hadja spoke like an advocate. Finally, the first policeman intervened with an even-handed resolution. A policeman indicates lack of interest with a display of Solomon-like wisdom.

Let the young lady speak for herself, he said.

There was a pause while Sulima stood back and prepared to speak.

I wish to stay here with my fiancé, she said. I am very sorry to have caused all this trouble and I thank you all for being so concerned. Massoud and I are going back to Iran next month to get married. Thank you very much again for your concern, but everything is quite in order. Massoud is my future husband. He is looking after me.

But what happened to your face? Hadja interrupted.

It's nothing, Sulima said calmly.

Is this what you want? Hadja said again. Think it over. Do you want to remain a captive for the rest of your life?

Sulima smiled, as though the question was irrelevant.

I have pledged my life to Massoud, she said, looking around at him. I am very happy.

Policemen indicate boredom with wide grins. The people on the landing began to look at each other. Policeman No. 1 looked at Policeman No. 2. Hadja looked at me. There was nothing more she could say. The first policeman handed the identity cards back to Massoud, allowing him and Sulima to withdraw into their apartment. Before Sulima disappeared again, she said goodbye to Hadja, kissed her on both cheeks and told her she would phone her after the wedding, when she got back to Berlin.

The crowd dispersed slowly, muttering. The policemen turned around and moved towards the lift. Policeman No. 2 pressed the button to call the lift.

What can you do? the first policeman said quietly to Hadja. You can't help those who don't want to be helped, can you. You can't force them to catch up with us overnight.

There is really only room for three people in the lift. But the policemen indicate their good manners by letting us in first and then letting themselves in after us. Four of us in a lift designed for three. And Hadja's leather bag seems to take up so much room. We couldn't turn, once inside. I could feel Hadja's breasts squashed up against me. Her stomach against mine.

8

Oil, Quark and Obedience

Helen is obedient. Every movement of her body responds to instruction; eyes, mouth, fingers; all obey hidden commands. Everything she does is in response to her situation. She raises a spoonful of Quark to her mouth and becomes momentarily aware that she is obediently feeding not only herself, but a voracious lineage as well; the nascent city inside her. Helen desires only what received instruction permits. The taste of Quark is cool and tart. She cannot stop thinking about Quark. The letter to her parents is unfinished. She cannot stop thinking about her parents. The pen with which she was writing now lies on the table. The need to tell her parents about her situation in Berlin is like the need to eat Quark. The way buses need passengers and books need readers. The taste of Quark is cool and tart. In response to instruction, Helen gets up from the table, leaves the unfinished letter and goes to the fridge in the kitchen to refill her bowl.

What is this Quark stuff? Is it a soft cheese or is it yoghurt? It's Helen's discovery. Her appetite has been reduced, or enlarged, to the extent that she often eats nothing but bowls and bowls of this Quark, which she mixes with fruit; apples, chopped bananas, peaches, pears, or fresh strawberries. There are lots of fresh strawberries out now. *Erdbeeren!* Helen knows the German for all kinds of fruit as a result. She's learning German with Quark.

Helen is also attending ante-natal classes, where she goes once a week to lie on a foam mat and obey unquestioningly the voice of a bombastic instructor. There are around twenty women lying on the floor at the ante-natal classes, all responding unquestioningly. Each woman is lying on her own foam mat like an island. Each woman has a small cushion placed under the small of her back and waits for the voice of the instructor.

Now . . . *meine Damen* . . . You are lying on your backs and I want you to bend the knees so that the feet are flat on the floor.

Helen has a mental picture of her own knees bent. She has a mental picture of her own body and her own life in Berlin.

Meine Damen . . . I want you to place your arms loosely on your chest and place the feet slightly apart.

Sometimes a mental picture is not enough. From time to time Helen raises her head to see if her own position correlates with that of twenty other women in the class, all pregnant and all positioned in the same direction like weathervanes. Helen's understanding of German is limited.

Now, *meine Damen* . . . what I want you to do is to get complete control over the pelvic floor and vaginal muscles. Take a deep breath now, and in a moment I will ask you to raise your buttocks off the floor. The object of this exercise is to strengthen the thigh muscles and buttock muscles as well.

Helen has a mental picture of her own buttock muscles.

Now, take in a deep breath once more. *Tief, tief, tief!*

OK! Now, slowly lift your bottom off the floor. Lift . . . Lift . . . *eins, zwei, drei, vier* . . .

Now, tighten your buttock muscles and pubic muscles all at once. Tighten, tighten, tighten. *Eins, zwei, drei, vier* . . .

Helen tightens. They all tighten together.

Wunderbar!

Again. Once more, ladies. I want you to tighten the vagina like a fist. *Eins, zwei, drei, vier* . . . tighten, tighten, tighten.

They all tighten together.

Very good . . . now, relax. *Und locker lassen!*

Helen began to look pregnant, too. Not obviously heavy or pregnant, but round and warm and calm, as though she had been filled up with down feathers, or Quark. Her face was brown, with freckles around the nose. Her eyes were clear and round. Her hair was lustrous. She looked better and better, and often behaved either like a three-year-old or like a small, humorous old woman.

The summer in Berlin had come into its own. The windows in the apartment in Sonnenallee were left open day and night. At night, the warm breeze shook the leaves of the tree at the centre of the courtyard. By day, it carried in the hazy noise of work from the scaffolding outside like the sound of a distant shipyard. The warm wind blew through the streets as well, occasionally lifting with it the smell of *Würstl* stands, bakeries, or just the collective exhaust at an intersection. Occasionally, too, the wind carried drizzle, warm city rain like tap-water, which made people sitting on terraces and in outdoor cafés cover their drinks with beer mats. Anyone who had a balcony to their apartment made the best use of it. Balconies in Berlin are like remote corners of the Schwarzwald or like glossy white yachts anchored off tropical islands. When the red sun goes down in the evening, you see people toasting and clinking glasses.

Helen got a great tan. Her freckles multiplied across her back and shoulders. The heat of the summer, trapped in the streets, seemed to infuse her with a languid confidence; sometimes it made her face red in the evening and made her belly rise like a cake.

The *U-Bahn* was often cooler than the street. I began to go everywhere with Helen. Once a week, I accompanied her to the clinic for the ante-natal classes. She was slower, but we always walked. Her full round stomach was not so noticeable in the street, not when she was dressed. But you could see it in the way she walked with a slightly rigid stiffness in the spine, as though her movements were affected, or manipulated, or obediently operating on strings.

We walked through the warm streets looking through clothes shops, antique shops, toy shops, video, hi-fi, and even bicycle shops, never buying anything, just looking. Helen bought nothing but Quark. In the middle of the street, she would stop me and tell me how much she longed for Quark. It was lust. We got into the habit of making sure there was an endless supply in the fridge.

On Saturdays and Sundays we went to markets; *Trödel* markets. Never bought anything there, either; just looking through junk. Then we went to the park, to the *Tiergarten*, or out to Schloss Charlottenburg, or even once out to Tegel, to the lake, armed with a plastic container of ready-mixed Quark and pineapple, which I would hear her spoon lazily into her mouth while I lay on my back looking at the blue Berlin ceiling overhead.

It was a slow summer. It seemed everything had been reduced to the pace of a Sunday, and Helen's round stomach would stay there for ever. I wanted nothing to change. I loved the shape. I loved the sound of Quark inside. And the occasional tremors of life. We wanted nothing to progress. Helen wanted to keep the baby inside as long as possible. And I wanted to avoid a possible encounter with Dieter as long as possible. Occasionally, I raised my head and looked with one eye to make sure her stomach was still there, swollen and radiant. Helen was so tranquil and disinclined to get up from the grass that I sometimes fell asleep, knowing that her weight had pinned her to the floor of the park. I would wake up, shocked and excited to see that her stomach was still there, like a round mountain, as were the trees around the park and the golden angel of the Stern monument, and the frisbie players and the chariot of horses on the Brandenburg Gate, which seemed to be charging away across the top of her stomach. As long as Helen was pregnant, nothing would change.

Walking home one Sunday, I noticed she was carrying a letter. Was it the letter to her parents? I wanted to know. It was the only thing that bothered her, this letter to her parents, which she had written over a week ago and still failed to post. We had passed enough yellow post-boxes since then. But she lacked the resolve to throw it in; something in the irreversible action of posting a letter that held her back.

What had she said in the letter? I asked finally, as we walked back towards the sunset over Charlottenburg.

Helen looked thoughtful. She had a mental picture of her parents. Whatever happened to her, whatever way she lived her life in Berlin, she didn't want to alter that mental picture of home. She didn't want to hurt them with information.

I told them everything, really, she said. I think they have a right to know, don't you? I think I should let them know.

Your parents are important to you? I said.

Yes, they are, she said. I don't want to hurt them. They're very fond of me. They've been very good to me.

From time to time during the summer, Helen went silent for no reason. I never liked that, when she went quiet and occupied herself with mental pictures of the past or the future. Now I knew one of the things that made her quiet. She seemed reluctant to send anything to her parents or to commit anything to the post, in case it would cast her for ever into some inadequate explanation. Letters are limited. The words would limit her life to a brief description which she might have to bear for ever.

Everything would be reduced to words. The whole glowing summer would be reduced and abridged to one thin, ineffective prosaic report.

But what exactly did you say in the letter? I pursued.

Well, I told them I was pregnant, for a start, she said.

Yes, but did you tell them who the father was? Did you mention Dieter?

They already know about Dieter, she said.

Did you tell them about me? I asked.

No! she said. How could I? I don't think it's fair to confuse them. I left it all very vague. I don't want to hurt them any more than I need to.

Then, realizing what she must have said, Helen clung to my arm with both hands and walked with her head against my shoulder. The pace of pregnancy allowed it. We walked towards the reddening sun. And somehow it made me feel like an altruist, which is the last thing I wanted to be, approaching the *U-Bahn* station at Ernst-Reuter-Platz.

Post it, I said.

The evening sun was bursting red with confidence. Amid the noise of traffic coming up from Bismarckstrasse, we found a yellow box. There's nothing to it. She plucked the letter from her little bag and threw it in. Normally you hear something. We didn't, with all the Sunday traffic.

Everything became irreversible. We turned and walked down to get the *U-Bahn*.

The distance from the *U-Bahn* station at Neuköln back to the apartment at Sonnenallee seems endless. I feel as though I'm crawling beside her. We walk so slowly, it makes us look like an old couple returning from a brass-band concert at the park. It's an infuriating pace. I could run back and forth from the station to the apartment at least twenty times in the space of time it takes us to get there. Helen is tired after the day in the heat. Her pace is reduced to a stroll, holding on to my arm for support. Her nose is red from the sun. She makes me feel like running. She makes me feel like dancing around her in the street with all my energy. She had a firm grip on my arm and looked up at me.

I slow you down, don't I, she said, as though she had been listening to my thoughts. What did she mean?

I'm in no hurry, I said.

As soon as we got up the stairs to the apartment, Helen decided to have a bath. She must have had a mental picture all along of herself in the steaming water. The bath-cum-shower in Sonnen-allee is no more than a cupboard really, which has been seques-tered from the kitchen. She ran the bath, took off her clothes and hung the green towel in readiness on the cooker. Then she tested the water with her foot and got in. She told me from the bath that the baby had set up a strong reaction to the heat of the water.

I looked at a newspaper, made a phone-call and then came back to the kitchen to prepare something to eat. Food should be attractive, to disguise the fact that people are trying to kill each other with it all the time. I placed a bottle of wine on the table as well.

Helen sat at the table with a towel wrapped around her. She ate everything. We sat around for a while after that. It was getting dark.

Will you do the oil? she asked.

It's something I asked to do once and Helen insists on my doing ever since. After every shower or bath, she always rubbed oil on to her stomach. She takes excellent care of herself. She said it was to prevent the skin from looking stretched and abused after the pregnancy. It was important. We never missed a day.

I followed her into the bedroom and laid the towel out on the bed for her. The room was balmy. There was heat lodged in the walls. There was heat still trapped in the courtyard outside, and we could hear the tree lisping in the breeze. There was heat trapped in the sand underneath Berlin. She lay down on the towel with her large, round shape bulging upwards like a copper dome. I kissed her stomach first, so as not to shock her with touch. She was looking up at the ceiling with her arms clasped behind her head. She might as well have been still lying on the grass in Tiergarten. I wanted to kiss her under the arms.

Helen had a mental picture of my hands unscrewing the lid of the oil bottle. I poured some of the oil on to the apex of the dome. Helen shrieked at the coolness of the liquid, which began slowly to roll down the sides. I put down the bottle and caught the rivulets of oil in time, and began to disperse them with circular motion. I placed the cap of the oil bottle on her breastbone and continued the circular movement of my hands.

Her stomach felt like a perfect globe. Helen has a mental picture of continents and oceans. Her navel at the top seemed to be the only peculiar shape to me. It had become taught and strained; like a lizard's eye. It used to look like a marble just dropped and submerged in fresh pastry. I poured more oil on her navel, and had to work faster this time to catch the rivulets escaping down the side. I spent a long time circling around with my hands, occasionally feeling the twitches and tremors inside.

I had a mental picture of a large round cake. The room filled up with the rich scent of oil and I was sure it was drifting out through the window all over the courtyard too. I pulled the sheet over her and she soon fell asleep. For a while I stood at the open window with my hands in the air, covered in gloves of precious oil.

9

Marauders

Once every second month, the city of Berlin turns its pockets out.

As with most other German cities, the inhabitants of Berlin have the opportunity every odd month to dispose of any personal belongings, no matter how large or small, simply by placing them out on the street. This special municipal collection is made quite independently of normal weekly refuse collections, and is intended for hardware and junk, unwanted furnishings and renovation debris, more than for ordinary domestic waste. Items that have lost their appeal and practicality against the forces of change and the incremental forces of well-being. Items of descending value, bashed in by familiarity and outwitted by fashion. It's all got to do with desire and the law of superseding desires. The constant rate of replacing the personal environment.

Before the actual collection takes place, people are free to look through the mounds of disposed junk on the pavement to see if they can salvage anything worth-while. Which they often do. I know people who have furnished their whole apartments with salvaged junk like this.

Not that this would in any way reflect squandering or neglect of personal assets in Berlin. Far from it; people don't like throwing things away. It hurts to discard. And shortages since the war have provided the inhabitants of Berlin, young and old, with a strong tradition of respect for second-hand items with life still left in them. It hurts to see somebody contentedly carrying off something you have just thrown out.

The general collection in Berlin is normally fixed for a Tuesday. Which means that early on Monday evening, and right through the night of Monday–Tuesday, a quiet, manic exchange takes place across the city. Sacred interiors are revealed. Old dog-baskets, doors, bicycle wheels, broken fittings, bedding and kitchenwear all find their way on to the pavement in an orderly fashion. Ridiculous items, too, which people often bring back from their holidays abroad and never wanted in the first place.

Berlin trades privacy for practicality. The city exposes its personality in piles of unwanted possessions. Private lives are unfolded in junk, laid bare for all to see as groups of people drift through the night; foraging, examining items of marginal value and exposing former owners to final twinges of regret.

It is the immigrant in Berlin who often benefits most from this exposure. Certainly, most of the furniture and fittings at Grossbeerenstrasse, the house owned by Hadja's father, would have been rescued from street clearances like these by silent marauding gangs. Turkish women with headscarves and multi-layered clothes will be seen jumping down out of the backs of vans to evaluate prey. Sometimes the women stay inside the vans and simply nod their heads at items held up by their men on the pavement. Jugs, plastic containers; that kind of thing. Nothing is too worthless to be assessed. And sometimes it's the men who nod while the women with coloured headscarves avidly examine the exposed history of Berlin's interior life.

There is a silent panic in the way that people's belongings are examined by street light in the middle of the night. The city falls into a phase of polite mania. Very little is said. At most, a whisper of dissent or delight at discovery. A smile of appreciation at an item worth keeping. By Tuesday lunchtime, the official collection will have been carried out by the city's disposal teams, and Berlin recovers its complete privacy.

There is really only one person in Berlin to whom Hadja can pour her heart out and expose herself. Only one person in whom she can truly confide. That's Kristl König. Former schoolfriend whose parents own the König flowershops. And it's not as though Hadja and Kristl are great bosom friends; they don't even meet that often. But the intimate bond between schoolfriends has never been broken. Perhaps Kristl is just a good listener. Perhaps Hadja still trusts her because Kristl is a tireless advocate of good fun. Perhaps Hadja just needs to get something off her chest badly enough to trust Kristl with the most sensitive details of her own biography. Maybe it has to do with the fact that Kristl is currently having an affair with her brother Konrad. Kristl is an excellent listener. She nods appreciatively. Her attitude is humorous and enthusiastic, supported by the simple tenet that life is too short, marriage is too long, men are too fast, love is too slow and a dog is a woman's best friend. Kristl owns a dachshund called Tristan.

At Kristl's apartment in Schöneberg, where she normally lives alone with Tristan, Hadja now pours her heart out. Wolf's infidelity, love, loyalty, the meaning of relationships, being wanted; that kind of thing. *Die ganze Gefühlskiste*: the whole trunk of feelings, as it is known. Hadja feels some momentary twinges of regret while parting with all these explicit details of her personal affairs. But Kristl is such a good listener. So is her dog, Tristan, curled up beside her on the sofa. Kristl has a way of putting herself on your side. She nods continuously, and her blonde hair falls down over her face, forcing her at intervals to throw back her head and begin again from the start, nodding continuously. Konrad says she's like a flower, a daffodil in the wind, the way she throws her head back. Hadja says Kristl is the kind of person you tell everything.

Kristl's three-bedroom apartment is generous on space. The commanding feature at the centre of the living room is the broad Persian rug, on which stands nothing but a low black ash coffee table with one of those half and half dishes with compartments of *Salzstangen*: pretzel sticks and peanuts. Two bottles of Beck's beer straight from the fridge are still smoking from the nozzle alongside two frothy blond glasses.

Sag'mal, Hadja! That, I just cannot believe, said Kristl, throwing back her head. Wolf? Can it be true?

But I know it's true, Kristl.

Wolf? I can't grasp it, Kristl exclaims with lavish amazement. Did you catch them at it or something?

No! But Kristl, I know when something is going on.

But not Wolf. Seriously, I never thought he was the type. Believe me, Hadja, I know a womanizer when I see one. I know the way men look at you while you're looking away. The side glances. I know when a man is interested, believe me. Wolf, he never seemed the type to me. Always thinking about things; music, culture. I just can't believe it, Hadja.

Well, look, I was twice as surprised as you, Kristl. I can tell you that.

Wolf? Kristl says thoughtfully, shaking her head from side to side. There I was thinking he was an idealist and a true artist, the furthest thing from a womanizer . . . *Na!* . . . Another lost chance.

Kristl, don't joke about it.

No! Honestly spoken, Hadja, I really did not expect that. I know Wolf is extremely handsome and all that, but I'm stunned. How long has it been going on?

Ach, I don't know, Hadja said. I'm quite sure it's over now. But I can't let him get away with it, can I?

No way!

Kristl leans over and picks up one of the pretzel sticks and begins to break it into pieces while listening to Hadja telling the whole story. Kristl never eats pretzel sticks. She gives them to her dog. *Hier Schatzelein, hier Tristan.*

Are you sure it's over? Are you sure this Lydia is the only one? Kristl wants to know, flinging back her head again. Is anything ever over?

It's over for her, Hadja said. I scared her away. I gave her such a fright, she won't be back. At the Aula concert, I got one of the spotlights turned on her. I'll tell you, she must have wet herself with shock.

Echt, Hadja, Did you do that?

Kristl listens with exaggerated interest to Hadja's calm description of the spotlight trained on Lydia at the Aula. Kristl laughs heartily, slapping her knee, but underneath, it gives rise to her own fears of being caught like that in a spotlight. She is also a surrogate. Caught in a frail relationship with Hadja's brother Konrad, who will never leave his wife and whose wife will never leave him. *Ersatzliebe!* At present, Konrad's wife is away in Ulm visiting her parents.

Kristl discusses Wolf's affair with Lydia. No matter who you talk about, you end up describing yourself.

Echt, Hadja, I wouldn't have the nerve. Wonderful! You did the right thing. I mean, it's not as though you and Wolf were not getting on or anything. You and Wolf are made for one another. You make love, *nicht wahr*? It's not as though you don't give him what he needs.

Take Konrad and myself, Kristl continues. That's an entirely different situation. Men need constant love. At least, Konrad does, and he doesn't get it. You know yourself, Hadja. She's cold. She's good for business but no good in bed. And men need that, otherwise they look around. That's not the way with you and Wolf, now is it. You give him what he wants, *nicht wahr*?

Not now I don't.

But why? Have you not made up?

Not yet. I feel I have to get him back for it.

Yes, but not like that, Hadja. This won't work. Believe me. What you should do is have a little fling yourself. Make Wolf appreciate everything more. Have your own little affair and that will even things up. Hadja, even if you don't want to, you have to balance the scales. Honestly spoken, that's my feeling.

No matter what you say to a dachshund, he'll believe you. Advice is self-justification. When Kristl talks about others, she speaks about herself. Women's laughter agitates a dachshund. Tristan sits up and wags his tail at the loss or expectation of personal attention. Hadja and Kristl discuss men, eyes, smiles, availability; that kind of thing. They talk about exploitation, sexism in the workplace, and reverse manipulation.

Kristl König knows how to manipulate and how to be manipulated.

At five o'clock on Saturday evening, she takes the *U-Bahn* into the city to meet Konrad at the new flowermarket; he wants to show her the latest of his enterprises. Following the much discussed success of the Weinstube chain with wine bars, he has acquired an old flowermarket where the women of Berlin used to collect their flowers and sell them in the streets. The building work has already begun. Men from Grossbeerenstrasse have already begun to chisel and work on the walls, and Konrad intends to give the cellar its former splendour and open the place as a new, exclusive wine restaurant with live classical music; quartets and quintets.

The *U-Bahn* is quite crowded at that time of the evening on Saturdays. Kristl doesn't normally travel on public transport, but decided that it would be more convenient this time, since she can then get into Konrad's car and go back to his house in Charlottenburg. His wife is away in Ulm. She's already seen the flowercellar. As yet, Kristl has not seen the flowercellar or Konrad's house.

At Eisenacher Strasse, where Kristl gets on the *U-Bahn*, there is little room in the carriage, and she has to stand. She decides to keep Tristan on her arm because people are pushed up against one another. Tristan is wearing a light tartan coat; blue. Kristl is wearing her new green dress, high-heeled shoes with small silver bows at the heel, no tights, costume *diamantés* and a necklace that hangs low, emphasizing the warmth of her bosom and the warmth of the weather; perhaps not exactly the right choice for the *U-Bahn*, she thought to herself. She feels a little exposed on public transport.

The normal rules of *U-Bahn* travel apply on Saturdays. Everyone looks preoccupied, staring into the distance as though at some far-away sunlit canyon. Expressions of fierce concentration or glazed sadness. One woman looks as though she's lost something. Another passenger beside her looks like he's remembered a private joke. Even Tristan looks preoccupied with his own personal life. Nobody speaks.

At Fehrbelliner Platz, the carriage became less crowded and she let the dog down, continuing to support herself with one hand gripping the vertical bar, the other holding the dog's studded blue lead. Two men got on, slightly drunk it seemed. One of them held the same bar as Kristl, but she ignored the intimacy and continued to employ the preoccupied, almost poetic stare into distant land-scapes, pretending to be absorbed by a full life. Pretence is provocative. The two men glance at her and speak loudly to each other, threatening communal privacy with indirect speech. The second man leaned with his back against the doors as soon as they shut, and though everyone knows he won't fall out, he looks precarious and dangerous. Danger is disgusting.

Nothing can stop these men smiling and looking at Kristl; looking at her dog and looking at her legs. Nothing can stop them talking in the third person. Nothing can stop them from imagining her undressed in front of them. No law against the imagination.

Was duftet hier so schön? What's that beautiful smell on the *U-Bahn* today? They must be spraying the carriages with a new disinfectant on Saturdays, *wa*, Hans?

The men smile at each other. Nobody else dares to look at them in case they draw attention to themselves.

Yes, it smells just lovely around here.

Absolutely!

Must be the dog. What do you think?

They looked down at the dog. But Kristl turned away, pretending almost that the dog did not belong to her, hoping still to belong to the general public. An elderly woman suddenly spun around in her seat to take a look at the dog for herself, and then looked at Kristl too, as though she were responsible for all this talk on the *U-Bahn*. The man leaning at the doors is doing all the talking.

And the little fellow is so nicely dressed, too, in his blue coat. He's probably going out for dinner this evening? What do you think, Hans?

Kristl began to look up at the advertisement display along the side of the carriage, at high-speed secretarial services, gallery exhibitions, BurgerKing and at the distant landscape beyond a solitary if not forlorn Marlboro smoker on horseback. She began to study the sequence of *U-Bahn* stations and was reminded that she still had two stations to go.

Very valuable dogs they are, too. Full pedigree, you can see that.

The quieter of the two men is laughing to himself.

One thing I can tell you, Hans, they reproduce at a ferocious rate, those dogs. It's true.

Kristl continued to look up at the ads with intense interest. At the next station, very little changed in the ratio of passengers; some got on and some got off. A woman moved over into an empty place by the window and felt the heat left behind by a former passenger. Kristl contemplated getting off a station too early, and when the train got back into motion again, regretted that she no longer had that option. She felt debarred from looking down at Tristan, her own dog.

Say, Hans, I think the dog is smiling at us. Such an honest smile. Very loyal they are, too, those dogs.

The man with his back to the doors began to move unsteadily towards the dog, throwing the passengers on the *U-Bahn* into a self-conscious frenzy. Instability is disgusting. The man crouched down and began to make faces at the dog, which reacted with a positive and affable tail-wagging that Kristl was powerless to forbid. Nor could she forbid direct communication between her dog and the stranger.

What a loyal little fellow you are, the man kept repeating. Repetition is disgusting. Or is it a sign of begging? Kristl continued to ignore him like a beggar, though he was obviously not one, no more than men normally are.

Schnukelein! Come here. What a loyal little fellow you are.

The man began to pet the dog. Physical contact is disgusting. He then began to make loud sucking noises which could be heard throughout the carriage. Labial smacking, which became clearly audible above the screech and whistle of wheels, throwing the passengers into a frozen shock of heightened interest. But the dog betrayed, responding to the man's voice with unmistakable signs of willing friendship in his tail. *Schatzy, Schatzy, Schatzilein*, the man kept saying. What is your name? Little *Schatzilein*. He crouched down only inches away from her bare knees and bare legs, on which tiny, invisible hairs stood out. A glance downwards would have confirmed that the man had a circular bald patch on top of his head. Vague fumes of alcohol reached her nostrils. The sucking noises started again. She could have knocked him over with her knee. Could have shown anger. She could have smiled downwards and said the dog's name was Tristan. She could have sighed in public reproof. Instead, she pulled again on the lead and continued to fix her ecstatic gaze on distant Marlboro canyons.

Can you get closer to Kristl than that? At the old flowercellar, Kristl felt impatient and told Konrad she was cold. A rash of goosepimples erupted on her arms, so they went for a drink, and afterwards for a meal. Tristan conducted himself as usual with admirable behaviour, though as soon as they arrived in Konrad's house in Charlottenburg, he did seem a little restless, naturally, being his first time; he sniffed around anxiously for a while before settling down on the sofa. Kristl was not a little excited herself. It was her first time ever in Konrad's house, too. Normally they met at her apartment in Schöneberg. This time there was a sensation of filthy fascination as she entered the home life around Konrad's house. A wild thrill of being wrong.

It was only when Kristl walked into the bedroom that she realized what strange privileges are granted to the surrogate. What powers of comparison. Invasion. Judgement. It was only when she watched Konrad's head between her thighs that she first noticed a faint bald circle on his crown. Only then that she began to see things the way Konrad's wife sees them.

Later, she left him asleep, and walked around the bedroom listening to his faltering snore. This was Konrad's wife's bedroom, Kristl thought to herself. Now it was her privilege to examine everything with judgemental pleasure. She wouldn't have chosen the wallpaper. Or the lampshades. The bedspread was pretentious. She opened drawers and examined documents, letters, jewellery, underwear, scarves and hats. She felt the silent marauding delight of this unhurried invasion of privacy. And privacy is founded in comparison, so she went on lashing out comparisons while Konrad's breathing achieved increasing regularity behind her.

The next time the general collection came up, I couldn't help noticing a large pile of broken and twisted cane screens outside on the pavement along Sonnenallee. There were some blackened pots outside the house as well as a broken ironing board.

Helen and I were looking for some bits and pieces for the apartment at the time; extra chairs, a press for my equipment, which is always in boxes on the floor. We were also looking for a cot. We would need a cot very soon. Late in the evening, we went out together and walked along the streets to see what we could find. Nothing. Nothing that I could see, anyhow. Except other people's junk. But we were there with all the other unseen and silent groups combing through the back streets of Berlin. In some places, we came across disturbed piles of junk that had clearly been gone through already. In another street, we saw a man alone sweeping the pavement with a household brush. We heard an alarm, but never passed the building or found out where exactly it was coming from. In one street, a non-functioning street light gave the impression of a bend in the pavement. And once, as we turned a corner, we saw people closing the back doors of a van and driving away.

10

Von Hinten

I thought I knew everything about Helen.

Until every time I watched her doing something like spreading butter, absently biting her lip, leafing through a magazine, brushing her hair, talking to herself, saying: Put my shoes on now. Until I once saw her staring at my shoulder while I was telling her something. Until every time I met her again. And every time it was night.

This is the way I imagined it would happen. At any moment I expected her to come in holding a baby.

I thought I knew everything about Helen. I knew what her weight was. What her weight should be after pregnancy. Height. Date of birth. Parents' names. Brother's name. What school she went to. Her vocabulary. I knew the way she yawned.

I thought I knew everything. I still brought Helen to the clinic once a week. Went with her and brought her with me as much as I could, to the Bar-o-Bar café, and other bars, and to Wolf's electric rehearsals, where Helen said the bass guitar seemed to drive the baby wild inside her. Until she talked about the baby like this. Until one day I met her in the street along Sonnenallee and we first looked at each other like strangers and then smiled idiotically. Until she told me later how she had passed by a sex shop somewhere along her way and seen all these foreign workers standing outside playing with beads in their hands, and how one of them half blocked her way and asked for something she thought at first to be directions or the time. How she was preparing to answer when he offered her 30 marks and she recoiled in shock, not so much at the offer or the idea of the offer, but at the thought of herself being so obviously pregnant. Really? she kept on saying afterwards.

What can be the attraction of a pregnant woman. Is it the calm prediction of the future? Is it the sight of life beginning all over again? Or is it the radiating image of pregnancy as a sheer confidence trick? Why does everybody like a pregnant woman? Is it the absence of threat?

Is it the unmistakable declaration of former coupling?

Until Helen began, in the days after that, to laugh at the whole idea of 30 marks, and kept on saying to me: There you are now, mate. Better watch it. I can get at least 30 marks any time I want. I'll never be stuck for money in Berlin by the looks of it. Until I noticed that Helen's sense of humour was always very close to the truth.

Then one day she came back with a small radio which I had never seen before and which, she explained casually, she had left in for repair while she was still living with Hadja and Wolf, and only remembered to collect that day. She placed it on the table to see how high the volume would go, and played with the frequencies while I reacted with open surprise. The radio was something she had never told me about. Until that day. Until I began to realize that Helen contained an endless collection of arcane things that would emerge one by one, day by day, month by month.

I thought I knew everything about Helen until I saw her blink. What is it about blinking that makes people look lonely? And vulnerable?

I thought I knew everything about her until she told me about Dieter and herself in the Shelbourne Hotel in Dublin. Until she told me how the two of them had booked into the hotel and said they had just arrived from London for a few days. They arrived with two travel bags, had dinner, went out for the evening, had champagne breakfast the following morning and left without paying. By lunchtime, they had gone, leaving two empty travel bags in the room behind them.

As usual, I rushed her with questions. What if she and Dieter had been caught? What did they do after they left the hotel? The most irrelevant things I wanted to know. Whose idea was it? What do you think Dieter is doing now? If not still leaving debts behind him in hotels? What would you say to Dieter if you saw him in front of you now?

I wouldn't like Dieter to see me now, she said.

She stopped to think for a while, and then looked up.

No! Not at the moment. Not now.

I thought I knew everything about myself.

Until she talked about Dieter. Until I began to realize that she still talked about Dieter in the present tense.

Until one afternoon on my own, I walked into a second-hand Trödel shop around Nollendorfplatz and bought a pink cot for Helen and her baby. Purely on impulse. Not because she needed it as much as because I needed it. I paid far more than anyone should pay for a pink second-hand cot, because it was an antique dealer with half-glasses who sold it to me, and because I bought it as though it was the last cot in Berlin. The way I always buy things in a complete emergency. And I told the man looking over his half-glasses that somebody would collect the cot within a day or two, because I had Hadja in mind; I knew I could rely on her to do me a favour for once.

Until I saw myself behaving more and more as though I too had been following stage instructions. Screenplay instructions choreographing each movement with an overbearing, almost tumescent significance: for the benefit of an omnipresent observer. If the phone rings, I look at the phone. If there is a knock on the door, I look at the door. At the end of a telephone conversation, I hold the receiver in my hand and replace it only after a significant interval to emphasize the weight of the final words spoken. I hesitate frequently, as though at each moment I am about to step into a new life, or an unforeseen calamity from which I still have the opportunity to turn back. As though the omnipresent viewer already knows what's good for me, even though I continue to move on as part of a plot.

Pedestrians appear as part of the plot, each person knowing exactly where to go without being told. Objects in the street seem to reflect on my earlier decision to buy a pink cot, as though these objects possess more than their normal qualities. As though each shop I pass bears some significance. Clocks accuse. Mosaic pavements make you dizzy. Everything is full of potential, even an overhead crane on a building site nearby. Everything is swollen with meaning. When I hesitate outside the *U-Bahn* station, the omnipresent observer will see that there is such a thing as choice, if only you knew the plot, if only you knew about the options of life in advance.

On the *U-Bahn*, I stood while there were empty seats. After a while I sat down as though I now intended a longer journey. Then I got up confidently and walked towards the doors with the obvious intention of getting off at the next stop. But when the train burst into the brightly lit station, I was left on the wrong side, facing the wrong doors with my eyes only inches away from the glass. There are some things you can't fake. I now had to wait until the next station on my side of the train in order to maintain my inner resolve.

And later, when I walk into a café, I want everyone who might be watching me to be confused about my intentions and confused about where I have come from; as though I am the last man who might have bought a pink cot. The café was empty except for one table at the far end, at which an old woman sat watching me as I entered. And I walked directly towards her all the way across the empty café, looking her in the eye all the time until the last minute, when I chose a table elsewhere and turned my back on her. I ordered coffee. Then ignored the coffee when it arrived. Then drank the coffee a while later with a thirst more appropriate to beer and, before a reasonable time had elapsed, left again as though I had remembered something. Paid for the coffee and stepped out into the street and turned left, only to pass back in front of the café in the opposite direction moments later, thinking at all times what the women inside the café must be thinking.

From now on I feel like answering questions with questions only. Speaking in double negatives. But there are things left of which I cannot pretend to be the opposite. There are some things you can't feign. Like an erection. Death. Surrogacy. How can I pretend not to be living with Helen? It's written on my face. How can I pretend not to be the father of her baby?

Until the afternoon when Hadja delivered the pink cot for me and Helen answered the door to find Hadja standing there, slightly breathless, in the company of a young curly-black-haired man carrying the cot. I was out at the time, rehearsing with Wolf. And Hadja explained to Helen that the young man with her was a Turk, just recently arrived in Germany, called Mehmet. She ordered him in Turkish to carry the cot inside. Then asked Helen where exactly she wanted it, and Helen merely said: Oh, anywhere at all. Against the wall for the moment. Which the young Turk understood without any need for translation. He propped the cot against the wall and stood back promptly, looking at both women for further instructions.

Helen began to thank them for bringing the cot. Hadja dismissed it as nothing with a downward flap of the hand. And thanking the Turk was superfluous, since he was merely doing his job. Hadja began to walk around the apartment as though it was her own. It was once her own; still is, any time she wants it. She looked out of the window at the courtyard, and then spun around to look at the room.

Nice the way you have it, she said. Compliment or accusation? There's been a strain between Helen and Hadja for some time.

Why don't you stay for some tea? Helen offered.

The strain is measured in gestures of polite friendship. They say the ape first discovered friendship as a weapon. Thus intelligence. Hadja is reluctant to stay for tea. Says she has to push off and drop Mehmet back to work at the flower cellar. But Helen insists. And before Hadja had the chance to tell Mehmet to wait in the car for her, Helen pulled out a chair for him and made him sit down. He couldn't refuse, even though he checked with a quick glance at Hadja. And Hadja signalled approval by slowly taking off her leather bag and placing it on the floor beside the window.

This was Hadja's apartment. Helen cannot forget that. Nor can Hadja forget that this is now Helen's apartment.

To add another genial dimension, Helen began to speak to Mehmet, the curly-haired Turk.

How do you like Berlin? she asked, but the Turk simply erupted in a fit of gesticulation and shoulder movements.

He doesn't speak a word, Hadja said. Mehmet. He's only recently arrived in Germany. Speaks nothing but Turkish.

Hadja sat down at the round table. Just a quick cup then, she said. She has a way of sitting down sideways, cross-legged, turned to the right with her elbow on the table. It has the effect of placing Mehmet almost behind her, even though he is sitting at the same table. She has a way of speaking almost from behind her mass of dark red hair, across her jutting left shoulder.

How is Dieter? Have you heard anything from him already?

No! Helen answered from the kitchen.

Is he still in Berlin then, you think?

I don't know. I'm sure he is.

There is no reason to suspect anything but genuine inquiry from Hadja, and when Helen came back in carrying cups and saucers, she began to give Hadja the up-to-date picture.

We found his bag in a hotel near Potsdam or somewhere. But you know that, Helen said. All it means is that we know he's definitely here in Berlin, although sometimes I'm even beginning to doubt it myself.

Then, with one look at Hadja's complacent way of sitting, Helen feels the urge to retract what she said. Surprised by her own honesty, she wishes she could have described a more positive state. No sense in giving Hadja ammunition.

Ach . . . I don't even care much at the moment, Helen said, going back out into the kitchen. But Helen is a bad liar. Hadja knows it.

When she came back in carrying a pot of tea and a tray of biscuits, she moved faster than her shape allowed, as though in front of Hadja, and Mehmet too, perhaps, she wanted to conceal her pregnancy. Another bad lie. Women can smell politeness like gas or burning rubber.

In a completely honest gesture, Hadja takes a biscuit from the tray without being asked. Greed is honest.

Helen poured the tea.

Look, Helen, if you want me to find Dieter, maybe I can still help you, Hadja announced, now about to take her second biscuit.

Du . . . You know what, Konrad has a private detective. I can ask him to have a look for him if you like.

Oh no! Not at all, Helen said. The thought of a detective chasing Dieter around Berlin was too much for her to grasp. In any case, she was reluctant to accept any more favours from Hadja. Already felt too much indebted.

It's just an idea, Hadja said. Think it over if you like. It wouldn't cost anything, since Konrad uses him a lot for business deals.

Helen was anxious to change the subject.

How is Sulima these days?

Ach, Sulima, Hadja said. She's gone back to Iran to marry this idiot.

So I heard. But is she coming back to Berlin then?

I really don't know, Hadja said.

There is little else for them to talk about. Each subject seemed to have a dead end, either ending up in annoyance for Hadja or tacit hostility from Helen. Until Helen found the one subject she could be totally honest about and began to describe to Hadja how difficult it was to get up the stairs; if there were a winch or a crane in the courtyard she would use it to come in the window instead. Until Hadja said it might be a good idea to find an apartment with a lift after the baby arrives.

How long do you have to go? Hadja asked.

Any day really, from now on.

Until Helen seemed eager to talk about herself for once without any inhibitions, and began to describe her heartburn, the way she could eat nothing but Quark now, and as soon as the baby was born she was going to go out and have a decent curry or something. Until she described the baby waking her up in the middle of the night with kicks, like a football match going on inside.

Hadja accepted another biscuit. The last one, she said. And then leaned back.

It must be difficult, Hadja said, with half the biscuit in her mouth. She can be very diplomatic.

Helen can be effusive. Too eager to talk.

It must be difficult to make love these days, Hadja asked, pushing forward her left shoulder again.

Helen stopped in her tracks; couldn't answer.

I mean, it must be so difficult and very awkward for you, Hadja went on. I am wondering all the time: how do you manage it?

Helen looked nervously across at Mehmet, but then it was quite obvious that he hadn't understood anything. Hadja kept talking.

I mean, everyone must bounce from time to time. Even a pregnant woman . . . *nicht wahr*? Honestly spoken now, I think this is the only thing I would have against being pregnant. Really, I'm interested now. It must be so difficult. How do you do it?

Hadja, come on! Helen began to pour tea-leaves. Hadja began to answer her own questions.

I suppose it's no use straight on then? And I could imagine that sitting up could be dangerous, for the foetus, that is. How do you do it? Oral love, is that it? You can always resort to oral techniques when you are pregnant, but that can't be so good in the long run. I suppose the only way is *von hinten*, am I right? *Von hinten*? From behind it must be as good as ever, is that so?

Helen is more amazed than annoyed that Hadja can go on like this.

Von hinten also! But all the time from behind can even get a little boring after a while, I would imagine.

Hadja, come on. Give it up, Helen said.

Hadja was smiling now.

Would you like to do it *von hinten* with this young man here from Konya? Hadja said, shaking her head over her shoulder in the direction of Mehmet.

Mehmet recognized the name of his home town and responded, looking up at both women with a brilliant white smile.

Shit, Hadja, give over.

Until words create havoc. Until Hadja's words were left behind in our apartment in Sonnenallee like some market survey between us. Or more like a psychological questionnaire which continues to irritate until it is either completed or thrown out. Hadja's words are like a double-blind trap of veracity. In Germany, any answer is a good answer.

Please answer as accurately and as honestly as you can.

I thought I knew everything until I got home late and Helen started telling me what Hadja had said about *von hinten*. Until I saw the pink cot leaning against the wall of the living room, unassembled. Helen had made no attempt to put it together. There was no rush.

How anxious are you to find out what Helen has been up to all day? How anxious are you to hear what Hadja and Helen have been discussing?

Place on a scale of priority, the following attributes in a pregnant woman. Warmth. Healthy complexion. Ability to talk like a non-pregnant woman. Ability to walk in the park without frequently tripping on irregular pavements. Ability to keep the baby inside her as long as possible.

Does the approach of birth increase or diminish longing for beer? Would fatherhood and ensuing pride alter your choice of beer?

I placed the can of beer on the table. I sat down with a tired expression and placed my feet like a bridge on another chair and my elbow on the table. Normally, this would have been the sign for Helen to come and sit on my legs but she has become temporarily too heavy for that and sat instead on a chair at the opposite side of the table. Both elbows on the table. She laughed.

Stupid cow, she said. I wouldn't mind it coming from anyone else but her.

Helen speaks about *von hinten*. With confidence? With difficulty? Does Helen have the ability to brush off obviously intended insults? Is Helen capable of laughing off the truth?

Place in order of least consequence the following properties in a pregnant woman. Skilled application of make-up? Ability to communicate to large groups of people? Buoyancy in sea water? Permanence of address? Who the father is?

Helen listened to the sound of bubbles and beer escaping down my throat. *Von hinten*, she said giggling.

It reminds me of that litany we used to recite at school, I said. What was it? Saint Patrick's Breastplate. *Von hinten. Von vorne. Von oben. Von unten.* Christ below me. Christ above me. Christ behind me.

Describe Helen's laughter. Schoolgirlish? Adult? Like gunfire? Tearing cloth? Airlocked plumbing? Or does it sound like wine bottles being decorked? Describe Helen's response to amorous advances. Uncontrollable laughter? Ocular acknowledgement? Indifference?

With which of the following would you associate greater pleasure? A woman's laughter? Ocular acknowledgement? A kiss on the temple from a pregnant woman?

Rank in order of viability under the Geneva Convention, in order of maximum support to the German character and progress towards the notion of an integrated Europe, the following range of alternative final solutions. The simultaneous floating of all pregnant women (seven to nine months) belly upwards in man-made swimming pools or lakes? The instant translation of all English pop songs into German? The repatriation of all immigrant workers outside the EEC? *Von hinten* for all EEC members?

Helen walked into the bedroom. Obedient to the laws of minimal discomfort, she removed all her clothes, threw her slippers in the corner and kneeled down on her hands and knees. Instantly, she felt the great release of weight from her spine. She says it's like dropping a heavy bag. Her head hung forward and the curls of her hair fell loosely down from her neck. She was still laughing like decorking wine. The light from the living room and whatever light came in from the courtyard outside illuminated the sheer pleasure of weightlessness in her spine. The cessation of pain or constant pressure can make you laugh sometimes.

From above, Helen looks as though she might not be pregnant at all. Except for the missing curve at the waist. Any contact with her spine is for her at once frightening and immensely soothing. I kissed the knuckles of her spine. At the small of her back, I licked a flat space and left a cool mark like a wet leaf.

Describe your mode of conduct with a pregnant woman. Your reaction to imagined contact with the foetus. Hostile? Degrading? Primitive?

I think it's beginning, Helen said.

I knew exactly what she meant, but I couldn't move.

I think it's beginning, she said again.

11

Before and After

Even as late as late October, the weather in Berlin stayed mild, perhaps uncharacteristically warm. There was nothing to announce autumn. At lunchtime, customers still sat outside at tables and restaurant terraces along Kurfürstendamm and Savigny Platz. People still found summer bargains in the shops. The sun slanting along the streets still occasionally blinded a pedestrian in the wing mirror of a car, or across the surface of an outdoor café table-top, and still occasionally illuminated, with inspired malice, the ill-defined silhouette of a woman's legs underneath a cotton dress, walking down some side-street.

And outside the city centre flower cellar soon to be transformed into a new exclusive wine cellar, the workers still came up at lunchtime every day to sit along the pavement in the sun with their sandwiches.

The owner of the flower cellar, Konrad Milic, for reasons best known to himself, discourages this congregation of workers on the pavement outside. But the foreman, Franz, is unable to stop them from coming up to take the air and lean their elbows against the disposal bin, quietly talking in Turkish. In this case they are all Turkish; all from Grossbeerenstrasse in Kreuzberg.

In fact most of the workers employed on the restoration of the flower cellar have no names. Their names, that is, do not appear on any list or register of persons existing in Berlin. Only Franz, the foreman, Rudi Schaeffer the subcontractor and Ali, one of the oldest and most loyal of Hadja's father's employees, are legally registered in West Berlin. The main reason for this is that the reconstruction work is still only in its initial phase. Later on, the subcontractor will require more skilled workers for plastering and interior decoration. The men now chiselling, drilling, breaking through walls and pushing wheelbarrows have been taken from Konrad's other building sites in Berlin, where they might be more exposed to casual checks by the immigration authorities. Men are easily hidden in a cellar. And it suits these workers too. Though they dislike being told not to come up for daylight at lunchtime. Even more so they don't like to be told to keep the Turkish music from the cassette player down.

One of the names only recently added to this group is that of Mehmet, though at present he is absent from the site, engaged in some other work for the Milic family. Over the past week, he has been helping Hadja deliver election leaflets, putting up some last-minute posters and transporting some antiques for her mother. Mehmet is a good worker. Hadja, foreman Franz and Konrad all agree that he has potential, and if he plays his cards right, he should be first in line for a full work permit in Germany, though Konrad has found in the past that a full work permit often means losing good workers to other building firms.

Hadja's parents have been persuaded to take a late holiday in Rome. It's where they were married and where they like to go at least once a year. Conveniently, it allows Hadja to get a few things done. There are certain jobs which she has promised to get done while her mother is away and for which Mehmet is very suitable. Hadja also needs to make some lengthy phone-calls around Germany to arrange the most suitable recording studios for Wolf's forthcoming album without running up her own phone bill. Wolf is still worried. All in all, even though he is busy every day with rehearsals on the new album, he keeps wondering; Hadja's frequent absences make him nervous. He keeps asking me what she's up to.

For the past few days Hadja has been able to do little more than issue instructions to Mehmet for clearing out a storeroom full of superfluous antiques for her mother. Mehmet is awestruck by the surroundings of his employer/landlord's house in Charlottenburg; feels he shouldn't really be there at all and moves with excessive caution at all times. The considerable wealth contained in some of the objects displayed around the house goes back to the post-war years, when people fecklessly exchanged such priceless items for basic needs; when people said things like: I'd commit a mortal sin for a cup of coffee.

In the study, Mehmet was busy polishing a wooden sculpture of a satanic goat. Hadja is pleased with his work and with his eager intelligence. She sat down in one of the armchairs and stretched out her legs, just missing the oblong shaft of afternoon sunshine from the window. She wanted to know if Mehmet had a career in mind. He seemed to be cut out for more than building work. His mere respect for the goat in his hands confirmed that much.

What do you want to be? she asked in Turkish.

Mehmet had never really thought about it before.

I want to make some money first, he said. Then maybe I can sit back and think about learning something. Maybe I'll become a chef or a manager so I can open a hotel or a restaurant back home.

Mehmet shrugged while he spoke. Hadja had expected more. She was a little disappointed.

You should think more seriously about a good career, she said with an encouraging smile. She told him to sit down in one of the other armchairs, which he did, holding the cleaning rag in his hands. He sat a little rigidly in the chair while Hadja began to discuss alternative careers. She said he had the brains and the opportunity to do anything he wanted; medicine, pharmacology, veterinary science; anything. Mehmet's eyes began to widen with enthusiasm. After a while, he almost began to believe that he would soon be starting on a brilliant career. He even stopped shrugging his shoulders habitually and began to imitate her determination, though he would never convince anyone else, she thought, while he still had the cleaning rag in his possession, tugging at it like a contest between his hands.

A strange idea had occurred to her once or twice before while she looked at him. This time round, it seemed like a brand new idea again. And now seemed like the perfect opportunity. At that very moment, she made up her mind and walked over to the window to close the blinds. The room was thrown into a blue and beige half-light. Mehmet sat up.

You have a great future, she said. You may not know it yet, but I can see success.

Hadja has often told me that Turkish women speak like fortune-tellers.

Hadja lay down on the floor in the middle of the room, continued to speak of the future and then instructed Mehmet to remove his clothes and lie beside her. Mehmet hesitated, but then he didn't want to hold back or inhibit any future promise with lack of co-operation. He did as he was told. Threw his clothes on the armchair behind him. Lay down beside her and began to embrace her instinctively. Began to assist her by taking off her clothes too, one by one, as though he were still dealing with precious objects. Placed his hands eventually between her legs, forcing himself to be more positive than his wildest imagination had ever afforded, and began to move with complete self-confidence only when Hadja allowed him to kiss her neck like an equal.

Before things proceeded any further, Hadja sat up and thoroughly inspected Mehmet's penis for any obvious blemishes. Nothing wrong here? she asked. And Mehmet shook his head, almost believing for an instant that this was part of every interview in West Germany; part of every code of conduct between employer and employee. He had only recently arrived in Germany. They resumed. Little was spoken.

In fact, the only interesting thing that I heard either from Hadja or from Wolf later on about this exchange was that Mehmet continued his infrequent, pleading words in Turkish while Hadja quickly reverted to German, underlining her employer status. She shouted words like *Feste*, *feste*, or *Schnell*, *schnell*, perhaps as some kind of dubious compromise since Mehmet was already familiar with some of these stentorian commands from the building site. There is little else to observe about the exchange except the fact that the employer/employee relationship eventually disappeared completely, and if anything became reversed in a swap of roles whereby Mehmet issued the final instructions while Hadja yielded to the luxury of complete helplessness. Otherwise nothing new. The sound was exotic, maddening. That's all.

It's really what happens afterwards that matters. Afterwards, the participants are inspired, and ready to change the world. Either that or intoxicated, sad; imaginative; resolved never to try and change anything. Somebody said they fell apart like two halves of a lopped melon. Afterwards it's everyone for himself.

Mehmet, just recently arrived in Germany, stood up and began to walk around the room with his confidence inflamed. He knew somehow at that moment that he could be anything he wanted. He turned around towards Hadja and sang two verses of a Turkish love song: a mountain love song. She couldn't believe it. Almost felt directly responsible for breathing the sheer dynamic of Turkish tradition into this young man.

She lay on her side and followed Mehmet's muscle movements

around the room. She liked the sound of his song, though two verses was as much as she could take. Hadja laughs at superstition. But she enjoyed the sight of air filling Mehmet's lungs.

Afterwards, there is no telling what a person might do. Your partner might leave, or decide to stay. They might want to kill you. Or declare themselves a slave for ever, or declare you a slave for ever. Where do you stand? Afterwards, like never before, the question of status returns like an incessant noise, like drilling on roadworks. Reassurances are sought and given. Was I good? Do you love me? Never leave me! I will love you for ever! Afterwards, while things slowly revert into a shared order, partners look back in disbelief at the equilibrium achieved by passion. Afterwards, some people believe it is possible to achieve the same equality in real life and sadly cling to the suspended status of sex. Why try to re-create it? Afterwards, like never before, everything appears to be reaffirmed in roles. Postmen continue to deliver the post. Ambulancemen still rush to the scene of accidents. Objects that appear before your eyes are alive like never before in the limits of their own identity. Afterwards, everyone rushes out for explanations. Where do you stand? Afterwards, it's everyone for themselves.

Afterwards, everything beforehand is a prophecy. And everything that follows seems inevitable.

Afterwards, somebody said: That's it! Lovely! Somebody said: Isn't it amazing how history repeats itself! That's the beauty of it! Somebody speaking on the phone said: You can depend on me! *Aufwiedersehen!*

Afterwards, you discreetly remove a pubic hair from your mouth and wonder whether you should keep it like a souvenir or curse all attachment to transient matter.

Afterwards, the sound of your partner's final gasp will fade away slowly like the clear shriek of a parrot somewhere close by in the rainforest.

Equality breaks out like a tropical lull which then recedes into the old order of killing chaos. Afterwards, everything has to be reassessed. Nothing can be taken for granted.

Afterwards, Wolf normally falls asleep, only to wake up again a short while later bursting with the need for music, which can send him out to the living room for hours listening under the head-phones, as loud as he can bear it, holding back the volume of reassessment.

Afterwards, Hadja likes to prolong the truce by declaring herself hungry. Bouncing makes you hungry, she announces frequently. It's a weakness she reverts to. And food is always something you revert to, like being neutral.

With Lydia, Wolf once sat up in bed afterwards with the same desperate urge for music. He found a rubber band which he spanned across thumb and forefinger and across Lydia's big toe, making her shriek at first. Then, turning the rubber band into an instrument, he played an endless, monotonous tune while they listened with blank expressions like a tribal couple, the urgent pulse in their throats still beating like primitive percussion.

Like never before, Helen felt like crying. She also felt like laughing.

Like never before, Dieter felt like swimming.

Like never before, Kristl worked her way through Konrad's wife's clothes, examining everything, eventually deciding to try on an evening dress.

Like never before, Sulima opened her eyes and looked up to see the poster of Khomeini above her on the wall. It must have been six in the morning because Massoud, her husband to be, was already up. She sat up herself, and saw with shock that he was kneeling on the floor of the bedroom with his forehead touching the carpet in the direction of Mecca while his naked anus looked back at her, like a secret eye, watching her. She lay back down again, consumed with respect.

Afterwards, Helen felt she could swim herself; felt if somebody had flung her into the sea at that very moment, she would have known exactly what to do, the way you know how to cycle or drive a car long before you actually try it. She wanted to tell Dieter how she imagined herself swimming, but then she fell asleep, only to wake later with a start, some electrical build-up in the muscles which made her think she was underwater.

Like never before, Dieter must have felt like disappearing.

Afterwards, in their flat in Mountpleasant in Dublin, where Dieter and Helen once lived, they lay awake in bed one morning surrounded by half-light. Helen had to go to work, and got up

119

slowly, dragging her body across his arm, her thigh making the last contact with the palm of his hand. Dieter's eyes remained closed. His limbs stretched out. He listened to Helen wash herself. The basin was in the bedroom. He heard the towel rubbing against her skin. The sound of her clothes. He knew the order in which she did things. The unzipping of a bag. The lull while she hastily applied make-up. The sound of her feet walking across the room and the sound of the wire hangers on the door as she walked out into the kitchen. Cups and spoons. He heard the sound of the kettle switching itself off. Soon she came back in again with a cup of tea and whispered in his ear: There's some tea for you! Her voice seemed to come from both near and far away. He groaned in answer but left his eyes shut. He felt a kiss on the temple and tried to pull her back down towards himself, but she escaped saying: Bye! Then he heard the hangers on the door again. Her footsteps on the stairs. Then the sound of the hall door slamming, as though it came at once from both inside and outside the house, the sound of the gate, the sound of her bicycle setting off along the street. With his eyes shut, he could follow her long after the sounds had disappeared.

Afterwards, Dieter left without a word.

Afterwards, Mehmet thought he knew everything and felt himself incredibly useful in the world. He filled his lungs and sang out his mountain song, uninhibited by the surroundings or the possibility of unappreciative audience.

Afterwards, all Berlin went out to vote. The candidates looked inspired, rapturous, ready to change the world. An old couple walked into a polling station together, though once inside they approached separate booths, and it cannot be assumed that their votes went in the same direction either. Voting is an inspired task. And once the vote was cast, they felt better, more individual, less precious.

Afterwards, everything broke out in a rash of aspirations. The balance of power. Justifiable homicide. Innocent until Irish. German until proven Turkish. *Vorsprung durch Technik*. Peace at any price. United Germany. Afterwards, all kinds of utopian concepts were dreamt of. Rubber bullets safe for children. Stammheim. Assimilated immigrants. The NATO umbrella. A green Europe. Fire without smoke. Afterwards, everything became civilized by rhetoric. There was a better understanding. All minds were numb; going to work, to war, or whatever else, to stop the world from changing.

Afterwards, drivers in cars, momentarily held up at Innsbrücker Platz, experience a trancelike immobility, the impossibility of reverting and a brief illusion of freedom as they race up the link road on to the *Autobahn*.

Afterwards, Mehmet sang his brief song in the beige and blue half-light of Hadja's parents' house in Charlottenburg. Hadja watched his strong arms and his lungs and then listened to him recounting stories and gossip from his home town. She lay on the floor while he stood above her. At one stage, he took on the pose of the satanic goat he had been polishing earlier on. But after that, his self-confidence seemed to slip again, because Hadja laughed politely and said very little. Mehmet became increasingly aware that he was standing naked, looking down at his employer/landlord's daughter on the floor. Hadja reached up and pulled him down towards her, down on his knees. She looked intimately into his eyes and told him that she was about to give him a very important piece of advice. If he ever so much as breathed a word about this affair to anyone – ever – then it would be all over for him in West Germany. He would be on the next flight back to Turkey, possibly with a criminal record. Understood. This was a secret between them, she warned, looking him straight in the eye. We understand each other, *nicht wahr*.

Afterwards, a new understanding was reached.

Afterwards, everything became so vulnerable that it needed protection. Warnings were given. Secrets were kept. Illusions believed. Words like FOR EVER and NEVER AGAIN became necessary to fight off misunderstanding. Everything became either the biggest or the smallest. The first or the last. Nothing was allowed the escape of mediocrity. Nothing was exempt from the contest; the competitive arena which slowly dawned on Mehmet as he looked into Hadja's eyes, on his knees, sinking back on his heels. He had the COLDEST sensation when his buttocks met his heels.

Afterwards, I heard Helen say: I think it's beginning. She got up and went to the phone. Came back a little later and said she would have to go. It sounded almost as though she assumed she would go alone. But I jumped up and went with her.

It was the middle of the night; night-club hour. The driver of the taxi seemed angry, and reflected none of the panic and urgency which I felt in the back seat. Each time the taxi stopped at traffic lights, I glared at him silently. Helen heaved at intervals, but even that didn't seem to make the Mercedes sound any faster than it already was.

Can you go as fast as you can please, I urged again. *Schnell!*

Ja, ja, ja!

A small ornamental monkey hung suspended from the rear-view mirror, and kept bouncing as well as circling laterally on its spring. There was a sign saying: *Nichtraucher*/Non Smoker. Clipped to the dashboard was a passport photo of the driver. I could not imagine him at home talking enthusiastically about anything. In my mind, he remained forever solemn.

I held my hand on Helen's stomach all the time. As though it would be the last time. As though somehow I could still keep everything from taking its course. And at times I couldn't understand why I was in such a panic, until Helen began to heave again and bite her lip. Helen was as calm as ever, even calmer than the taxi driver. Perhaps it had something to do with her frame of mind: She thought it was beginning, while I thought it was ending.

At the clinic, I was confused. Whether to run around and open the door for Helen or pay the taxi driver first. I helped her up the steps and carried the shoulderbag which had been ready for the occasion for weeks. She paused and stiffened again half-way up and then a nurse came to meet us at the door and took Helen's elbow from me. Reluctantly, too, I gave away the bag. I was told to wait, and in situations like that you obey out of confusion. Helen stopped and objected; tried to persuade them to allow me in as well. But I understood what the nurse was saying in German: as I was not entered as the natural father, I could not be admitted. Why don't you go home? the nurse said. It will be quite a while yet. We knew nothing. We accepted that. The nurse asked Helen to remove all her jewellery; she could leave it either with me or with the reception for safe keeping. I was given her watch, ring and the frail gold necklace which the nurse helped to unclasp at the back of her neck. Now and again, the nurse nodded or spoke quietly to another nurse. Everything seemed so slow and formal. I watched the nurse guide Helen towards the lift. The doors prised open and they stepped inside, turning around just in time for Helen to smile back at me before the doors closed over again. It seemed like the last time I would ever see her.

Outside on the street, I hesitated and looked back at the clinic, as though I was expecting some sign from the windows above. Just to be doing something, I began to walk. There were election posters everywhere. It would have been impossible to ignore the fact that elections had been held in West Germany that day. Here and there, batches of leaflets chased each other in a breeze along the pavement. At the end of the street I came across a poster of Helmut Schmidt which had been defaced with an aerosol can. It must have been done very thoughtfully and discreetly because only the light reflection in his eyes had been touched in with black paint, making him look demonic and vicious. It was only when I came to the next poster of Helmut Schmidt with the light source in the eyes left intact that I was sure I knew the difference.

I kept walking, trying for some reason to pretend there was no election, trying to preserve Helen's last smile from the lift as though she were in danger of becoming submerged in election smiles. After a while, I could only remember the expression on her face as she heaved, biting her lip, holding back. But even that was better than the confusion of faces on posters in the empty streets. At the end of each street, I was faced with the choice of going left or right or straight on. At one stage, I stopped and thought I should go back to the clinic again. But I was no longer sure then whether I could retrace the route. I felt the watch and chain and the ring inside my pocket and thought it was all that was left of Helen.

Hadja got up from her place on the floor and went into the kitchen to make coffee. Mehmet soon followed her with all his clothes on again. She offered him coffee and a white roll with strawberry jam, which he ate very quickly. When this short meal was over, she told him to wait for her in the car while she made a phone-call.

Hadja took a shower and then sat down to make her phone-calls. She was concentrating on recording studios in the south of Germany. Felt it would inevitably be more productive and creative an environment for Wolf to work in. People who deal with Hadja on the phone are stunned by her charm and her flawless memory. She has a cool manner and a spontaneous turn of phrase which diffuses tension. She is direct. Uses phrases like: Come on, I'm not playing Tischtelefon. Or something like: Spare the deep breathing, Karl. How much will it cost?

With Wolf, she is equally businesslike. She wants him to make a choice of studios so she can phone back and make a block booking. Wolf is hostile on the phone. Wants to know where she's been for the past few days.

Come on, Wolf, Hadja said. Spare me the long silences. Right now I'm talking to you as your manager. I want to know which you prefer: Stuttgart or Freiburg?

Wolf answers with further silence.

Wolf, *Schätzchen!* Why so *touchy* today? she said. Look, I can meet you later and we can speak ourselves out. Right now I'm busy. I'm your manager. I want your decision: Stuttgart or Freiburg?

Stuttgart!

See you later, *baby*.

Hadja often uses English vocabulary to emphasize her fast, businesslike approach.

Mehmet waited in the car, not knowing where he would be going from there. Finally, Hadja came out and drove back to the city centre to the flowercellar. She led the way down the steps into the damp underground smell of sand. The noise of drilling and hammering stopped and started. The foreman Franz came to meet Hadja and she told him that, if possible, Mehmet was to be given some very easy job to begin with. Ali, the old man, was standing with a wheelbarrow in his hands, half hidden in the darkness of an alcove, smiling. Mehmet was given a chisel and a lump hammer. Foreman Franz called Ali and told him to show Mehmet where to begin. Hadja made her way back up the stairs into daylight.

12

Perfect Progeny

Hadja is a perfectionist.

When she swept into the clinic to visit Helen, the second day after the baby was born, she looked around as though everything could be improved. The paintwork could be renewed. Doorways could be widened. Flowers could look fresher. Nurses could be friendlier.

Is perfection a virtue or an affliction?

Helen looked a bit grey. She could have done with a few more visitors. Calcium? Iron? Multivitamins? Lots of steak and spinach, Hadja recommended. You could see that Hadja was glad to be the first, apart from me, of course, to visit Helen; she got there before Wolf and that's what mattered. She congratulated Helen on the fine baby boy, and was about to congratulate me too when she reconsidered, stopped short and seized the moment to dig into her leather bag for a well wrapped present. Soap and talc. It was the right thing to bring. Helen thanked her and placed them beside the bottle of champagne I had put on the bedside cupboard the day before. Champagne was the wrong thing to bring. Would have indirectly given the baby wind problems through breastfeeding.

Helen asked Hadja to pull up a chair and sit down. But Hadja couldn't stay. Said she had somebody waiting for her outside in the car. Instead, she sat on the edge of the bed for a moment with folded arms and her shoulder jutting forward. Helen instinctively pulled back her foot, like a clear gesture under the blankets. The movement was an over-reaction. But hospitals erase malice.

I hate hospital smells, Hadja said.

Somebody could have pointed out to Hadja that this wasn't a hospital but a maternity clinic. Somebody could have pointed out that the sun was shining through the window or remarked that the heaters were on and that such heat was superfluous. Somebody could have noticed that flowers in vases were crying out for water. The windows were crying out to be opened. The polished floor on which the sun was reflected in a white sheen was crying out to be skated on in socks. It could have been said that Hadja was only half sitting on the bed. Or that the baby looked the image of Helen. Remarks could have been made about religion, education, fluid retention, soil erosion. Somebody could have spoken about the impulse of self-perpetuation. Fear of extinction in the city.

Hadja wanted to know about birth. Pain? How long did it all take? she asked. Helen spoke slowly, as though each detail forced her through the ordeal all over again. She played it down; said it was a spontaneous birth and that the baby was born no more than an hour after she arrived at the clinic. Somebody could have remarked how easy it is to say things with hindsight. I was still trying to work out how far I had walked that night.

Hadja wanted to know about breastfeeding. Somebody could have remarked how easy it is to ask questions about things that don't concern you. But then Hadja assumed the answer and began to tell us how she had read that thousands of West German mothers would not breastfeed because it ruined the shape of their nipples. And that many women were now opting for caesarian sections at birth, voluntarily, she said, just to maintain virginal perfection.

Progeny is an admission of failure. Children are born to shoulder blame and responsibility.

Remarks could have been made about childbearing hips. Somebody could have spoken about the dissoluble role of the father. Somebody should have said something about the dangers of forming attachments. Stretching the imagination. Outstaying your welcome.

Hadja picked up her bag and got ready to leave. She leaned over the bed and kissed Helen. I walked out as far as the corridor with her. She told me there was something she wanted to discuss with me. She used the word *eigentlich*: actually. What it was, she wouldn't say. But she made arrangements to meet me at café Trödel the following day.

I went to the clinic twice a day to visit Helen. I met Wolf at the clinic, too, and it seemed like a place to congregate. One of the nurses recognized Wolf and asked if he had come to sing a song.

The following day there was a letter for Helen, so I dropped in earlier than usual, earlier than I was meant to. I knew the letter was from home and that she would be anxious to see it as soon as possible. But there is something about mothers that dissolves panic. She didn't make enquiries about anything. She didn't need to know about the election results. She felt everything was irrelevant. Calm. She could have sat through an earthquake. The only thing that bothered her was the heat. Why do they have the heaters on so high in maternity wards? Her skin was dry.

Do us a favour, Alan, she asked. Open the window.

I looked around at the other women in the ward. They seemed to have understood Helen's request because they all looked back with a sleepy, hostile look. Forbidden, they seemed to say.

Go on, just a fraction, Helen urged.

I was the only possible culprit. Why does everything have to seem like crime?

The letter was not from her parents but from her brother David. Helen could tell that from the cover. After a pause, she opened it and began to read. Nothing was desperate. I watched her while she read. The logic of her eyes skipping across the lines of familiar handwriting. I waited for something to show in her eyes and then saw her drop the letter into her lap and look away towards the window.

Any news? I asked.

She seemed not to hear me. With an unrelated movement of her hand, she pushed the letter along the bed towards me without saying anything.

I read quickly. Read it yourself, she must have said to herself. I had difficulty with the handwriting but I swallowed the lines whole.

Dear Helen, it said. Do you realize what you've done? This house has been dead like a morgue since the news of your condition. What a pity you didn't think of your parents before you got yourself into this mess. Nobody speaks around here any more since your letter arrived. Ma keeps disappearing up to her bedroom to cry about it at all times of the day. And Daddy goes out every evening to sit outside in the back with his head in his hands, just thinking. I know they'll get over it. But I think it's a shame you didn't take them into consideration. They had such hopes for you. They did everything for you and they really deserved better. Don't you know what it means to them? You ruining your life like this.

And as for that German bastard you're living with, I would love to tell him what I think of him.

The letter was signed Dave. I read it twice. A hasty construction, I could see that. But enough to make me want to rush to Helen's defence.

He's got no right to talk to you like that, I said.

Helen shrugged. At last she turned back from the window and looked at me.

It's what I expected, she said. It's just a typical reaction from a brother. I know how he feels. He used to be in charge of looking after me when we were kids.

But Helen looked back out through the window again and I knew that she had said it just to appease me. Who was defending whom? I knew it was something she couldn't discuss. Something she would only begin to think about when I had gone away again.

I think that's very rough, I said. I just don't think he should be saying things like that to you in a letter. I don't care who he is. I feel like writing back to him. I'll write back to your parents and tell them what things are really like here.

No, don't, Alan! It wouldn't do any good.

But they should be told.

No, Alan. I'm inclined to let them sleep on it for a while.

I knew that Helen just wanted to be left alone to think about home. She wanted to look out of the window and imagine her father outside on the bench at the back of the house with his head in his hands, looking out over the fruit trees. The dog sniffing around the garden. The midges dancing up and down between the apple trees. The familiar sound of water flowing from the kitchen into the drain.

I'll be back, I said, and kissed her. I couldn't get over the flatness of her stomach. Her hands lying loosely in her lap.

As expected, the SPD won the elections. The weather remained balmy. The airport at Tegel replaced the airport at Tempelhof. The residents of the apartment block at Sonnenallee had noticed Helen's disappearance and said congratulations. As expected, the newspapers reflected the optimism so clearly obvious in shops and supermarkets around Berlin.

Optimism is not something I was born with. Going to and fro

through the streets of Berlin, I had begun to sense a new dislocation, a problem with chronology. In Germany, where everything receives its proper title, and where everything like this can be placed among symptoms of a pathological condition, it would have been termed Chronology Shock. That's what Wolf called it, anyhow. I could no longer distinguish between events. What came before the birth and what came after. I knew it was a temporary problem. I had trouble with the outline of things. The boundaries of events and personalities became unclear and elusive. Where does Helen begin and Hadja end? Where does Mehmet end and I begin? Where does Dieter begin and I end? Nobody was in sharp relief any more. I felt I had become subsumed by whatever event or person stood in front of me. The more I watched somebody, the more I became like them. If I heard the biography of an explorer or a rock singer or a famous footballer, I could instantly believe the same tale would fit me as well. Whatever I see or witness describes only myself. Where do other people end and I begin? Does the sea define the land or land define the sea?

Hadja left nothing unfinished.

As expected, all cafés in Berlin have damson tart in October. Café Trödel is no exception. It's like eating the national flag. Hadja ordered two slices of damson tart with cream along with two coffees. Her address book lay on the table because she was about to make a phone-call. Hadja is always either on the way to or coming from a phone-call. Things are hotting up with Wolf's recording deal. As they have been on a personal level between them as well.

Hadja immediately gave me the details about Mehmet. Told me she had already informed Wolf. I pursued the matter with unenthusiastic questions. She was going to tell me everything, and for a moment I assumed that this was what she wanted to discuss with me.

What has it achieved? I asked.

Immeasurable respect, she said.

All friends again?

Yes and NO! But Wolf and I, we are beginning to understand us a little better now.

Hadja got up to make the phone-call. By the time she came back the flags had been served. Steam rose from the coffee. The hands of the waitress adjusted the white ribbon at the back of her head. The phone, which had only moments ago been in Hadja's hand, now fell into the hands of another customer. The table at which Helen and I had sat at our first meeting was now occupied by two women. The finger which had only recently dialled a number was now being used to hold a fork. Words that could equally be used to describe luck are now being used to announce imminent disaster.

I have news for you, Hadja said.

What's that?

You know Dieter, the father of Helen's baby. I have found him. He is living here in Berlin. I have seen him.

How do you know it's him? I asked.

I am absolutely sure. Trust me, she said. I thought it was only fair to discuss the matter with you first.

Words to express surprise fell unspoken. The way Hadja spoke implied that she was about to tell Helen the same news she had told me.

You haven't told Helen yet?

No!

That's good. Better not tell her at all in that case, I said.

But why not, *um Gottes willen*, Alan? Isn't that why Helen is here in Berlin? This is the news she has been waiting for.

I don't think so, Hadja, I said. Honestly, at this stage, I really think Helen doesn't want to know any more.

Hadja laughed. An expression normally used to show mirth was now used to show disbelief. How she can laugh and chew and show disbelief beats me.

Alan, she pleaded. Surely it's up to Helen to decide that. She asked us all to help her find Dieter. Surely she still has the right to know. Even if all she wants to do is tell him he's the father. Or tell him what a bastard he was to leave her in the first place.

No! Not now. She doesn't want to know.

And what about the natural father, Dieter? Does he not have the right to know about his little boy?

I began to despise the drama Hadja was feeding into a situation that had, after all, nothing to do with her. She was forcing me to put my own case, unequivocally. For once, life seemed inadequate for the words I had in mind.

For fuck's sake, Hadja. Can't you see that I'm living with Helen now? That it has become totally irrelevant where this man Dieter is from now on? I would do anything for Helen now. And I intend to bring up her baby as though it were my own. Nothing would stop me.

Hadja shook her head. Was it in surprise at my reaction, or in disagreement?

Alan! But you cannot keep this information from a mother.

She doesn't want to know, I repeated.

That's all right, then. She can make up her own mind. She can ignore the real father if she likes. It's up to her.

I knew it was futile to try and stop Hadja once she had fixed her mind on something. Every now and again as she spoke, she pointed her fork at me. An instrument used to convey food was now being used to convey meaning. The thought struck me that I should brandish my own fork and start fencing with her across the table. If I had finished my damson tart, it might have been an even match. If I could have remained more detached, I could have challenged her. If it hadn't been for this, I might have built up a permanent liking for damson tart.

Anyhow, I said, after a pause. How can you be so sure it's Dieter? There must be thousands of Dieters in Berlin. How did you come across him?

Casting doubt is a noble contest. But it's no match for resolve and determination.

Hadja began to explain how her brother employs the services of a private detective to access information on competitors and associates alike. He must study the background on every deal. Otherwise the JOB becomes too risky. She pronounces the word like CHOP. Said she gave the private detective the JOB of finding Dieter. Cost nothing. Only took an afternoon.

Jesus, Hadja. I don't believe it.

As expected, Helmut Schmidt became the new *Bundeskanzler*. Talks were held on improving road and rail connection through the East German corridor. New arrests were imminent in the fight against the Red Army Faction. Expectations on housing and accommodation were elevated. Unemployment and the immigrant problem were to be dealt with. The D-Mark strengthened on the open market. The past was erased. Every new government begins with a clean slate.

Where does the state end and the people begin?

When I dropped back to the clinic in the evening, the ward was full of visitors. New flowers had arrived, and new gifts. Visitors and patients were eating chocolates. The woman in the bed by the door had a large fruit bowl beside her and was surrounded by her husband and three children. The boy looked the image of his father. The girls looked the image of their mother. They were all eating sweets intended for the mother.

At the bed next to Helen there sat a woman in a green coat and a pine green hat from which a long pheasant plume shot gracefully backwards. It was the longest pheasant plume I had ever seen in a hat. It made her husband's head look minuscule. Every movement of the woman's head accentuated the movement of the plume, nodding up and down behind her with a silent swish.

Everyone spoke in whispers.

The woman with the plume treated her daughter like a baby until her daughter's husband arrived, out of breath, with more flowers, more chocolates. When the new infant was brought in, the plume went out of control. She shook her head from side to side saying *Schnuke – Schnuke – Schnukelein*.

All new babies begin with a clean slate. I wondered how free and unprejudiced babies really are. How much of Dieter was already in Helen's baby? How neutral can a baby be?

Near the door, the young boy got a clout on the back of the head from his father. *Lass das sein*: stop that, the father said out loud. Everyone in the ward turned on the little boy to see what he had been up to. Then everybody went back to their own business. Whispering. Cooing. Fathers found common ground with new fathers. Mothers brought out motherhood in other mothers. The plume kept cutting the air, up and down, left and right.

Helen gave me a drowsy smile. She said her breasts were killing her. They were bulging with milk.

They only let you feed the baby at appointed times, she said.

Helen looked as though she might have been crying. Or was that my imagination? I didn't want to ask. Perhaps she was exhausted. Perhaps it was over-capacity. Is the need to cry like the need to breastfeed? I asked about the letter instead.

Did you mind getting the letter from your brother?

A bit, she said.

Somebody could have remarked that I was behaving too much like a father.

We were whispering too. It was no time to discuss the future. The future is meant to be postponed with cooing sounds. All burdens are dispelled with new-born jubilation.

Helen, there's something I wanted to tell you, I said.

What?

I want you to know that everything is all right with me, I said. I mean, with the baby and all that. I will be perfectly happy to bring up the baby as though it were my own son.

Helen looked at me as though I had said something completely irrelevant. It sounded like a manifesto. Or more like a threat to the baby. I felt spurious not telling her the news about Dieter. And then I felt she already knew.

Helen took my hand. Then let go again.

The woman with the plume couldn't be dragged away from her new-born niece. She looked around the ward briefly, as though to make a quick comparison with other babies. Before she left, her head hovered a moment over Helen's baby like a woodland fowl. *Ach – ja*, a little boy.

I could steal any baby, she said, smiling at Helen. I could eat him up.

There are some things you don't say in maternity clinics. Somebody could have asked her where she got the feather. Somebody could have asked me where I came from.

Helen said her breasts felt like footballs, they were solid and sore.

If it was any consolation, I said, men must have taken over the duties of breastfeeding once. All right, maybe it was a long time back, but the anatomical evidence was there to prove it.

Helen laughed.

That's absurd, she said. And in any case, it's not more milk that's needed.

Before I left, before I was urged out by the nurses politely saying it was feeding time, I kept thinking there was something else I should have said to Helen. Something more jubilant.

I kept walking. A modest sign outside a *Gasthaus* caught my attention and I decided to go inside for a beer. Once inside, though, you don't stop walking for a while. The cadence in your feet continues long after you've stopped.

I sat down at one of the tables covered with white table-cloths. Over by the bar there was a noisy group of men and women; mostly men. Some were sitting at a large round *Stammtisch*. Occasionally, they raised their beers and hailed collectively. They were jubilant. Celebrating something, I thought. I was wondering whether I should get up and go to another *Gasthaus* when the barmaid came over to me with a large beer. She was dressed in a traditional *Dirndl*. Her bosom again emphasized abundance, jubilation, perfection. Pinned to the cut of her dress was an SPD rosette. The crowd at the bar wore the same rosettes.

Gratis, the barmaid said. On the house.

It was only then that I realized I had strayed into an election celebration. What luck? As I picked up the beer and drank, some of the men at the bar turned and smiled, raising their glasses in a toast. I obliged.

Two tables down from me there was a man on his own with a beer, feeding a gaming machine on the wall. He seemed to have separated himself from the crowd at the bar, creating his own luck. Every now and again he stood up to insert another 5 mark piece into the machine, which spun consistently, producing electronic phrases: always the same ones, again and again. Excited lights ran up and down along the machine as it spun. From where he was sitting sideways at the table, the man could comfortably press a triptych of HOLD buttons whenever they lit up. He wore a beige or mustard brown leather jacket. The top button of his shirt was open. The WATCH-ARM lay along the table with the watch clearly exhibited beyond the sleeve of the leather jacket. His wallet, cigarettes and lighter were neatly arranged on the table. He bore the expression of a man at work; fully in control and undeflected by bursts of mirth from the bar. His right arm was the PLAYING-ARM. He hit the HOLD buttons deftly, with a slack index knuckle.

The barmaid came around again, this time offering free *Würstl*.

A woman from the crowd at the bar went to insert money into the jukebox. Her face lit up purple as she leaned over it on both arms. Her hips swivelled around as she selected her choice of hits, and by the time the first song came up, she had already rejoined the group at the bar. The song was familiar to everyone. It obscured the bleeps of the gaming machine. ALL-I-NEED-IS-THE-AIR-THAT-I-BREATHE! The woman who had chosen the music knew the words. Others around her seemed not to hear it, and kept talking. She pronounced the words, AIR THAT I BREEZE! and began to dance on her own with her arms in the air. Her action was acknowledged without surprise. Ignored by the man at the gaming machine.

I took another drink from my beer. I felt the slow conscription of its effects. The march in my feet died away and became obscured by the march in my head.

Somebody could have said something about the white table-cloths. The transparency of glass. Somebody could have spoken about victory. *Wurst*. Velocity. The birthrate in Germany. Some-body should have said something about the chronology of luck.

13

Water, Pain and Land Reclamation

The city cries out. As the sea cries out for land. The Baltic sea will
return to reclaim the lost sea floor, and the buildings will become
submerged beneath the city. The houses of Berlin will be draped in
seaweed. The future will surge into the streets so fast that nobody
will be able to speak. Mouths will be left open. And people will
drift in and out of the buildings on a tide of desire. Fear will be
replaced by need. Skin will be exchanged for shell. Eyes for claws.
They will walk sideways to avoid each other in crowds. In the
cafés, they will swallow detectably as though they had gills on the
sides of their necks. Gossip will rise like bubbles. Trays laden with
damson tarts will rise and fall on their way towards tables.
Outside, the traffic will float silently. The city will sway.

The sea floor will be littered with everyday objects like supermarket trolleys and broken umbrellas, billowing plastic bags and
lost gloves. Algae will grow like graffiti. At airports and train
stations people will move towards each other and away from each
other. They will walk without moving. Stare without believing.
Eyes will fill up and fingers will tremble against the pull of longing.
Against the sway of human lineage. Friends will be held back by
friends. Father by son. Lover by lover. People will cling to each
other as they would cling to the rocks. As they cling to memory. It
will be difficult to move. And difficult to say goodbye without
swallowing. Farewells will be silent. And thought will be deep. At
the windows of apartment blocks, people will stand for hours and
watch the city drifting away.

I hope I'm wrong.

There has been an accident down at the flowercellar. A construction accident involving one of the immigrant workers. A man with
no name. A man who might have disappeared without trace except
for an accident. As yet, only scarce details have reached me through
Wolf. But he seems reluctant to talk about it.

It was Mehmet. An accident is enough to give you identity, a place in the world. A serious construction accident is enough to give you a name; and life if you survive.

Hadja spoke of inexperience. Unskilled labour. They had Mehmet working with a Kango hammer, drilling a vault into a thick wall, when the rocks began to fall. Mehmet must have been right underneath, drilling upwards, because the Kango hammer was pinned against his chest when they dug him out. Broken ribs, certainly. And a punctured lung. But Hadja was still waiting to hear from the hospital on the full extent of his injuries. There was some concern about the spine.

The old man Ali said it was the wheelbarrow that saved Mehmet's life. If it hadn't been for the wheelbarrow, which tipped over and shielded him from the worst, Mehmet would certainly have been crushed beneath the rocks. The basement walls in some of the buildings in Berlin are as wide as trucks. At the flowercellar, they are fifteen to twenty feet in diameter.

Mehmet's sudden presence in Berlin has thrown everything into a panic.

If it wasn't for wheelbarrows, there wouldn't be life. If it wasn't for rocks, there wouldn't be bones. If it wasn't for mouths, there wouldn't be dust. If it wasn't for panic, there wouldn't be pain. If it wasn't for shivering, there wouldn't be dampness in basement walls.

Also in Berlin again is the Iranian student Sulima. After her marriage to Massoud in Tehran, they have decided to return to Berlin. This time it was Sulima who sought contact with Hadja and arranged to meet. Sulima feels life needs to be explained. The wedding day needs to be recalled, photographs shown and the future of marriage as an institution put into perspective.

The marriage has changed everything, it seems. Vast emotions and feelings of security and purpose in life have been listed as some of the initial rewards. Among others: family acceptance, a place in society, cooked dinners, favours laid on, immunity from social diseases. In addition, Sulima and Massoud have come into possession of vast sums of money on account of their faithful adherence to Islamic tradition. They now have enough wealth to live in relative luxury for the remainder of their lives. Sulima now drives a red BMW. What else? Hadja says it's obscene. The colour red.

Marriage has also changed the basic ground rules. Certain threats have been obviated. Sulima has gone back to her studies at the university and Massoud has become more rational in his manner. In fact, he now insists on a certain level of openness and freedom within the marriage. For the moment, they have decided to play the European rules, with perhaps a little Islamic self-discipline thrown in. The faith will remain Muslim. Appearance and clothes will be European, however. Carpets will be Persian. The microwave will be German.

Hadja says it's indecent.

Kristl König has been let down by her own dog. She has been caught red-handed. Caught in Konrad's wife's dressing gown.

It always happens that way when precautions slip as a result of some unforeseen event. Blame it on the accident at the flowercellar. Konrad has been so concerned about Mehmet that he has neglected his own safety and that of Kristl. Konrad was thinking constantly about Mehmet's injuries, and about the whole nature of the building business. Kristl is the only person who can erase the fears from his mind.

Fearing an investigation of some kind as a result of the accident, Konrad forgot to fear an investigation by his own wife. Luckily, foreman Franz had the foresight on the day to send all the other workers home immediately before the ambulance and the fire brigade and the police arrived at the flowercellar. When the police got there, it was only Ali, the old man, foreman Franz and Mehmet who existed in the cellar. Though nobody was sure about Mehmet. Konrad took the precaution to dismiss all unregistered labour from his building sites for the present. It's going to hold things up seriously.

This was the lapse in concentration that exposed Kristl. An unexpected return. A woman's intuition. Whatever it was, Konrad's wife arrived back in her own kitchen, only to find Kristl sitting on one of the high stools on her own, drinking coffee and eating fresh rolls with jam. The immediate impulse is to offer a cup of coffee. But it wasn't Kristl's coffee. And it wasn't Kristl's dressing gown. Konrad's wife smiled and said: *Keine Eile*: no rush. Finish your breakfast in peace. Then she walked out again.

There was even less fuss after that. It seems Konrad's wife knew about Kristl from the very beginning. Divorce proceedings will be calm. There will be no hysteria. Proof will be adequate. Settlements will be generous.

It was Ali who kept Mehmet alive. All the time they were waiting for the ambulance and for the men with the lifting gear to free the injured worker, it was Ali who looked after him. Spoke to him in his own language and told him he was alive. Told him he was in Berlin. And Mehmet kept responding all the time with smiles of pain. Numb smiles and repeated efforts to raise his head. Ali told him not to move. Not to smile. Until there was no pain any more. Just the shock and disbelief at the sight of ambulancemen working at the rocks in the wall, clearing the rubble, speaking in fast, commanding voices. German words echoed around the cellar. Mehmet was shivering. Because they wrapped him in blankets and attached a tube to his arm. Because all the time he could smell the sand underneath.

Helen came home from the clinic. Initially, Hadja had promised to bring her home when the time came, but there's been so much going on lately, it was impossible. Hadja has been up to her eyes since the accident.

We got a taxi instead. The nurse carrying the baby out to the taxi would not let the infant out of her possession until Helen was actually sitting down in the back seat. Something to do with insurance, perhaps. Or mistrust.

Helen asked that the taxi driver go over Gleisdreieck, her favourite patch in Berlin. She had a sudden need for disused railway stations. Crumbling buildings and remainders of the war. Pockmarked walls, that kind of thing.

Helen has developed a whole new set of cravings since she had the baby. Wine. Music. Geography. Suddenly she wants to know where Brunei is. And Port Moresby. She despises Quark. Has taken up pitta bread and dips instead. Cumin and coriander are high in her value system. So are lifts in apartment blocks. Cars with childproof locks and baby seats. Silent nights and sunburst mornings. The patient and sober hands of a father.

It's great to see the baby asleep in the pink cot. It terrifies me to hear it crying. Fascinates me how Helen can so easily appease and reduce the cries to sighs and exhausted sucking noises. The baby's lips are pink white or milk pink. There is always a little pearl or marble, or so it seems, on the baby's upper lip. Right in the middle. Always a pink pearl there after breastfeeding. I keep wanting to place my finger in the baby's mouth. But it's not my baby. And anyhow, my skin has begun to feel scaly and crustaceous of late. It's lovely to see the baby's eyes open. It's lovely to hear Helen talking like a baby. And lovely to see the baby gripping a finger with its hand.

Sometimes Helen wakes the baby up for no reason. Just to see it move. Whenever the baby is asleep, which is most of the time, it seems, Helen asks me to go and check. Make sure he's breathing, she says.

Between Wolf and Hadja, things could be said to be going as well as ever. Good and bad. Wolf is obsessed with his music. Hadja is obsessed with strategy.

On a professional level, things have never been better. Hadja has managed to sign Wolf on with a recording company in Hamburg. Things are set to take off. Dates are set to record the album in a studio in Stuttgart after Christmas. And after that, Hadja has arranged a small tour of southern cities.

On a personal level, things have never been worse. Do they have any contact at all? I wonder. My only gauge for the relationship between Wolf and Hadja is the permanence of my own job and the stability of my own address. Hadja has been talking about the possibility of having to repossess the apartment at Sonnenallee. It's something she feels she has to fall back on. She's been thinking of turning Sonnenallee into some kind of studio or rehearsal room for Wolf. Somewhere he can put all his instruments and machines. She's fed up living with his music. She wants a home.

Music keeps them apart.

The volume will be turned up. Music will be loud. No song will be unsung. No mind will be left without an opinion. It will be difficult to move without idols. It will be difficult to say goodbye without swallowing.

I may be wrong.

Hadja has a mental map of Berlin. She can see every street and district of the city below in her mind. She can mark the places she thinks about with an X. She has a mental image of the hospital and what will happen to Mehmet. She has a picture of Sulima and Massoud in their Steglitz apartment. She has a mental picture of Oranienstrasse; a new apartment to replace the one I'm in with Helen in Sonnenallee.

Hadja has a mental map of Berlin on which there is an X for the spot where Helen and Dieter will meet.

If it wasn't for maps there wouldn't be cities. If it wasn't for streets there wouldn't be reunions. If it wasn't for sons there wouldn't be fathers. If it wasn't for Helen. If it wasn't for me. If it wasn't for Dieter. If it wasn't for buildings you could walk as far as the eye could see.

Ali, the old man, has been like a father to Mehmet. Went to visit him without fail at the hospital every day. If it hadn't been for Ali, there would have been no wheelbarrow. And there would have been no visitors at the hospital except Hadja.

For three days in a row, Hadja has gone to visit Mehmet. He is out of danger. There are no serious spinal injuries, as first suspected. But Mehmet has now become a danger; a burden on the Milic family. A casualty. The frequency of Hadja's visits to the hospital have to do with her efforts to establish Mehmet's existence in Berlin. She's been in with application forms, asking for details of parents' names, birth certificate, passport number as well as other information. Luckily, she has been able to register Mehmet retrospectively for insurance with the *Krankenkasse*. For the moment, the bills are being paid. Konrad says it's important to keep up appearances.

Ali brought writing paper and a stamp so that Mehmet could write home to his parents. Ali has no family of his own. So he knows what it's like to have a son. At a men's shop not far from the hospital he bought Mehmet a shirt. A white shirt with vertical thin green stripes and button-down collars. Ali says Mehmet's future in the construction industry is finished.

Hadja knows everything there is to know about people. She knows everything about me and about Helen. Everything there is to know about Dieter.

She's been following Dieter. She is excited about the task. Driven by endless stamina for new roles. Roles with a challenge, like private investigators. By now she knows where Dieter works, where he drinks, how often he goes to the cinema, whom he meets, the parties, everything. One night, she even managed to get herself invited to a party at which Dieter was present. Just to get a closer look. Now she can predict almost every movement during the day or night.

Hadja has an X on her mental map for the place where Helen and Dieter will meet. She can imagine a reunion on counterflowing escalators, or somewhere in a city centre street. Hadja likes to mix strategy with chance. Fate with plan.

I could never be quite sure from then on whether Hadja had already spoken to Helen about Dieter. Sometimes I thought Helen had already met the real father somewhere secretly. Sometimes I thought she was so involved with the baby that it became totally irrelevant. Now and again I asked her questions without letting on that I knew anything more than she did.

Was she still anxious to meet the real father?

More than ever.

More than ever she needed material proof of her own existence in Berlin. Something to declare reality. She needed a father to acknowledge the baby. She needed parental acknowledgement. The present is never enough to establish reality. She needed memory. She needed a new view of the future. And old comparisons. She needed Dieter.

Helen said the baby's buttocks were the image of mine. What can you say to that?

I could see that Helen had become fundamentally unhappy. There's nothing you can do about it. We talked about it from time to time, but it was no use. I suggested language classes. Adult education. There were so many things she could start in Berlin. But there was something wrong. I couldn't put my finger on it. Happiness, for what it's worth, is something for the converted. Jokes. Beer. Luck. Nothing works if you're on the wrong side. Fun is for the initiated, the way Catholicism is useless if you're not a Catholic. And the Islam is a beautiful mistake, if you're not a Muslim. And Europe is a joke.

Helen didn't get the joke. Whenever she laughed, it was at something else altogether. All the time, her mind seemed to be occupied with something else. It was the baby. Babies make everything irrelevant.

One night in bed, she began to laugh hysterically. She couldn't stop. I asked her what she was laughing at, and she just shook her head. She couldn't even answer. And you get angry when you don't know what people are laughing at.

It's nothing, she said eventually, before bursting into further fits of laughter.

I tried to work out what she could possibly find funny. But I must have been way off the mark. Was it me who didn't get the joke?

No, it's nothing funny, she said. I'm sorry. I just can't stop laughing.

She tried to suppress it with her hand. Her body kept shaking beside me. Her shoulders leaping up and down silently. Every time she tried to say something, it only made it worse. I lay there, just looking up at the ceiling, at the light cast in a diamond shape from the courtyard outside. I kept staring at the ceiling until she stopped shaking beside me and fell asleep.

If it *wasn't* for laughter, there wouldn't be bouncing. If it *wasn't* for fingers, there wouldn't be light-switches. If it *wasn't* for history, there wouldn't be repetition. If it *wasn't* for bouncing, there wouldn't be public order. If it *wasn't* for fast food, there wouldn't be fingers, and freedom of choice. If it *wasn't* for music, you'd hear mastication. If it *wasn't* for news bulletins, you'd feel there was something wrong. If it *wasn't* for jokes, you'd be laughing at nothing. If it *wasn't* for immigrant workers, you wouldn't be laughing.

Mehmet was discharged from hospital close to lunchtime on a Friday morning. Hadja was there to collect him. There was no need for Ali to be there as well. Mehmet had his arm in a sling and a collar around his neck. He moved reasonably well on his own across the car park, without any help. The only thing that gave him great difficulty still was turning his head around without turning his whole body.

Mehmet felt different. He felt the street outside was unusually bright. Unusually broad. Berlin had changed. Something about it. He was seeing things for the first time since his accident. It had definitely turned winter, for one thing.

Hadja had spoken to the doctors. It would be quite a while before Mehmet recovered fully. In the medical records at the hospital, the name of Hadja Milic had been entered consistently as the next of kin. The doctors found it easier to explain things to her. The need for further treatment. Physiotherapy. Adequate caution and no sudden movement.

How are you feeling now? Hadja asked in the car.

Oh, fine, he smiled. He was forced to talk to the windscreen in front of him.

The doctors tell me you have to have a lot of physiotherapy from now on.

Yes. Mehmet tried to turn towards her. To see her eyes. Because eyes say more. And injury prohibits communication.

You have to look after yourself, Hadja said. You have to be very careful with your back from now on. No hard work and no lifting.

Yes.

And no bouncing, she added.

Mehmet struggled to turn. He wanted to see if she was smiling. He could only see straight ahead through the windscreen. He could only smile his broad, white, magnificent smile like a man who understood the joke.

It's a matter of presentation.

On Saturday afternoon, Hadja arrived at the house in Grossbeerenstrasse with an envelope for Mehmet. Of course, Mehmet was there. He wasn't moving around much. She knocked on the door and was let in by one of his room mates. Mehmet was sitting on the bed. There were signs of celebration around the room from the night before. Mehmet's room-mate stood back and asked if he should leave. Hadja said no: please stay. She sat on the edge of Mehmet's bed holding the beige envelope in her fingers. Mehmet was still a patient, still injured, so there was nothing strange about Hadja sitting on the edge of his bed. She asked him again how he felt. He acknowledged her concern with an embarrassed nod.

Mehmet, she said officially. In view of your unfortunate accident and all you've been through in the past weeks, we have decided to make a gesture; to help you out financially.

Hadja paused. Time explodes.

We have decided to give you a thousand marks. Enough to see you through the foreseeable future, at least.

Money screams. Mehmet was visibly surprised. The amount was obscene. Mehmet's room-mate shuffled on his feet with embarrassment at the idea. Within five minutes, the news would have gone around the whole house. The generosity of the Milic family. The loyalty to its workforce.

I know it sounds like a lot of money, Hadja said. But we felt it was only right in view of your injuries and the fact that it will be a while yet before you can return to work.

Mehmet wished he had put on a good shirt. You should be well dressed to receive money. He pulled back his right leg on the bed. Hadja swung the envelope in her fingers for a moment, slapped it against Mehmet's knee and said: Take it. You deserve it.

Mehmet was reluctant, almost frightened, by the envelope he held in his hands. It seemed an insult to open it immediately, so he kept it still in his grip and nodded continuously with sincere thanks. His room-mate echoed the hysterical gratitude with a rigid stare. Mehmet couldn't speak.

We also felt, Hadja continued, that you would want to visit your parents and spend some time at home with your own people. So we arranged to give you a flight home as well.

Hadja pointed to the envelope, commanding him to open it. Mehmet discreetly began to open the envelope. It looked as though he had never opened a letter before in his life. He tried to open it the way envelopes are closed, with thumb and forefinger, by understanding the nature of envelopes, not by sticking his finger in like a knife and ripping it open. The crisp banknotes shone. The blue and yellow Lufthansa colours were reflected like a light on the inside of the envelope. A one-way ticket.

Things will be left behind. There will be expression of regret. Sadness at squandered moments. There will be no time for celebration. Things will be given away. Burdens will be inherited. Everything will appear at the last minute. It will be difficult to speak. It will be difficult to spend all the money. It will be difficult to say goodbye. There will be general movement towards the boarding gates. There will be no turning back.

Ali, the old man, went out to the airport in the car with Hadja and Mehmet. He sat in the back seat. The conversation along the way was stunted. Bravado. The way men talk on building sites. The way people talk when they know each other superficially. Hadja kept the conversation going. The men were mostly silent.

At the airport, Ali spoke to Mehmet like a father. Told him he was going home. Told him never to come back to Germany.

This is no place for you, son, he said. I wish I could change places with you.

Mehmet defied like a son. I'll be back, he proclaimed.

It is difficult for men in Berlin to embrace without attracting attention. It is difficult to slap an injured person on the back.

If it wasn't for water, you wouldn't have to swallow. If it wasn't for sand, you wouldn't have to blink.

14

Milk Love

It was a desperate idea from the start.

Helen said she wanted some photographs taken. To send home. She wanted her parents to see proof. Pictorial evidence that she was still alive in Berlin. I ignored it. I knew Hadja had a camera I could easily borrow, but I had no enthusiasm for it.

The thing that is meant to record for posterity, to fix the present, has the opposite effect in reality. Photographs kill. What's meant to be a method of making something permanent on paper is really only a way of saying goodbye. Photographs dismantle reality. Snapshots are farewell.

Is there nobody around with a camera? Helen asked me first thing again after Christmas. There still hadn't been any word from her parents. I need to send them some photographs of the baby. I want them to know we exist, Helen said.

Of course, Hadja has everything. At first she was reluctant to part with her Pentax, but then she conceded that she had used it only a half-dozen times since it was given to her by Wolf. All that Hadja could find to photograph was Wolf. And there was a limit to the possibilities there.

Three days before I was due to leave for Stuttgart with Wolf and Hadja, I borrowed the camera. Wolf is due to start recording his album. It is to include the well-known song '*Atlanticsucht*'. I've got the job of studio assistant.

Helen bought three 36-shot rolls of colour film. That was overdoing it, I thought.

I was present when Wolf and Hadja discussed business; whether they would need me in Stuttgart. I was always present when they made plans.

I could do with Alan in Stuttgart, Wolf said. *Mein* ROAD CREW.

Hadja didn't object. I was included in the budget.

Helen needed photographs badly. For three days before I left, we made our way around Berlin with the baby in the buggy. The buggy had been a gift from the *Hausmeister*'s daughter, who had no more need for it. Three days we wandered around the city with the camera around my neck. I told Helen we were beginning to look like tourists. In February?

At the *U-Bahn* steps, I usually lifted the front of the buggy while Helen held on to the handles. Most of the time the baby was asleep. Whenever there was an escalator, Helen would wheel the buggy on to the moving steps and then hold up the handles to maintain equilibrium. Whenever we went down, she had to bend forward to hold on. She was getting good at it.

We didn't know where to take photographs at first. It was very cold.

I was usually present, too, when Wolf and Hadja discussed personal matters. You can expect the worst. They stop at nothing. They can switch from business matters straight into a personal row about infidelity. Wolf and Hadja can be vicious.

Vicious!

All the way down to Stuttgart in the car, they either fought or said nothing at all to each other. They assault each other with silence. When they fight, nothing is spared.

I'll take a picture here, will I? When we came out of café Trödel, I held up the camera as though we'd forgotten about it.

Why not? Helen said.

While Helen got the baby ready, I turned myself into a professional photographer; conscious all the time of what would go into the background; conscious that I should be getting the blue and white canopy bearing the name café Trödel into the frame. Conscious that if I didn't, café Trödel might disappear for ever. The baby was wrapped in a chequered rug and could hardly be seen at all. Helen winced with the cold. It had been so warm inside the café. She looked impatient as I focused. A little hostile. A little camera-shy.

For three days, I saw nothing that wasn't framed in terms of a photograph. Everything had slipped into the past. Everything looked photogenic. All over the city, things appeared as they would on prints; durable images that would outlast either of us. Fixed images that would turn up years later among piles of letters kept secretly in a drawer. Everything we saw in Berlin for three days was trapped into a stare. Photographs are like staring matches where nobody is allowed to blink or look away.

Hadja and Wolf stop at nothing. I have witnessed almost every flare-up, every insult and every sly lustful look with which these battles are erased and forgotten. They say irreversible things. I hate you. I love you. Yes. No. *Liebling. Schatz. Arschloch.* Anything. Things I would never dream of saying to anyone. Hadja has been badgering Wolf about moving his music and his whole practice arrangements out to some kind of rehearsal room in future. She wants to lead a normal life when he comes back from Stuttgart.

Wolf calls her *Schweinefresse.* He does his best.

Hadja laughs. Instead of walking out insulted, they now wait for things to continue. They believe in perfect openness.

I hear them talk about the value of intimacy. You have no idea what a woman needs, she shouts. No imagination.

She looks at me to make sure that my presence redoubles the insult. But Wolf knows how to return. He picks up his saxophone and blows a profane riff, at which she turns around and slams her foot on the floor.

Everything is irreversible.

Even before we got to the checkpoint on our way to Stuttgart, I felt like getting out of the car and making my own way back on the *U-Bahn.* I wanted to see what Helen was thinking. I wanted her to know I hadn't intended it that way. And that I was furious with Hadja at the way she had treated her. How could I travel all the way down to Stuttgart with somebody like Hadja? But I said nothing.

Wolf said nothing either.

And Hadja was impatient. I could hear it in the engine. She's an aggressive driver. Honks needlessly. Makes out that all other drivers are idiots. At one stage, she found herself stopped behind a parked car.

Mensch, she shouted. What idiot parks his car there?

Wolf snorted. That only makes matters worse.

After the checkpoint, of course, there's no way you can get out. Theoretically, while travelling through East German territory, through the corridor, you're not allowed to stop. Even in emergency.

You must keep going until you reach West German territory again. You're not even supposed to stop for a piss, Hadja says.

Hadja is the only one talking in the car. She says she wouldn't mind if the East Germans could build decent roads. East Germany is sneered at among friends.

As soon as we got past the checkpoint on the open road of the corridor, Wolf switched on the music again. Loud. Hit the road, Hadja shouted over the music, touched by excitement and freedom.

Wolf slapped the dashboard with both hands, acknowledging the new mood without a word. Then he placed his brown leather boots on the dashboard and slipped down in his seat so that his head was much lower than Hadja's. Travelling makes you feel small again. Staying in one place makes you swell up. More than ever, I wanted to jump out of the car. But the motion of the car began to reduce the swelling, and I couldn't hold on to my anger.

In the afternoon, the light is reasonably good in the apartment in Sonnenallee. That's what I think. I was able to get a few shots of Helen beside the window with her face turned away from the camera towards the light. Then we reversed roles and Helen took some shots of me. I stood looking down at the courtyard. We could hear the *Hausmeister* below but I couldn't see him anywhere. And you never know whether he's shouting or just talking.

I wanted a picture of Helen breastfeeding. Helen said no. But then she agreed.

The following day, we took some shots along Kurfürstendamm. At one point, I allowed Helen to walk on with the buggy. I pretended to be doing up my shoelace. Then I caught up and took some shots from behind, taking in the whole street; cars, pedestrians and café awnings.

Alan, that's a waste, she said.

Why?

Well, what's the point in taking pictures of somebody from the back. For God's sake, Alan, that's wasted.

No it's not, I said. It's a picture of you from the back, isn't it?

What use is that? Helen laughed. Who is going to recognize me from the back on the main street in Berlin? She laughed again.

We'll know it's you. You'll know.

Don't be daft, Alan. That's a complete waste of film.

The landscape along the corridor through East Germany is flat and white. With the strength of the music playing inside the car, the landscape seems to belong to the beginning of some movie. There is a line of grey trees in the distance. Occasionally we pass pine woods bordered by single birch trees or sometimes small groups of birch trees. They look odd in the country. I've only seen them in gardens.

Now and again you see a hawk. I want to say: Look, a HAWK. But I let it pass. The sky is slate grey, I suppose. It's like being in the cinema with the white land slowly passing. All the time, you expect something to appear, something to happen on the horizon, some shape to distinguish itself on the flat surface.

Wolf took out a large purple-coloured bar of chocolate. The size of a number plate. There was a picture of a cow with a bell dancing on the wrapper. Wolf uncovered one end of the chocolate and held it up.

Want some? he asked.

Hadja glances at the chocolate.

Take me off a piece.

Wolf and Hadja have learned all their English from pop songs.

He broke off a piece of chocolate and placed it on Hadja's lips, and then pushed it in with his finger. She chewed. He then broke off a piece for himself and held the chocolate back towards me.

No, no, I'm fine, thanks. I leaned forward to say no thanks.

In Germany, if you say no thanks, that's it. You won't be asked again.

Hadja points to a can of coke lying next to the gear-stick.

Make it open! Make it open!

Wolf opened the can and took a sip before passing it to Hadja. Hadja drank without taking her eyes off the road. She rinsed her mouth with coke and handed back the can. I had a mental picture of a mixture of coke and chocolate swirling around Hadja's teeth.

Helen wanted to get the baby registered. She had decided on a name. Daniel. I told her I like the name. She asked me. And I went with her to find the registry office. The baby went along, as though for proof.

The clerk at the registration office handed Helen an index of German names. She told him she had already chosen a name. There was a problem then about the father. The clerk didn't understand the situation; he took it for granted the man with Helen would be the father. He was led astray by intuition. Helen took a long time to explain. The clerk had little English and I didn't want to intervene with my German.

The clerk pointed across the counter at me.

Who is this man then? he asked.

Helen spoke quietly. The registry official always speaks with incumbent confidence. At all times, he seemed to be speaking to an inquiry which might be instituted after the event, at which he might have to account for himself. His voice was much louder than Helen's, as though he had to keep other people in other rooms informed as well. As though he had to seek a consensus of opinion.

Is this not the father? he asked.

No. Helen told him that she was not married. That the child was to be given the mother's surname. But this was more than the clerk could take.

Who is this man here? He pointed over at me again.

He's a friend, Helen said. She turned around and smiled at me.

A friend? the clerk repeated.

Yes.

Not father?

No!

In Germany, everything must be explained.

Wolf and Hadja like to make everything painfully clear. They don't seem to mind that I know everything about them; everything they've eaten over the past year. Why Wolf never drinks milk. Why Hadja avoids yeast. Every snooze in the afternoon. When they discuss matters, everything comes out.

Hadja feels she needs more space to herself. Wolf encourages her to speak about it. In Germany, there's no sense in hiding anything under the carpet. Hadja feels Wolf should get some kind of studio for himself where he can rehearse and blow his instruments. She wants a home.

Hadja feels squeezed in. Her back is against the wall, she says.

All day, everywhere, this music. It makes her feel unnatural. We must talk about this, she says. The end of every conversation concludes with that phrase. We must talk about it again.

In Germany, anything unspoken is ignored. Anyone not registered hardly exists. And anyone without feelings is not alive. Like unexpressed opinions. Unsent postcards.

Anyone unphotographed is missing.

The *Hausmeister* at Sonnenallee liked us. His daughter gave Helen the buggy. He registered his congratulations. He's never been this friendly before and I can only assume it must be the baby. The baby makes everyone equal, gives you status. The baby has placed me on the *Hausmeister*'s level because he now feels he can talk to me, man to man.

I returned to the house alone one afternoon, only to meet the *Hausmeister* on the stairs. I felt he must have been waiting for me.

Ach . . . there he is at last, he said. The new *Papa*.

The *Hausmeister* took me by the hand and led me down the stairs into the basement without a further word. There was nothing I could say. No time to explain. In the basement, he opened the door to a small cellar filled with racks and rows of wine bottles. He took one of the bottles and placed it firmly in my hand, looked into my eyes and winked.

Für den Papa! he said.

Then he told me where he gets the wine. In the south. He pointed to where he thought the south was. Beyond the walls of the cellar. Out there somewhere. He wanted to show me on the map. *Die Landkarte*, he shouts. I smiled and tried to thank him for the wine. He didn't even give me a chance to thank him. He wants me to come and meet his wife. His daughter. And his daughter's husband.

Come you inside . . . IRISH *Papa*.

We took so many photographs in Tiergarten, there was nothing else to photograph. Park benches. With trees. In open green spaces with trees in the background. Helen had her hair tied up. She wore her tweed coat and a black beret. She looked well. Better than ever before. When we came to the Berlin Wall, she said she wanted one or two shots of herself against it. The Brandenburg Gate in the background. Sentry towers, that kind of thing. The Berlin Wall suits her.

I laughed at the idea first.

Come on, Helen, I said. Nobody in Berlin would dream of getting their picture taken by the Wall.

Why not?

We're not holidaymakers, are we.

Who cares? she said. I need proof that I'm here in Berlin.

Helen stands in the foreground with hands clasped in front. The wall with all its graffiti forms the background. The base of a sentry tower is just in the picture. Helen is smiling. Without baby. Her head is tilted to the south.

Every year, thousands of visitors take photographs of the Berlin Wall. There will be nothing left of it soon.

Helen and I stopped for a beer, not far from the wall: Potsdamerstrasse. Helen would be able to tell you the name of the bar. She has a memory for things like that. All I remember is that it was an old bar, a part of Old Germany, with a brand new aluminium door and tinted brown light shining through the frosted glass like carrot juice. In other parts, the windows had been widened to allow more light.

There was only one man in the bar at the time. Helen decided to risk breastfeeding. You wouldn't notice the way Helen did it. Then, when she was finished, she put Daniel back into the buggy and began to drink her beer. I could only think of the idea of fluid replacement.

Helen held up her beer for a toast and I decided to take a photograph of her in the bar. There seemed to be enough light from the windows. And it was only afterwards that I noticed two large round stains on her dress where the milk had begun to seep through from her breasts.

I think you're leaking, I said in a whisper.

Why didn't you tell me? she said, looking down. You'd happily let me walk around like that.

She put on her coat again and discreetly stemmed the flow of milk with tissues. I had to get more tissues from the bar. They had the crest of the bar on them. That's probably why she would remember the name of the bar so well. And probably why she was laughing at the time. I offered her a beer mat as well, but she threw it back at me saying: Get lost.

We had walked almost half-way down Potzdamerstrasse by the time I noticed I had left the camera behind in the bar. I ran back and found it still there on the table. I was relieved. But the sight of the empty bar made me uneasy. The idea of going back to see the place where we had been sitting together only moments before made everything seem strange to me. I expected something familiar. That's probably why I don't remember the name of the place any more. I caught up with her along Potsdamerstrasse. I felt very hot, from running, from the beer.

The camera is a lethal weapon. They used to shoot wild life; now they photograph it. The camera takes everything in the present and places it in the past.

Wolf says it's like those antlers they have hanging on the wall all over Germany. Or butterfly collections. His parents had antlers in every room of the house. Staring down over the dining-room table. Over the bed. In the hallway by the coat stand. It was life after life. Photographs are dead animals.

This is the way you make love for the first and last time. Milk love.

Helen asked me to check on the baby. Check on Daniel, she said. Make sure he's breathing.

I made sure that the baby was covered. I put the light out in the sitting room and banged my knee against a chair on the way back. I ignored the sharp pain, the way players ignore things on football fields. For a long time, we lay on our backs looking up at the diamond shape of the window-frame cast against the ceiling by the courtyard lights outside. We lay there talking about things. About nothing really. The pain in my knee drifted away. At one point it felt as though my limbs had drifted away. I could feel them somewhere at the end of an expanse of landscape. Further than that.

Helen sat up, threw her hair to one side and lay on top of me, allowing her body to descend slowly. Weight is not something you can measure. Helen is very light. And there was nothing urgent to this. The diamond frame was on the left side of her head. Now and then, she threw back her hair and looked up at the window, at the sky outside maybe. Except that her eyes were shut. Imagining the sky, maybe. And then I felt milk running across my chest. It was like being under a warm tap. Milk ran down my chest, along the side, under my arms, and formed pools underneath. It was like being under a cool tap on a hot day. There was a babyish smell; a milky, babyish smell. And then she realized it herself. There was milk everywhere. Once she allowed her full weight to descend on my chest, she noticed the milk all over.

Oh look, she said. Why didn't you say something?

That was the last time. Next morning, I left for Stuttgart with Hadja and Wolf.

Everything seemed so quiet and slow before they arrived. Time was exaggerated. There was so much time to spare that I sat on the bed watching Helen bathing the baby. She plugged in a heater to keep the room warm. Then she brought in the white plastic bath tub filled with water. Now and then, the baby's arms and legs went rigid and he would try to clutch on to something with star-shaped hands. Helen anticipated every movement. Every time she picked up the soap or put it down again, she seemed to do it with extreme caution. She wrapped the baby in one of her white towels. The water looked blue and milky in the tub. Almost drinkable.

Once Hadja arrived to collect me, everything was thrown into a huge hurry. Wolf was waiting in the car. Hadja immediately talked about driving time to Stuttgart.

We MAKE A MOVE, ha!

I carried a small box of equipment down the stairs while Hadja carried my bag. On the way out of the door, Hadja saw the camera on the table and picked it up.

I'll take the camera back, if that's all right, she said. We want to take some photographs in Stuttgart.

It's not finished, I said. There's still some shots left on the roll.

Hadja said she would give us another roll after Stuttgart. She would give us the prints or come to some arrangement. I let it go. Things seemed unusually rushed. There was no time to argue. When I came back upstairs to say goodbye to Helen, she had come out of the bedroom with the baby in her arms, all dressed.

156

Where's the camera? she asked immediately.

Hadja needs it for Stuttgart, I said.

But the roll wasn't finished.

I know. But that's all right, I'll get the roll off her in Stuttgart and get it developed.

Jesus! Helen shouted. Hold the baby.

She ran downstairs and out to the street, where she found Hadja already sitting in the car. Hadja had put her sunglasses on. She was doing the driving. There was snow in the street.

Can I have that camera, Helen said. I want to finish the roll of film in it.

There's no time now, Helen. *Schatz*, Hadja said. We have to MAKE A MOVE now.

Helen got suddenly very angry. Far more angry than you need to be over a roll of film.

Hadja refused again. Said there was no time. And Helen raised her voice. Helen's voice echoed in the snowy street.

Then Wolf intervened. For FUCK'S SAKE, Hadja, he shouted. Give her the camera. Wolf was far more forceful than you need to be over a camera.

When Helen had the camera back in her hands, she was stuck for words and didn't know which way to move. She was surprised to have put up far less of a fight than she expected.

Hadja signalled to hurry up.

Helen panicked. She ran upstairs again. It was far too dark to take any shots inside, so she told me to bring the baby down into the courtyard. I wrapped the chequered rug around the baby and followed her down the stairs. I took some shots of her and the baby in the courtyard. Helen took some of me. I must have looked bewildered in some of them. And then Helen got the idea that there should be some photographs of both of us together, so we went out into the street, where she asked Wolf and Hadja to take some. Hadja got out and took the camera. She decided it would be quicker if she did it herself.

The snow on the pavement was half melted; half slush.

Helen stands beside me, on the left. It was very cold. I was holding the baby in my arms. We stand in front of the double doors of the house on Sonnenallee. I am taller than Helen. Helen is smiling. The baby's eyes are open. My weight is on my left leg. Helen's head is leaning towards mine.

Transit vehicles are not permitted to stop. No matter how much I might have wanted to jump out, I couldn't. Along the corridor through East Germany, there is no opportunity to stop. Even at Helmstedt, on the border back into West Germany, I wanted to get out and go back.

As we approached the checkpoint, Wolf switched off the music and took his feet down off the dashboard. The road signs are unequivocal. Heavy traffic. Cars. Buses. Hadja handed three passports out through the window. It's a mistake to assume that three passports together mean anything. The border guard bent his knees to see our faces in the car.

Further up ahead, there was a sign for the West German *Autobahn*. And more road signs for Hamburg, Bremen, Hannover, Frankfurt. It's a mistake to think that road signs mean anything.

Hadja gave another shout as soon as we drove on. HIT THE ROAD GUYS. Wolf switched on the music again. Hadja accelerated. Again, the white landscape of Germany took over, like the end of a film, swollen with significance. Wolf smiled and handed back my passport. It's a mistake to assume that the occupants of a car travelling together along the *Autobahn* are content.

It's a mistake to take anything at face value. It's a mistake to believe what photographs tell you. Later that day, when the snow was cleared from the footpaths, Helen walked into a shopping centre to get the films developed. She walked around for an hour to kill time. She watched a woman demonstrate the virtues of the vegetable slicer. *Meine Damen und Herren.* A vegetable slicer is the same in any language. Then it was time to collect the photographs.

I never saw any of them.

After Helmstedt, there was nothing but fighting in the car. First it began with penetrating silence. The music didn't help any more. Music in cars and restaurants and shops is designed to keep people apart and create an illusion of space.

This time, it's Wolf who begins. I suppose you'll miss your macho Turkish boy with the big pectorals, he says.

Hadja is surprised, and loses ground. It takes her a moment to retaliate.

Come on, Wolf, you can't say it's my fault now when it was you who started it all. You and that little student bitch.

Wolf snorts.

You should have thought about it when you started kicking around with her.

So it's revenge, then, is it? Wolf shouted. For you it's all a matter of getting your revenge. You can't even do what you want to do because you do everything to get even. You have to pick up some young Turk to pull the knickers off you. I suppose we're quits now. Is that it?

It is misleading to compare like with like or to confuse pleasure with success.

How can you tell me we're quits? Hadja shouted. Her rage is complete. How can you compare what you did to me with what I did . . .

You're so small, Wolf shouted back. You still want to get even. That's all you can think about, isn't it.

Well, look, how do I know? How do I know when I'm quits with you, you bastard? How can it ever be the same after what you did?

Revenge is all you can think of.

Hadja changes the subject. The driver can do that at will. She says she wants Wolf to take over at the wheel for a while. She's fed up driving. He refuses. She insists. From Braunschweig on, you'll have to take over.

It's a mistake to think that driving is a pleasure. Can you achieve equality along the *Autobahn*? With snow in the fields? With an audience in the back seat? Isn't revenge meant to be sweeter than anything which started it? So Hadja must be getting a better deal after all. Is it better to be equal in misfortune or unlucky in better circumstances? Superior in squalor or disadvantaged in affluence?

What does it matter – THE – FUCK? Wolf shouted. What does it matter who gets what? You might as well start keeping a scoreboard. How many times before breakfast. How many times after breakfast. Is that what you want? Fellatio: five. Others: three. Is that it?

Yes . . . *meinetwegen*. Why not?

Ach – come on, Hadja. Alan doesn't want to hear all this.

Alan doesn't mind, do you?

Hadja looks back in the mirror at me. I wish they would leave me out of it. Very soon, they begin to compare details. Hadja wants to know about Lydia's competence in bed. Wolf wants to know what Hadja did with Mehmet.

Wolf listened with a raging stare while Hadja described her adventures with Mehmet, the Turk. Wolf kept looking out over the white fields as though he were seeing it all on screen.

From Braunschweig to Göttingen, they fell silent.

Somewhere around Kassel, we stopped for something to eat. *Schnitzel* and *pommes frites*; that kind of thing. Wolf sits sideways, cross-legged, and swings his leg while he eats. As soon as he's finished eating, he inspects Hadja's plate to see what she has left.

Outside, in the car park, Wolf stretched and kicked his legs out. We got into the car and waited while Hadja went to the washrooms. *Damen*. Wolf sat in the driving seat this time. When Hadja came out, she had her hair done, and when Wolf saw her approaching the car in the rear-view mirror, he drove forward suddenly, leaving her standing behind in the car park. Then he reversed again. But just as Hadja leaned forward to reach for the door, Wolf drove away again, laughing. This time he reversed once more and let her in.

Du FUCKING *Arsch*, she screamed, when she got into the car.

She lost colour. I've never seen her so pale.

It's a mistake to make a noise with the back of your nose. Dangerous to suppress mirth or to shudder silently in the back seat.

Du FUCKING *Arsch*, Wolf, she repeated. Then silence. You could hear the noise of cars along the *Autobahn*. If you ever do that to me again, she said, you'll pay for it. Don't underestimate me.

From Giessen to Frankfurt, things were relatively quiet. Wolf put on this old tape of B. B. King.

From Darmstadt on, things began to simmer again. From around Mannheim on to Karlsruhe, it all erupted once more. Worse than ever. Vicious.

We arrived late in Stuttgart at a small house in the suburbs. There was a low wall of pine trees in the garden; dark green if not black in darkness. By street light I couldn't see the roof of the house, but I felt certain it was made of red tiles. It was the ideal setting for Wolf. For uninhibited creativity. Hadja felt it was right. She's a thorough manager.

Hadja and Wolf were giving each other looks.

There was a smell of cooking from the kitchen downstairs. *Sauerkraut*. Or maybe it was caraway seeds or even *Knödel*.

On the way upstairs, Wolf slapped Hadja's backside.

Rauf, rauf, he said.

I carried in some of the luggage and equipment from the car. I helped Wolf with his instruments. Carried in one of his guitars, and as I walked into the bedroom, I discovered them already lying on the bed. Hadja face down. Wolf pulling at her clothes.

Hadja was laughing. Wolf was slapping.

Auf, auf!

I brought the guitar into the room and leaned it against the wall in the corner. But even then I found it difficult to leave.

15

Lovers Turn into Shoppers

I was afraid of that.

Berlin went under. The city welled up with a new sense of prosperity. A new post-recessionary realism. An optimism matched with discipline and practicality. There was talk of a second economic miracle in Germany. Talk about revaluing the D-Mark. There was talk about waste. Talk about global warming. Clean industries.

Hadja left Stuttgart after a week and drove back to Berlin on her own. Now she had Berlin to herself. She had a mental X marked with a red felt pen for the spot where Helen and Dieter should be reunited. Hadja knew exactly how Helen should look. Natural. How she should be dressed. Coat. Black beret. Not too much make-up. *Immer natürlich.* Hadja knew exactly how two people should accidentally meet after a long absence. Think coincidence, she kept telling Helen.

Hadja also thought it would be a good idea for them to meet without baby the first time. Just to see what Dieter's reaction would be. I was afraid of that.

Sulima and Massoud have bought themselves a new apartment in Schöneberg. They have been throwing parties for all their new friends almost non-stop ever since.

Konrad has all but moved in with Kristl. All but left his wife Gudrun. For practical reasons, he still considers himself at home with Gudrun, even though the nuptial arrangements have come to an end. There is talk of divorce and de-involvement. But for practical reasons, the idea of legal separation has been put off for the moment. It would complicate inheritance. Konrad stands to inherit so much more as a securely married man.

Helen got a letter from her mother. The photographs must have worked. Finally, her parents have acknowledged her existence in Berlin; her condition and her new baby, Daniel.

For some reason, Helen's parents are convinced that she is living with Dieter, a Berliner. They have been urging marriage. They want Helen to come home on a visit with the baby. They want to see the little boy. But they want her to be married and to arrive with a husband.

There was talk about a living city. Living art. Berlin became a capital for artists and alternatives. There was talk about theatrical innovations. Berlin had discovered the sloping stage, with living birch trees implanted as part of the props. Due to public demand, there was talk of the Schaubühne theatre bringing back its record-breaking production of Maxim Gorki's *Sommergäste* for another run.

Hadja knows everything there is to know about Dieter. Within limits, that is. Dieter is tall. Drives an Audi. Seems to have something against driving a current model. His occupation as a motor mechanic allows him to maintain an old car. He spends a lot of time in hi-fi shops, record shops, and in Berlin's largest swimming pool. Enjoys the freedom of movement through water and time. Seems to crave anything that offers imaginary space, and doesn't differ from most other inhabitants of the city in that respect. Lives alone in Kreuzberg. Has few guests. None staying overnight. Speaks only when necessary. Has a great capacity to stay up late at night and turn up fresh for work at the garage next morning. Has lately turned to artistic pursuits. Sculpture.

I was afraid of that.

Helen has decided to learn German. If she was going to settle in Berlin and bring up a child in Germany, then she thought she might as well learn the language. She wanted to be able to explain things. To ask questions. She wanted to be able to speak out.

Kartoffel! Brot! Milch! Wurst!

She wanted to be able to make equations and comparisons and call things by their rightful names, instead of endlessly pointing the finger at objects in shops, gesticulating and smiling wildly at old women who stop her in the street to admire the baby. There must be a shortage of babies in Berlin, Helen thought. Helen wanted to talk to the old women who look at the baby with the same longing with which they speak of the past, of life before the war when Berlin was still Berlin.

163

Helen thought about the best way to learn German. Not by shopping in supermarkets, where few words are ever exchanged beyond the requisite minimum. She decided that the best way was through the newspapers. The evening papers seemed most appropriate. Everything is simplified. There are plenty of pictures, which usually tell their own tale.

Feuerwehr kam zu spät, sagt Witwe! Fire brigade came too late, says widow!

Helen always had an ear for languages. She can hear things spoken as she reads them. She could add the right plaintive or outraged Berliner tones to the headlines she picked out. Helen had also begun to see her own life in more simplified terms. Her own situation and the events of her life had become titles from evening newspapers. Even the simplest events of daily routine screamed back at her in headlines.

Window left open! Baby asleep! Book lay on table! Spoon used as bookmark! Natural father found! Accidental meeting arranged!

Each event in her life became at once tragic and funny. Her situation appeared to her as it would to millions of readers. Everything stood at once accused and defended. Answerable to collective opinion; one moment dead set against her, next minute sympathetic, even sorry for her. Each situation, each daily action profiled Helen before the readers of Berlin.

Young, Attractive, Alone! In search of a father! Parents urged marriage! Traffic on Sonnenallee to be diverted! Berlin water leaves film on teacups! Coffee becomes national drink! Household addiction; doctors warn!

I knew it.

There was talk about need. There was talk about for ever and talk about marriage. Family. Role of parenthood. There was talk about not being able to live without things. Cornflakes. Sausages. Love.

Helen had a bit of luck. She had gone down to the local supermarket to get some groceries. Helen has always paid for everything she got. Almost always. Once or twice she had slipped something into her bag. But no more. It made her nervous. Crime is attractive until you need it. Otherwise, Helen had never got anything free. Never won anything in her life before. So she couldn't believe her luck.

She walked around the supermarket aisles on a Saturday morning, dazed like all other shoppers. Shoppers are unaware of the presence of other people. The supermarket had a red and white colour scheme. It registered only subconsciously. Relationships with other people are subliminal. A husband passed his wife without either of them noticing each other. A famous face was ignored. Cut-price offers attracted more attention than beautiful legs. People forgot about love and concentrated on shopping instead. Lovers turned into shoppers.

When Helen got to the checkout, she placed her groceries on the conveyor belt behind the sign; *Nächste Bedienung*: next customer. She moved in parallel with her own ingredients. She knew herself by her own shopping items. And as soon as her groceries were checked out and paid for, an alarm went off.

Immediately, Helen was surrounded by shop assistants and managers, all smiling and beckoning her. At first she thought she had done something wrong. But then she eventually understood from the hysterical smiles around her that she must have won something. She was a winner. The millionth customer.

Yes, yes! Now come you with us, somebody said.

The shoppers, who had been so torpid and dreamy up to then, woke up at the thought of how close they had come to winning. The manager of the shop took Helen by the arm. A shop assistant pushed her buggy with the baby in it. And somebody else carried her groceries for her. They brought her to a stand where her name was taken and where it was announced that Helen Quinn from Ireland had won herself a two-minute shopping spree at Tenglemann's. She was to come back any other weekday that would suit her.

Helen couldn't believe her luck.

Something that Helen knows about Dieter and Hadja doesn't. Something only Helen knows. Dieter is generous. Helen still cannot believe that Dieter left of his own free will; she continually wants to give him the benefit of doubt and believe that something drove him. She knows that he never got on with his own father; had few conversations with him. That he once applied for a visa to the USA but never went. That he was always fond of Irish brown bread. That while Dieter was living in Ireland, he slowly got the impression that everything in the world had already been said. He began to think about the countless men he saw on the seafront, gazing out to sea as though they had seen and heard everything. It became important to give the impression that everything was known. Every day when Dieter went swimming, he saw men sitting on benches, stone walls and concrete battlements, looking at the sea. Men ate sandwiches furtively on blue benches along the seafront. The wind blew paper around. A ship crossed the bay. By evening, the seats had all been reallocated to newcomers; some with ice-cream cones, some with cider bottles.

That was the day before Dieter left Ireland. Helen knew what was on his mind when he left.

The X on Hadja's mental map where Dieter and Helen are to be reunited by fate is at the corner of Lietzenburger Strasse and Bleibtreu Strasse. Since Helen would have the advantage of prescience, Hadja thought it would only be fair to give Dieter an equivalent advantage of seeing Helen coming towards him from a distance. Enough time to think, but not to avoid reunion or run away.

Helen had nothing to lose.

She stepped out of the shower on to a towel she had placed on the kitchen floor. Somewhere she had read that baths and showers have negative and positive ions, but she didn't know which. She preferred the shower and was afraid that more information might change her mind.

She dried herself quickly and walked around the apartment, wondering if she could be seen from the scaffolding in the courtyard. She assured herself that as long as she heard the sound of work, she was safe.

Helen's physical perfection had been restored. She had every reason to be proud that there was not one single line or mark along her body which could prove that she was a mother. She still rubbed oil on to her stomach every day, but she could now confidently stand naked in front of anyone knowing that they would never guess. She is afraid of nothing. Occasionally, a drop or two of milk would still escape from her nipples, but the likelihood was remote. The baby had been weaned. And nobody

166

would have believed she even had a child unless Daniel was there beside her.

Helen placed a mirror sloping against the window-frame as soon as she was dressed. She applied some make-up. Very subtle. Made sure that she looked natural. *Immer natürlich.* She then found another mirror so that she could examine the side of her face and the back of her head. You need two mirrors.

On the evening that Helen and Dieter accidentally ran into each other in the city centre, there was a mild breeze. The first of spring. The kind of evening that makes people think and re-evaluate their wardrobe. Helen and Hadja walked together down Lietzenburger Strasse, unrehearsed and natural. They were going for a drink together like any two Berliner women when they saw Dieter walking towards them along the mosaic pavement of the inner city. Helen couldn't believe her eyes. Nor could Dieter.

In that first moment after such a long absence, anything can happen. Things could have gone either way. They might have taken one look at each other and decided to cling to memory rather than reopen their discourse in the street. After a long absence like that, everything has to be instantly reappraised. As they walked towards one another along Lietzenburger Strasse, it was touch and go. They might have embraced unreservedly. Or walked past one another, furiously.

As it was, they both smiled awkwardly at a distance of around six or seven metres. Lopsided smiles. From there on they walked towards each other mechanically; it was more like walking side-ways. And when they came level, they embraced each other without a word, the way you sometimes see people embracing in the street or at railway stations, indefinitely, without inhibition, which makes the observer think there must be a long story to it. Helen's feet came off the pavement. Hadja stood back. A motorbike ripped along Lietzenburger Strasse behind them.

I don't believe it, Helen eventually said.

Sag mal, Helen!

The embrace was more crushing than necessary. Helen still had the irrational anxiety that such embraces would force milk from her bosom and make circular stains on her dress. It went on longer than necessary. Embarrassing to anyone looking on. Neither of them, Helen or Dieter, wanted to be the first to stop or to pull away. Hadja stood about two metres away, getting impatient. A man emerged from a building right next to them leading two small dogs on two thin leather leashes which were bound to become plaited and knotted the way the dogs pulled and crossed over, dragging the man off in the direction of Ku-damm.

Helen pulled back to look up at Dieter. He is much taller than she is.

I don't believe it, she said. Where have you been?

Ach – Helen, you don't believe how much you are in my head.

Are linguistic errors venial? Helen didn't know whether to laugh or retaliate. It's a matter of presentation. And a matter of what you want to believe. Helen and Dieter looked each other in the eye, but at such close range, they must have been sharply out of focus. There was a sweet smell of beer. Helen's back was arched, leisurely on Dieter's arm. There was a short burst of questions and answers, mostly unintelligent, mostly irrelevant.

You got not my letter, Dieter said.

No! Where did you send it?

Mountpleasant! To our address in Dublin, Dieter said. But it comes back to Berlin after three months.

I never got it.

How long are you here in Berlin?

Almost a year, she said.

Aber – Helen! This cannot be true. *Wirklich*?

It is true, Dieter. I picked up your bag from the hotel; what was it, Potsdam? I still have it.

Ist das möglich?

All questions and explanations suddenly become irrelevant, the way they often are between people who know each other so well. Former intimacies short-circuit reappraisal. Explanations were postponed. Helen suddenly realized that Hadja had been left standing in the street on her own. She pulled herself away from Dieter and began to introduce them. Hadja and Dieter shook hands.

Hadja suggested a drink. A quiet bar just around the corner. She was expecting some kind of confrontation between Helen and Dieter. But Helen and Dieter began to talk as though they had never been separated. There was talk about Berlin. And talk about

Dublin, about Dieter's mother. Letters. Work. So far, nothing was said about the baby. There was talk about Kreuzberg. Distances to and from work. The convenience of public transport in relation to motoring. There was talk about insurance premiums. And life insurance.

Nobody had the presence of mind to order a drink. Once they sat around a table in the next bar, it was Hadja who had to do all the thinking. She ordered three beers. She burned with anger. She couldn't believe that Helen could give in so easily, without a showdown of some sort. No accusations. No hostility. No tears. Maybe all that would follow, Hadja thought to herself.

There was talk about old friends in Dublin. There was talk about the flat in Mountpleasant. Helen explained that her brother David had cleared everything out and even paid off the rent that was due. In recompense, her brother inherited Dieter's hi-fi system and records.

Schluss! Hadja said abruptly. Dieter and Helen looked at each other and then at Hadja.

Schluss jetzt, she said again, slapping her hand on the table. I have my nose full of this.

Hadja broke into German and began to accuse Dieter of all the things she expected Helen to bring up. Why had he left her? Why had he treated her like that? Did he think he could treat women like dirt and get away with it? Without so much as an apology?

Helen couldn't understand all of what Hadja was saying. But she knew she was being defended. And she hated being spoken for. Hated the idea of being thrown in with all other women. Why do people always have to speak for each other? She pleaded with her to stop.

Let me finish, Hadja said. Hadja had a courtroom voice. She continued to accuse Dieter with the palm of her hand turned upwards, pointing like a spade towards his face.

Hadja, come on, stop it.

Now it looked as though Helen was beginning to defend Dieter, which made Hadja even more furious. Dieter was twirling a beer mat on an axis beneath his finger. He knew Hadja was speaking out of turn.

The waitress wore sensible shoes. It's regulation. The beer has no artificial chemicals to keep the froth on top. Regulation. Helen looked into her glass with one eye shut to see what it was like for somebody with one eye to look into a glass. Mothers do that. She tried not to listen to Hadja's tirade. If it hadn't been for Hadja's tirade, she might have been more hostile herself.

Hadja stood up. Looked across the table at Helen and nodded her head.

Come on, Helen, she said. I give you a lift home now.

But Helen didn't move. She said she would make her own way home. Hadja turned and walked out, furious.

How would you know somebody was a mother? How would you guess? Not by physical appearance. Occasionally, you can tell by the roundness of the stomach. But not with Helen. How would Dieter have guessed? Not from Helen's body. Or the way she walked, or the way she spoke. Is it the calm, lingering look in the eyes that disposes of all fake platitudes? Or is it that her mind is somewhere else?

Mothers do that. She can be irrational. She can behave in an erratic way, quite justifiably, without offering an explanation. She can get up suddenly and want to leave. She can change her mind for no reason. Get bored. Become noticeably uninterested in current affairs and conversations about new books, new films. She can pretend there are more important things in life, always something more important. She can get momentarily frightened and want to leave. Her imagination can play tricks on her. She can hear baby cries where there are none. Baby cries where there are squeaking doors and baby cries where the waitress in rubber soles turns a ninety-degrees angle.

Dieter drove Helen home in his old Audi. He is a fast driver. There was a sweet smell in the car which reminded Helen mostly of toothpaste. When they arrived at Sonnenallee, she didn't want to bring Dieter inside. For lots of reasons. Not that night. She wanted to think.

Come back tomorrow, she said. I've got something to show you.

What is it? he asked.

Tomorrow, she said.

Helen would say no more. She wanted Dieter to drive home and think about it. She wanted the idea of the baby to come to him slowly on the way home. She wanted him to guess himself. Like the game they used to play: Guess who I saw today? She wanted him to think of it on his own, and if he came back the next day, it was because he had decided to come back, because he believed he could be a parent. It was a test.

Helen was suddenly reminded once again that she was a parent and had a baby waiting for her. How could she have stayed out so long? Can a mother do that? She ran upstairs to the apartment. She had asked the Frau Brab, the old woman across the corridor to listen out. But how reliable was Frau Brab's hearing? Helen had left the door ajar. She expected to hear her baby crying as she ran up. She heard nothing. Danny . . . Danny, she called as she ran through her own apartment leaving the doors open behind her.

Mothers do that. They repeat the name of their own baby for no reason. She switched on the lights, picked up her boy in a wild panic, woke him up, opened his eyes and stopped breathing herself to listen and make sure he was alive.

Frau Brab came out in her dressing gown at the sound of running on the stairs. She could see right into the apartment where Helen stood under the light kissing the baby and holding it in a terrifying embrace as though its bones would soon break; as though all the air were being squeezed from its tiny lungs. She kept repeating his name. Danny. Danny. Danny. As though he couldn't hear her.

As soon as Frau Brab heard baby sounds, she shook her head and closed her door again. Helen sank on to her knees, whispering into the baby's ear: I'll never leave you again – never.

Dieter did come back the next day. He picked up his own son as though he had been longing to see the baby all night. Longing to see a baby for months. Daniel, he kept on repeating. Daniel, Daniel. As though he needed a name to believe what he saw in his arms. In fact, Helen and Dieter met every day from then on. He wanted to see more and more of his son. And more and more of Helen. There was talk about their getting back together. Talk about Helen moving in with Dieter. Packing. Cooking for two. Three. Talk about installing a baby seat in the Audi. There was talk about marriage.

I was afraid of that.

171

* * *

A Tuesday morning had been arranged for Helen to go back to Tenglemann's supermarket for her prize of two minutes' free shopping. *Millionen Einkauf*, it was called. As much as she could fit into a trolley in two minutes. Tenglemann's shopping spree. It took Helen a while to dress up and get ready.

Dieter decided to go to the shop with her. He slipped off work for an hour in order to drive her back to the Neuköln shopping centre. He parked in the underground car park. While they sat in the car, Dieter, who had already been to the supermarket to check the location of all the goods, drew a hasty map of the aisles for Helen. He told her what she should go for; where the meat counter was, wines, smoked salmon, tinned delicacies. There was no use throwing big family-size packets of cornflakes into the trolley once she had the chance. Two minutes is not a long time, he kept telling her. You have to know what you want.

At Tenglemann's, everyone was waiting for her. There was a large banner spanned across the ceiling inside the glass doors of the supermarket: *Millionen Einkauf*. Underneath stood the manager and some of the shop assistants, all greeting her with generous smiles as she arrived. The manager introduced himself and began to explain the rules of the prize to her. There were people from the press there as well, from the local district newspaper, the *Neukölner Anzeiger*: Neuköln Informer.

The manager held the trolley ready for Helen. She wished there was less fuss about all of this. She would have preferred something more leisurely. The manager held a stopwatch in his hand and made a sign with thumb and finger: *Zwei Minuten*. Dieter held on to the buggy with Daniel in it and stood behind a barrier which had been placed across the first aisle. He gave Helen last-minute hints on where to find the meat counter and the wine section.

Achtung – fertig – los!

Dieter saw her running straight down the first aisle ignoring everything until she got to the end and turned left. She had the whole supermarket to herself. Now and again there were glimpses of her galloping across the junctions between the aisles. Now and again she was seen stopping right in the middle, looking around her as though she were lost. Panicking. Running. Knocking down as many goods as she managed to get into the trolley. Two minutes is not long, and she was soon back at the starting line again being congratulated by the manager and all the staff.

You were very good, Dieter whispered into her ear as soon as he got the chance.

The trolley was almost full to the top. The shopping spree was counted up at one of the checkouts. It came to 342 marks in total. There was a round of applause from the staff and from the customers who were waiting to do their own shopping. The manager announced the total. He remarked, in a carefully phrased speech punctuated by pauses, that Helen, the girl from Ireland, had done extremely well. She had chosen the right things. But he was proud to announce that, despite everything, she was still only able to score 342 marks, which must mean that the Tenglemann prices were as low as ever. Everyone laughed. There was another round of applause.

Helen was still out of breath. It was the excitement more than the physical effort. She saw Dieter standing behind the barrier with Daniel in the buggy. For no reason, she began to cry. Mothers do that. She couldn't explain it herself. She didn't know why. The onlookers felt for her. Everyone felt for her. There was talk of Kleenex. And one of the staff, a small fat woman with a red face, held a paper tissue towards her. Helen was overcome. It was understandable. When she recovered herself moments later, the photographer began to take more photographs of her beside the manager, shaking hands.

Then it was the reporter's turn to take some details for the *Neukölner Anzeiger*. She was from Ireland, the reporter already knew. What was her full name? And in that moment, Helen didn't know what to answer. She thought of her mother just then. She thought of the sea and of ships. For no reason, she thought of home and of a rusty toy wheelbarrow at the end of the garden, half buried, sloping, from which the dog always drank when the rainwater lodged in it. Mothers do that. Her mind was elsewhere. The reporter asked her once more. He made himself clearer this time.

What is then your full name, Helen?

Instinctively, she answered Helen Penzholz, because that was the first thing she thought of there and then. And that's how it appeared the next day in the *Neukölner Anzeiger*. Right under her

173

own smiling picture with the manager and the full trolley. Trapped in her own headline. Her luck.

ONE IN A MILLION. Helen Penzholz.

16

Sand

From then on, most things were done purely for appearances. The Dresdner Bank got a facelift. Sonnenallee was resurfaced. Further inner-city streets were selected for pedestrianization and repaved with mosaic stones. Street sculptures were added. And street furniture for pedestrians to sit on. The newspapers began to imitate the mind of the pedestrian. Strategy was given the appearance of innocence. Public inquiries became show trials. Terrorism was promoted by media fear. The hamburger bun was authentic only if it was sprinkled with sesame seeds. Production of the VW Beetle was abandoned. The breast was replaced by Milupa. The leotard swept Europe. The Pope began to travel. Disposable nappies were genderized.

Helen began to shave her legs. She began to answer the phone in German: *Guten Tag. Bei Penzholz*. She did something to her hair, though nobody could be sure exactly what. A sailor's outfit was bought for the baby boy Daniel, even though there was little likelihood of his ever becoming a sailor. Helen received a family christening robe in the post from her mother; an ancient lace christening garment which had gone slightly yellow with age and had been in the family for over a hundred years. The parcel had been registered and insured for a thousand pounds. Nothing could replace the appearance of age. And nothing could replace tradition. The appearance of things the way they always have been. Dieter and Helen decided to get married. On reflection, they thought it was the best thing they could do. Helen had received nothing but support and total commitment from Dieter since the reunion. He was a real father.

At the end of February, Helen contacted me in Stuttgart about this. We had been on the phone a few times briefly, just talking, and laughing mostly. But this was something frightening. She had left a message for me to ring. And I rang from a public phone-box. I must have turned pale as she began to speak.

Alan, there is something I have to talk to you about, she said quietly. Helen was a different person on the phone. There was something in the statement that was like an immediate warning. Something in her voice that sounded alarming.

Don't tell me, I was about to say. But I let her speak for herself.

Alan, I don't quite know how to put this, but I think it would be grossly unfair to you if I didn't tell you immediately. I have met up with Dieter here and we have decided to get back together again. We're going to get married. I know this sounds awful, especially on the phone. But it has to be said . . .

My first reaction was silence. Then I tried to stop her.

Why, Helen? I asked. You can't do this. You can't just walk away like that.

I looked around, out through the glass panel of the phone-box, to see if anyone was waiting to get in. To see if I was being unreasonable.

Alan, look, this is very difficult over the phone. I can't really talk about it. It's unfair to ask me to explain.

I suppose I should have known, I said.

We stumbled through a half-dozen badly formulated responses, hurried and half pronounced. There is an innate panic on long-distance calls at the best of times. Is it the risk of being cut off, the money running out suddenly before things have been said? Is it the urge to say witty things that people will remember you by? Is it the unreasonable panic on long-distance calls that makes the other person sound a lot closer than they really are, almost in the next room, as though I could touch her? The line was so clear. Even when the credit had only dropped to 17 marks, I pushed in another 5.

I feel terrible about this, she said. Really awful. I hate myself for doing this to you. But I can't see any way out. There is no sense in denying what's happened.

Helen, I can't let you do this, I said.

There was somebody waiting outside the kiosk now. There were these ridiculous silences. I counted 7 marks' worth of silence at one point. Then her voice leaped back. Clearer than ever.

No, Alan, don't ask me to change my mind. I won't. I can't.

The thought occurred to me that I should race back to Berlin immediately to stop her. I couldn't let her go on with this.

Helen, wait. Don't do anything. I'm coming back to Berlin. Wait. You can't get married.

No, Alan, don't. Please. It wouldn't help.

The christening took place at the nearest Catholic church in Kreuzberg. A vast church which the priest complained was under-utilized. People don't even know there's a church on Grossbeerenstrasse unless they look at it and say to themselves: There's a church. Inside, the sacred surroundings added to the furtive nature of baptism; silent, in broad daylight, with no witnesses, and the distant impervious traffic outside. The priest coughed as he approached the baptismal font. Coughing in church is done for effect. The baby hardly fitted into the christening robe, and the photographs of the occasion, this time taken with Dieter's camera, show an obvious late baptism. After the ceremony, the priest asked Dieter and Helen to wait for a while because he wanted to fill the church with music. He told them he was a keen organist and rarely had such a fine opportunity to play with purpose. Again, he spoke of the fall off in attendances. There is a strong aggression in organ music which is hurled along the walls of the church; a defiant death touched by an instinct of comic glory, ignoring everything beyond the walls of the church, drowning the city traffic and everything else that kills God.

I didn't go back to Berlin after all. I couldn't. Wolf had just finished recording and was about to start touring southern Germany. I couldn't very well desert him. Besides, I was no longer sure it was a good idea to go back to Berlin and change Helen's mind. It would have achieved nothing. I mean, how could I ask her not to marry Dieter if I wasn't prepared to marry her myself? I wasn't prepared to offer what Dieter was giving her. Future, family; all the appearance of settled life. That's what I believed. I wasn't prepared to believe that she had chosen to go back to Dieter for any other reason. I couldn't live with any other explanation.

I called her the following day from the same phone-box. It was she herself who brought up the subject.

Alan, listen, I don't want to be put in a position of making a choice between two men. I don't wish to trade you off against

Dieter or to compare you both. As far as I'm concerned, you are two totally different people.

Except that I'm in the past and he's in the present.

Alan, look. She paused. Didn't know what to say for a moment. Alan, you were very good to me and I'll never forget you as long as I live.

Come on, Helen, I don't want to hear this.

Alan, I've got to be honest with myself, she said. You wouldn't have married me. You wouldn't have been a husband and a father, now would you?

What makes you so sure? I said. Anyhow, what's so important about marriage? What the hell does it matter? Who gives a damn whether you're married or not?

It does matter, Alan.

There was a pause. When somebody keeps calling you by your first name, you've got something to worry about. Either you're being under-estimated or else you're just a bit simple.

Why? I asked. Give me one good reason.

Alan, you don't understand, she said. I need to know where I'm going. I need to be able to see the future a little. I have a baby that needs a father and a mother. A secure home.

Come off it, Helen. You can do anything you want in Germany without being married. You could make a secure home on your own, without anyone else's help.

But that's just it, Alan. With you there was nothing certain, nothing permanent. I never knew from one day to the next where I was going. I loved you for it. With you I didn't want a future. I didn't want anything to be all organized and planned. That's what I liked so much about you.

But why does everything have to turn permanent all of a sudden? It's a phobia, Helen. Half the country is divorced, and you're still trying to set up the everlasting marriage.

Helen stopped talking for a moment. She came close to saying what she wanted to say. What she hadn't said. Again, I counted silent money disappearing; 15, 14, 13. I didn't care about that. I pushed in more coins. I could have stood there for hours saying nothing. All I wanted was to keep her on the phone.

Alan, you won't let me explain, she said. I don't want to argue with you over the phone. It hurts me and it hurts you. It's not fair.

178

So it all boils down to marriage and security, then, is that it? I asked. I was surprised at my own hostility and bitterness, because all along I wanted to appear reasonable and humorous; I wanted to be remembered well. Whether it was over or not, I wanted to be remembered well.

Stability, is that it?

No, Alan, it's not that at all. To be honest, I didn't know what I wanted until I met Dieter again.

There was nobody waiting to use the phone that day, and I could have spoken to her for hours. I wanted to stop her from explaining everything. I could have stood there and listened for ages, to nothing. The line is so clear. I wanted her to say nothing more. I just kept her on the phone. For the first time in her life, Helen knew exactly what she wanted. That much was clear. She wanted Dieter, not me.

From then on, market forces were allowed to prevail. Black came back into fashion. Demand grew for Irish smoked salmon, British rock, French lingerie and Japanese technology. The colours navy and yellow were associated in the mind with Lufthansa, travel and freedom. The letter M caused subliminal hunger. The colour red was reserved in the mind for intimacy, fire extinguishers, lips and hearts. Why is blood red? A quirk of evolution became a graphic designer's dream. The accordion came back into music. Sex became a cliché. Bed manners became important. After you. The cliché worked better than ever.

The only question that remained unanswered was whether life reflected market forces or vice versa. Whether market forces were part of a natural order. It was also unclear if marriage could be called a natural institution.

There was absolutely nothing secure about my apartment in Sonnenallee any more. While Hadja was on the phone to Wolf she asked to speak to me, and explained that she had to make a decision to take over the apartment again. She must have known Helen had moved out. Hadja said she had found a nice little apartment for me in Oranienstrasse. She would be turning Sonnenallee into a rehearsal room or studio for Wolf. With my permission, she wanted to begin the renovation and ask workers to start

179

soundproofing the walls. The removals could be done in time as soon as I arrived back in Berlin. I didn't have much to move.

Dieter and Helen got married. They would have had a church wedding if there had been any relatives to invite. Dieter's mother is far too old and no longer aware of what's happening. Only Helen's parents would have been impressed with wedding cakes, flowers and limousines. And then only if the right people saw it. Instead, Helen and Dieter decided to go for a quiet ceremony at the registry office. It was insignificant, they told each other. Helen wore a navy dress. She had wondered if she should have bought a new one for that occasion, but decided not to in the end. She made a clear distinction between weddings and marriages. Ireland had always been a country for big weddings and small marriages. A small country with a big imagination. Marriage is in the imagination.

It was a formality. There were no unnecessary words spoken. There was no music. In fact, they could have had organ music if they wanted, for a fee. The administrator seemed surprised when Dieter said no. It was a marriage that started off with no fanfare. There were no friends. The only witness on the day was a fellow worker whom Dieter had asked to come, a Tunisian from Kahl Autowerkstadt. He signed his name, smiled and went back to work. The only sign of ostentation at the registry office was the red, or burgundy red, velvet seats. Otherwise, everything was simple.

Outside, a professional photographer took up his position ready to take photographs until he noticed that Helen was carrying a baby and that Dieter had begun to unfold the buggy. Dieter waved his hand. The photographer withdrew. Helen saw him smile. At the bottom of the steps, she put Daniel into the buggy, strapped him in and began to walk along the pavement. They walked for a while. Then they stopped for a drink, not to celebrate but to put the whole thing out of their minds. Marriage is something you put behind you. In broad daylight. Without a word.

I still called Helen, every day, almost. Somehow I couldn't leave it alone. It became a habit, standing in a telephone booth somewhere along the *Autobahn*, outside a stopover restaurant or in an unfamiliar street somewhere. I spent all my change on the phone. I got to know telephone booths. Like the one in Freiburg where I called her three times. Nobody can tell me that one telephone booth is the same as another.

Of course, after Helen got married there was less and less reason to talk to her. There were less and less things for us to say. She seemed to understand that I had to talk to her, that I needed to be weaned. It was an understanding that drew a silent rage. I know why telephone booths get vandalized. But then I always said I would phone her for the last time. Have the last word. I was full of last words.

And Dieter seemed to have the same considerate understanding, because he once answered the phone and seemed to know immediately who it was. He was polite. There was no need for animus.

Ein Moment, please, he said. I will bring her.

Helen and I no longer spoke about anything important. It was mindless gossip. We spoke only about current things. It became impossible to mention anything from the past. We talked about Wolf. The concerts. I told her about southern Germany. She said she would love to go some day. We talked about Hadja, who had come back down from Berlin to accompany Wolf on tour. We talked about music. I told her how Wolf had found a coin inside a sausage which almost broke a tooth; he was threatening to sue if he wasn't so pressed for time. It's put him off *Würstl* for life.

From Göttingen, from where I could see the university, I told Helen she was doing the right thing. What a thing to say to somebody like Helen. But somehow I meant it. Though I knew she didn't believe me. I told her I would be moving out of Sonnenallee when I returned to Berlin.

Alan, listen. Do you mind if I take the cot?

No! Sure! Why not? I said. You don't expect me to sleep in it, do you? It's fuck-all use to me, I said amicably, trying to be funny.

I'll pay you for it, she said.

Look, Helen, don't annoy me. I want you to take it. You need it, don't you?

But I've no key to the apartment any more.

Doesn't matter, I said. There are these workmen in there all the time now. You and Dieter can collect the cot any time you like. Just tell them you know me. Tell them Hadja Milic sent you.

Again, Helen threatened to pay me for the cot. I told her it would make me very angry. I wouldn't hear of it. For some reason, last words never sound like real last words. Not until you think about them.

Demand grew for holistic things: medicine, food, books, bicycles. Nothing was taken at face value. Former excesses were forgotten. There were reformed smokers and reformed junkies everywhere. Friends turned their backs on each other. People turned macrobiotic overnight. Demand grew for solicitors, programmers, auditors. People became professional to the point of no return. Obsessed to the point of no return by excellence, clean lungs and regularity. Logic entered the food chain. Logic and love were combined, too. Demand grew for baby oil. People became imaginative to the point of no return.

One afternoon, alone with Daniel in Dieter's apartment with the sunlight flooding in through the window, Helen began to think of her situation. She held her baby boy up to the sun and got the idea that her son's lungs were translucent. Somewhere in a book she had read that, unlike adults, a baby fills its lungs completely with clean air. She thought of her baby's lungs as pink. Something like a Chinese lantern, lit up.

Then she began to think about leaving Berlin. Going back to Dublin for a while. It was a thought she had always held at the back of her mind. But there had never been an opportunity to think of it before.

Helen went almost every day to meet Dieter, either at the garage or at the swimming pool, where he likes to swim for an hour after the day's work. At Kahl Autowerkstadt, the workshop is filled with the noise of spanners and the sound of the hydraulic lift. The music over the speakers helps everyone to concentrate. Occasionally one of the mechanics begins to howl along with a song, tilting nostalgia into comedy. Now and then, the music is interrupted by the voice of Mechtild, the receptionist at the office. The receptionist's blonde hair, blue eyes and red high-heeled shoes enter the minds of all mechanics as they work. It is easy to visualize the receptionist's mouth because her voice sounds so familiar and so near over the speakers.

With a mixture of terror and excitement, Dieter is reminded that Helen and Daniel are waiting for him outside at the reception. He is continually reminded of his role as a father, as though he had been conferred with an honorary title. With terror and excitement, he thinks of his own son, the most vulnerable part of himself, floating around the city in a buggy, breathing Berlin air like a pink Chinese lantern. A son exposes his father. A son makes his father think again. Dieter found he now had to examine all his old excuses to the world.

He walked out and met Helen. Wiped his oily hands on his overalls and kissed her. On the way home in the car, Helen mentioned the fact that she had been thinking about Dublin. Wouldn't it be great to go back and live there. It wouldn't be like going back, she promised. It would be like going forward.

Dieter stopped the car. He was dramatic like that. He turned to Helen and looked into her eyes. Why not? he said. Berlin is no place for us. Let's go back and live in Dublin.

It was like something that was waiting to be said. Once it was said there was an acknowledgement of perfect unity, an embrace, silence, a hand running through Helen's hair. There is nothing more that can be said when people think alike. Dieter restarted the car and pulled out into the afternoon rush hour.

Dieter is a good swimmer. Most days, Helen went to the pool to watch. Sometimes she held the baby Daniel up to the glass window for Dieter to see from the pool. Sometimes the baby smiled. Sometimes the glass was steamed up.

The swimming pool is blue or green? The splash of somebody entering the water is like a page of a book being turned in a quiet house or like a letter being torn open in a hurry? The strokes of a swimmer are a sign of panic or a sign of strength? When Dieter comes to the end of the pool, he dives downwards. His feet come up out of the water for an instant before he propels his body forwards underwater. Unless you watch closely, you could think he never takes air.

With a mixture of terror and interest, obsession and fright, Dieter has now become aware of the medium through which he has been pushing his body like a seal. He thinks of his new status as father. He has become part of a universal movement; a conspiracy, a self-perpetuating, self-protecting society like a swimming federation.

He has begun to think about water in a way that he has never thought about it before. With a mixture of terror and obsession, he now realizes that a vast number of ordinary things have become relevant to him as never before. Parents are forerunners.

He stepped out of the pool and the water fell off his back. His chest is designed for strength and mobility. He walks as swimmers do. His muscular thighs collide as he walks. Pearls of water cling to his biceps as they do to cans of beer just taken from the fridge. Even now there is little evidence that he needs to breathe.

Dieter looks angry and kind. Concerned and careless. He would do anything for Helen. And he would do anything for his son Daniel. He has become aware of a new responsibility. He now has to show respect for himself. Market forces prevail. Genes are pooled.

With a mixture of self-consciousness and habit, choice and duty, he began to dry himself with the towel.

Things moved forward. Only forward. Nobody looked back. Demand grew for culture and leisure activities, like windsurfing. The poise of the windsurfer became an art; half seated, half standing. It became important to forget. Stress was a key word. Anything to forget. Memory and progress were incompatible. Past and present couldn't live in the same room together.

What could I do but try and forget? It was impossible to put Helen out of my mind. I threw myself into my work. Hadja and Wolf remarked at how efficient I had become. The concert tour was becoming a great success. Everywhere people attach themselves to success. It's contagious. Everybody puts the bad things behind them.

For some reason, whenever I tried to forget about Helen, I began to remember other things, further back. Worse things. School, for instance. Home. Things I was hoping never to be reminded of again. Things that only Helen could help me forget. In Frankfurt and Mannheim, I began to think that nothing has happened to me since I left home. I'm still the same. Now I've begun to mutilate my memory. And Helen.

Logic and longing can't stay in the same room together. Everyone became creative to the point of no return. Everybody worked on his own personality. Nobody was himself.

The last time I spoke to Helen was from Munich. I phoned her briefly from the Frauenhoffer bar, and when she told me she was leaving Berlin, I told her to hang on, I'd phone her back. I found a more private place to phone outside the post office. Again, I had the urge to go back to Berlin immediately to try and stop her.

She told me that she and Dieter had decided to go back and live in Dublin. They were going to make a life there instead of in Berlin. The idea was that Helen would fly back first and visit her parents while Dieter would tidy up the loose ends in Berlin, pack all their belongings and follow later in the car. Helen was going to try and organize a flat in Dublin by the time Dieter arrived.

She was excited about going back. I told her she was doing the right thing. The thought crossed my mind that Dieter might decide not to follow her, but she seemed very confident and I didn't want to sound negative. I wished her the best of luck. I meant it, I told her.

You wouldn't do that, she said.

What?

Go back to Ireland.

No, I said. I suppose not. Never.

She told me how Dieter was full of enthusiasm for the idea. It was he who had made all the plans. She told me she would be sorry in a way to leave Berlin. There was more of this silence. Fumbling with coins and fumbling with answers.

I'd like to see you before I leave, she said.

I don't think so, I said. I can't. Maybe. No, better not.

Things were excessively well intentioned. Polite to the point of no return. Everybody was bending over backwards.

Tempelhof is the smaller of the two airports in West Berlin. Also the nearest to Kreuzberg. There was a strong wind on the day Helen left. Early April. A styrofoam hamburger box skipped across the open area in front of the airport terminal. Small twigs with premature blossoms and bright green leaves were broken off and blown on to the ground. The wind caught the suitcases. Sand blew upwards into people's faces. Helen ran across the open space, pushing the buggy against the wind, bending down with one hand over the baby's face to stop sand from getting into his eyes. In the end it was Helen who got a particle of sand or something into her eye, because once she got into the departure area, inside the glass doors, she couldn't see anything. She was like a blind girl. Rolling her eyes. Leaning over backwards. One eye was quite red from all the rubbing. Outside the tinted windows of the airport building, it looked like a real sandstorm. From the glass, it was possible to see that it had begun to rain as well. Helen was an intending passenger. *Abflug*. She checked to make sure she had her ticket and her passport. She said she had no book to read on the plane. She shrugged a lot and smiled.

Do you want any sweets? Dieter asked.

There was time to buy some sweets for the journey. Lemon drops. They looked at one or two magazines together. Then it was time to go and they looked at each other.

Und so, Dieter said. We will see us in Dublin then.

17

Music Kills

*Berlin is not Berlin any more. But then, maybe it
never was what it was.*

(Ageing Berliner)

Dieter could be declared committed. Married. Desired. Expected to
arrive back in Dublin very soon. He could be declared foremost in
Helen's mind, as she was foremost in his. He wasn't going to
spend a minute longer than necessary in Berlin. He had already
tendered his month's notice to his employers at Kahl Autowerkstadt. He had also given notice to his landlords and begun to
repaint the apartment walls white. Part of the tenancy agreement
stipulates that the walls are to be left white. Since many of the
inhabitants of Kreuzberg paint their apartments with shrill colours, white is generally regarded as a return to normal. Any
furniture which Dieter had collected was sold at the nearest *Trödel*
market. The pink cot was sold for far less than it was originally
bought for. Dieter decided to bring with him only what was
essential. As always, there were things he was sad to leave behind
and things he was glad to get rid of. There were maps, old maps of
Germany, which he was determined to take with him. He couldn't
wait. He felt a duty to have one last wild time in Berlin before
going back to Dublin; to collect some last-minute memories. But he
became too busy preparing for the journey. There were some
things he still had to buy.

It's hard to imagine Berlin without Helen. And hard to imagine
that I don't still occupy some part of her mind. As soon as I arrived
back, I began to think of going to Dublin; getting there before
Dieter, talking to Helen, getting her on my side for ever. Just the
idea of arriving on her doorstep might have been enough. Half of
me wanted to go and half of me wanted to stay in Berlin. Get on
with it. Forget. The same way that half of you always wants to
dwell on things, tell everybody everything, discuss it to death,

while the other half of you wants to keep your mouth shut and say nothing.

I arrived back in Zoo station on a Sunday afternoon. I had to talk to somebody. I had taken the train back because I couldn't face the journey all the way back to Berlin in the car with Wolf and Hadja together. And Sunday afternoon seems to be the worst time to re-enter any city. Everything looks spent, eaten, done. The bars look depleted and the intensity which you have associated with the city is only a shadow of itself; a let-down. A panic builds up. Sunday is a day to get some leisure done; relaxing like hell before the week begins again. The platforms at Zoo station were down to half capacity. The pigeons seemed to be aware of it and took more daring risks, flying low between the passengers. They walked freely among the round tables where people stand and hastily eat *Wurst* or *pommes frites* while pigeons pick up available crumbs, now and then hastily turning to mating rituals. I would have stopped at one of the round tables for a beer or something to eat, but I was in a rush to get back to Sonnenallee to sort things out and to see for myself how the apartment had been changed. I didn't recognize the place. All the walls looked thick; cushioned.

I rang Wolf from the apartment as soon as I got there. I thought he might go for a drink with me. Instead I got Hadja on the phone. She said I got them at a bad time. They were just about to have a private celebration for Wolf's new album. The record company launch was still to come. And Hadja's brother Konrad was also going to throw a special party for Wolf's new success. There were going to be plenty of public occasions, Hadja said; they needed a Sunday evening at home together for once. By which I understood they were just about to take a bath together, candles and candelabrum all ready and a bottle of champagne cooling in the fridge. Wolf has often told me that the combination of heat and the rush of carbonated alcohol has the most profound effect on the bloodstream and the mind. Hadja was brief on the phone. Wolf was obviously there in the background, striking the matches, damp from the steam, eventually transforming the bathroom with golden light. Hadja said she would call over to me the following day to help me move my stuff to the new apartment in Oranienstrasse. I said I'd be waiting for her. I got the impression that Wolf was standing in the background, impatiently nodding towards the bathroom with the bottle of champagne in his hand. Hadja's brown skin turning slightly pink with the heat of the water as she got in. And the champagne cork floating around in the bath between them; bobbing on the water as they laughed. I got the idea that the bath seemed a bit small at first and that neither of them knew where to put their knees and legs; Wolf opting to sit for a moment with his knees bent up and the frail glass of champagne propped like a monument on one knee, held between thumb and forefinger.

Dieter had to get a few things before he left. Helen had asked him to bring one of those wooden coffee grinders with the handle and the drawer at the bottom. She asked him to get a coffee pot while he was at it. Dieter spent the last of the three weeks in Berlin collecting small things for their new home. Items he knew he wouldn't be able to get in Dublin. There were things he had to get for his son as well. Something to help the baby learn to walk. Ducks and wooden boats for the bath. Wooden, non-toxic building blocks. He knew Daniel's first impulse would be to put all these things in his mouth; the building blocks would squeak with the baby's pure saliva and gums practising the act of chewing. Dieter also bought some children's books, though it might have been far too soon for that. *Max und Moritz*. He could remember his own childhood.

I met the *Hausmeister* early the next morning in the courtyard. We nodded at first, then he said *Guten Morgen*. He must have had something in his mouth, a toffee or some chewy sort of chocolate, because he had difficulty pronouncing my name as well. The *Hausmeister* must have known about all the changes. He must have known that Helen was gone. That the apartment had been turned into a studio. Perhaps he was unhappy about it, because he didn't ask me anything. I had expected curiosity. I volunteered nothing.

Dieter had to go back to the restaurant where Helen worked for a while to collect some tax documents she had never bothered to pick up. She was due a rebate from the time she worked in Weinstube. Dieter undertook to fill in the forms and make sure she got it. He called Weinstube on a number of occasions and was told by the manager that the documents were all at headquarters. He collected the documents there and went on to the tax office, where he was assured that the tax refund would be sent on to Dublin. He applied for a similar refund in his own case. He gave Helen's parents' house in Dublin as a forwarding address.

The apartment in Sonnenallee is completely transformed. It has been turned into a fully soundproofed studio. The inner doors are thick and heavy. They open and close with a swish like the door of a bank vault. The windows have also been reinforced, with heavy insulating shutters that block out all sound and light. The walls and ceilings have been covered with a three-inch thick foam skin which seals in all sound. The floor has been covered with a special spongy carpet. And these are only the minimal requirements to dampen the sound of Wolf's rehearsals. The residents are fussy about noise. All the furniture is gone. None of it was mine anyhow.

It's like standing in a vacuum.

In the music business, you have to be ready to move at a moment's notice. I had everything packed by the time Hadja arrived.

How do you like it? she asked, looking around the apartment.

Great, I said.

You will be able to store all your lighting equipment here as well, she said. You won't have to clutter your own apartment with these things.

Oh yes, I said. Great.

We will make a move then, she said.

I got on with the task of carrying my stuff out to the car. Hadja helped me with some of the smaller boxes. There wasn't much anyhow. We drove around to the new apartment in Oranienstrasse, which is on the ground floor overlooking the street. From the window I can just see the tops of people's heads as they pass by along the pavement. The new apartment is darker than Sonnenallee, but functional. It's smaller, too, but Hadja said it was only temporary until she found something better for me. She was going to keep looking out for a really good apartment for me.

This will only be for a small time, she said.

Wolf's album is called *Atlantis*. I've seen the artwork. A clever merger of images and graphic design. Pictures of Berlin, Kreuzberg and the Berlin Wall are superimposed around an image of Wolf-gang Ebers looking out across the Atlantic waves. His hair is blown back by the wind. The title of the album is written along the Berlin Wall as part of the graffiti. Wolf's name is written with an aerosol can.

In the last few days I've also seen a copy of the *Neuköllner Anzeiger*, the local paper in which Helen's picture appeared. One in a million. The article underneath her photo said more about Tenglemann's supermarket than it did about her, the winner. Most of the quotes were from the manager of the shop.

Dieter went to the Polizei Präsidium in order to de-register as an inhabitant of Berlin. Whenever you change address or leave for another place in Germany, you are obliged to notify the central authorities at the Polizei Präsidium. I'm going to have to do it myself one of these days for Oranienstrasse. Dieter filled in the customary forms for both himself and Helen. He put in a forward date; May the fifth, the day he was planning to leave Berlin.

I helped Wolf and Hadja move all their equipment into the apartment in Sonnenallee. Guitars, amplifiers, a new drum machine and a new hi-fi system, as well as some of Hadja's files. They are very pleased with the new studio. The walls of Hadja's new office are covered with the new record sleeve, *Atlantis*.

Wolf has been excited about the new studio. He's already talking about the next album. For me, the place seems very strange. I still can't get used to it. I keep hearing imaginary sounds of the baby. You can never eliminate everything.

Wolf and Hadja wanted to test the soundproof quality of the main room while we were there. Each of us went into the sealed chamber while the others stayed outside to listen, to hear if any sound seeped out. The windows were sealed with the shutters. They asked me to go inside and make as much noise as I possibly could while they listened outside. The main door was closed with a hollow swish. It seemed to change the pressure in the room, the way the pressure changes on your ears while travelling in the mountains. Hadja went down into the courtyard to see if she would hear anything from there. I was meant to shout something at the top of my voice. Whatever came into my head.

Sonnenallee . . .   Sonnenallee . . .Sonnenallee . . .   Lufthansa . . .
Tenglemanns . . . Tenglemanns . . . BVG . . . BVG . . . BVG . . .

Biography gets into everything.

Wolf came in smiling. Said he didn't hear a word. Then he asked
me to try some of the instruments and went out again, closing the
swish door. I blew a few crass notes into the saxophone. Then I
plugged in the electric guitar and strummed a bit. Nothing
musical. Just profane noise.

Dieter had organized everything. He even made sure to buy some
real German gifts for Helen's mother and father. Pretzels and
chocolate *Lebkuchen*. The last thing he had to do was to visit his
own mother. The afternoon he went to visit her, she hardly
recognized him. Her dogs didn't either. They barked hysterically.
He told her he was going back to live in Dublin. It all meant very
little to an old woman. She was glad to have her own son sitting
with her for a while. Dieter was impatient and uneasy. He was
reluctant to leave once he had made the effort to visit. It frightened
him to see her. And when he left again after an hour, she said very
little. She didn't beg him to come back, as he expected. She didn't
ask him to stay. The dogs started barking again. They were
jumping up and down off the sofa as he left.

It was decided to have an open-air party to celebrate Wolf's new
album. Out in Alt Mariendorf, a suburb of Berlin where Konrad
owns a large garden with a swimming pool and a tennis court. It
was to be the first barbecue. And the first Country and Western
club meeting of the summer. Every guest was meant to wear
country and western gear or contribute in some way, though Hadja
explained to me that I didn't have to. It was enough that I was a real
English-speaker. Hadja sent out invitations to all her friends. She
was determined to leave nobody out. She was also in charge of
organizing the bar and the catering. All on Konrad's account. He
insisted.

Dieter went for a long swim in the morning. He spent over an hour
in the water, swimming up and down the length of the pool. He
had forgotten how easy it is to swivel through the water. The
length of the pool suited him. When he got out of the water, he had

forgotten how strange it is to walk on solid ground, on non-slip tiles.

After lunch, he began to pack all his belongings into the car. He did it slowly, without any great urgency. He was excited inside. He had forgotten what Helen looked like. How strange it would be to hold his own son. To embrace Helen again. To sit down and talk for hours. He had forgotten what it was like to be so close to her.

It took all afternoon and early evening to get everything packed properly into the car. He had to lock the car every time he went back upstairs to get something else. You know Kreuzberg, he told himself. He packed things three or four times until they were just right. It's quite a distance from Berlin to Dublin. He made sure that everything was packed low in the back seat. He didn't want the rear view through the back window obstructed.

The night of the party, Hadja, Wolf and I drove down together to Alt Mariendorf, almost as far as Lichterfelde, where there is nothing but gardens and summer-houses. Konrad's garden had a log cabin with a metal smoke-stack. The swimming pool was lit from inside and looked blue, even in darkness. The garden itself was ringed with coloured lanterns, which hung from one tree to the next all round. The cars outside were parked half up on the pavement. The pavement was made of red sand, the kind of sand they often use for practice football pitches and tennis courts in Germany.

At the gate to the garden we were met by Peter, a man dressed as Davy Crockett with a fur hat and the clothes of a trapper. He spoke in English to Hadja at first, then reverted to German. He was in charge of the catering, Hadja informed me. In Germany, you shake hands with everyone. Most of the guests were standing on the lawn, holding glasses, occasionally dancing whenever the music became lively enough.

Beside the log cabin, there were two charcoal fires; a small one on which all kinds of hamburgers and sausages were being cooked. Over the larger fire, they were roasting an entire pig. The shape of a pig is even more like a pig when it rotates slowly on a spit. Now and again, Davy Crockett or somebody else standing nearby picked up a ladle out of a basin and poured something over the pig's back. Orders were mainly shouted in English, disfigured

English, leaning towards America. There was a broad woman standing over a pot of beans.

I was surprised to see Sulima and Massoud at the party. Hadja went over briefly to speak to them, and then rejoined Wolf and myself at the bar. I was introduced to Konrad and Kristl. Kristl said she had heard so much about me. But as usual, there's no chance to ask what she'd heard. Kristl's dog, Tristan, was attracting attention everywhere.

Drinks were being served from a table beside the pool. From where I stood, I could see Hadja's strong legs silhouetted against the lights of the swimming pool behind her. A woman with a single vertical feather, dressed in beads and a torn suede skirt, came over to us and introduced herself as Uschi. She seemed delighted to find somebody who could speak English. Wolf and Hadja normally separate at parties and arrange to meet again later. I was left talking to Uschi. Her legs looked much slimmer than Hadja's. I had to tell her to be careful not to step backwards into the swimming pool.

Dieter decided he was going to drive through the night. All the way through West Germany. The roads would be clear. He would arrive at Ostend, at the ferry, some time the following day. If there was any need for sleep, he could stop off at a layby and snooze for an hour. He set off close to midnight. Stuck a cassette of Bach into the car stereo and switched up the volume. Stopped for petrol before he got to the border. By half past twelve he was already travelling through the East German corridor.

When the food was eventually served, everyone seemed to panic. Important conversations were abandoned. People got the impression there wasn't going to be enough.

Somebody passed by with a plate full of food. Uschi and I became distracted. We forgot what we were talking about.

Oh – Waiija! she said. The food looks so good. It makes me direct hungry.

Uschi disappeared and came back with two plates laden with *Schweinehaxe*, sausage, salad and beans. I was able to follow her movements wherever she went by the vertical feather on her head. The feather was stuck into a thin sweat band.

Mmm . . . schmeckt aber, she said.

What more can you say? Uschi began to pick up the conversation where we had left off. She progressed to vegetarianism. She had often thought of becoming a vegetarian. I told her I had no time for vegetarians. I told her it was racism under another name. She moved on to animals. Seals. Whales. Vivisection.

I'm very for animal rights, she said.

Around half-way between Braunschweig and Hannover, Dieter drove off the *Autobahn* for a good, strong cup of coffee. He preferred to stop in a small town, rather than somewhere on the *Autobahn* itself. It took some time before he found an all-night café. The thought of food had not entered his plans up to then, but he decided to have a quick sandwich while he was there. When he was finished, he thought he had already lost too much time. He hurried back to the car and drove back towards the *Autobahn*. He had difficulty finding his way at first. There were new roads and flyovers being built at the edge of the town. When he eventually found it, he thought for a moment that he had chosen the wrong direction. But that was impossible. He was certain he was on the right side. The road signs confirmed it.

Uschi begged Wolf to sing a song. Then she begged me to beg him. In honour of the occasion, there was no way that Wolf could refuse. He picked up one of the nylon string guitars which had been brought for a free-for-all session later on. He sang one song: '*Atlanticsucht*'. There was huge applause, which travelled over the neighbouring gardens, swimming pools and tennis courts. There were cries for more. *Zugabe! Zugabe! Zugabe!* But Wolf smiled and pretended to stagger across to the bar. When it was clear that he really wouldn't sing any more, other people grabbed the guitars enthusiastically and began to play. Somebody produced a mouth organ. A girl sitting with her knees up thrashed a tambourine against her thigh.

A breeze blew up. Uschi asked me if I wanted to join in with the singing. I told her I couldn't. She understood that I didn't know the words of the songs, so she disappeared into the log cabin and came back with a stack of photocopies.

The TEXT, she said.

Dieter was driving in the right direction. What happened was that he drove on to a section of the *Autobahn* which had not been opened to traffic yet. How he got on to the ramp leading to an unopened *Autobahn*, nobody can explain. Questions would be asked. But accidents never make sense. Local residents said they heard something which didn't make sense either. Dieter drove up the ramp and thought nothing of the fact that there was no other traffic. It was the middle of the night. He accelerated on to the *Autobahn* proper. Decided to change the cassette. Put in something by U2. Turned up the volume again. Accelerated and drove straight into the first of a line of yellow roadwork machines which were parked along both lanes. He had time to see them but no time to stop. He struck a bulldozer. The impact of the car pushed the machine back into the next one behind it. He knew exactly what happened. He saw it coming. He remained conscious for almost two minutes. But he had no urge to move anywhere. Everything was silent and stationary. He was aware that none of the things packed into the back seat had been thrown into the front. He was concerned that some of the gifts might have been broken. He was alive for another twenty-five minutes after that. But he was only discovered at around six in the morning.

Hadja drove us back from the party. Wolf and I decided to stop off at Sonnenallee to listen to some decent music for a while. Hadja went straight home. She said she was tired.

I made some tea when we got upstairs. Everything was so familiar. I could do things blindfolded in Sonnenallee. Wolf began to look through his vast collection of tapes and albums. I brought in two mugs and set them on the floor in the middle of the room. Then closed the door behind me with a swish. There was only the floor and some cushions to sit on.

Wolf selected some cassette. The music came on loud. Turn it up, I said. It's got to be LOUD. The song was familiar to both of us. It was almost as though he had chosen it just for me. But you always think that with music you like. Wolf looked for acknowledgement in my eyes. He turned to me with a cruel expression on his face and punched the air in front of him like an imaginary stomach. Then he sat down on his cushions.

Your relationship to music is always basically the same as your relationship to alcohol, drugs, travel, people. You love it or hate it. It's based on need. It has to be LOUD.

I keep thinking about Helen. Waiting. I keep wondering what she must be thinking. I keep thinking about the presents arriving. And the tax refund.

The music has to be loud enough to eliminate thought. And loud enough to eliminate all desire for conversation. All desire for answer and expression. Loud enough to shake the pit of your stomach and send terror through your colon. Loud enough to kill all ambient knowledge. Loud enough to stop time. Turn it up. It's got to roar like a football stadium, or a river, or an *Autobahn*. Like an endless impact. Loud enough to break through the pain of twisting metal. Loud enough to make it impossible to move, or breathe. Loud enough to eliminate pulse.